Wiccan Mirror

by

Mark Rosendorf

The Witches of Vegas, Book 5

This is a work of fiction. Names, characters, places, and incidents are either the product of the author's imagination or are used fictitiously, and any resemblance to actual persons living or dead, business establishments, events, or locales, is entirely coincidental or the result of a witch changing reality.

Wiccan Mirror

Cover Art by *The Wild Rose Press, Inc.*

The Wild Rose Press, Inc.
PO Box 708
Adams Basin, NY 14410-0708
Visit us at www.thewildrosepress.com

Publishing History
First Edition, 2023
Trade Paperback ISBN 978-1-5092-5202-2
Digital ISBN 978-1-5092-5203-9

The Witches of Vegas, Book 5
Published in the United States of America

Sebastian always smiled when addressing the audience, but not this time.

"Ladies and gentlemen," he continued, "The Witches of Vegas are not just a show made up of talented magicians. We are also a family. Right now, a family situation has come up, so we must cut the show short." The audience groaned and booed. Understandable after less than fifteen minutes of "magic." But, damn, this may have been Isis' best use of the energy on the stage, and instead of a buzz in the air, all she heard were boos.

The lights in the theater came on. Isis could now see who was standing near the stage holding the family's attention. The older and well-built man with the blond ponytail made her gasp.

"Paul!" Isis exclaimed.

The vice president and head of the task force for New Salem. He had traveled all the way to Vegas to see their show once before, and he did it in support of a family under his charge. This time, he wore a far more serious and official look to him.

"Please accept our apologies," Sebastian said to the audience. "You will receive a full refund for tonight's show. We hope to make this up to you soon. Meanwhile, we ask that you make your way out of the theater in an orderly fashion. Thank you for your understanding."

"Dad," Isis whispered to him. "What's going on?"

Sebastian eyed Paul from the distance. "I have no idea, but for Paul to come all this way, and ask us to stop the show, something major must have happened in New Salem."

Praise

The Witches of Vegas
Winner of the 2021 RONE award for Young Adult Fiction

Winner of the 2022 Pencraft Award for Literary Excellence in Young Adult Fantasy and Science Fiction

Finalist in the 2020 International Digital Awards for Young Adult Fiction

Journey To New Salem
2022 RONE award finalist in Young Adult Fiction

1st Runner up in the 2021 National Excellence in Story Telling contest in Young Adult Fiction

Witch's Gamble
Winner of the Critter's Annual Reader's poll for Best Young Adult Book for 2022

Witch Way to Vegas
Recipient of the prestigious Crowned Heart from InD'Tale Magazine

"The Witches Of Vegas is simply screaming out to be a movie series. One can only hope that Hollywood snaps up this incredibly engrossing adventure."

~ Doctor Who Online

"My teen, Moxie, really digs The Witches of Vegas series and is looking forward to the next book."

~ Penn Jillette, Penn &Teller: Fool Us

Dedication

To Sue
The center of my universe

Prologue

Rico was never a smart man. That's why he always listened to his older brother without question. The guy was thirty years old—eight years older than Rico—and he always had the answers to their problems. When his brother wanted him to run drugs for his gang, Rico went along without question, even if it didn't feel right.

The result was a six-year stay in an upstate New York maximum-security facility's gang unit. To make things worse, Rico drew the short stick when it came to cellmates. Rico was Johnny's fifth cellmate in three years. From what Rico had heard, three of them ended up in the infirmary before getting relocated to other cells. The fourth went straight to the morgue.

It was just past midnight when Rico dozed, letting go of the day's stresses. He was yanked off the top bunk and dropped on his feet. Rico stumbled, unable to keep his balance, then fell, hitting the back of his head against the sink. "Johnny, what the hell, man?" He could have died right there if he hit hard enough, and the face staring down at him didn't care.

Johnny lifted Rico by the shirt and slammed him against the wall. Johnny towered over him and outweighed him by a good fifty pounds. With his build, Johnny would have been welcome on any athletic sports team, if he wasn't such a scumbag. "Too much snoring up there," Johnny growled. His foul breath almost knocked Rico unconscious. It actually smelled worse than the sweat his body seemed to produce all day, every day.

"Come on, Johnny, my man," Rico pleaded. "I can't help snoring if I'm asleep. I got a deviated septum in my nose—"

"You sound like a goddamned train." Johnny's massive hands tightened their grip. "Keep waking me and I'll rip your nose right off your face."

Yeah, the short stick for sure. Johnny was a lifer who intimidated everyone, even the guards. Rico wanted to tell him off, put the big man in his place, but he'd never last thirty seconds if it came to a physical altercation. Johnny had slammed guys twice Rico's size in the yard. It usually took eight officers to bring him down whenever he went off. He was so massive and so violent. So…

Rico's eyes flashed to the metal bars keeping him trapped in the eight feet by ten feet cell with this monster. They were being watched from the other side. Rico was used to getting peeked on throughout the day and night, but it was primarily by prison guards. The girl staring a hole through him, and casually dressed in a tank top and ripped pants, was way too small to be a prison guard. She was also way too young.

"What the hell?" Rico exclaimed. "Who is *that*?"

"What are you yammering about?" Johnny grunted. "You high or a nut or something?"

Rico motioned his hand past Johnny. "Dude, there's a girl outside our cell. It's a kid!"

Johnny finally turned his head ever so slightly. He eyed with confusion the girl who leaned her forehead against the bars and watched them as if they were animals in a cage. She was skinny and had Latina facial features, but her complexion looked like a light brown shirt that had been through the wash so many times its color had faded. The tank top was brown from age or filth, which made it hard to guess what its original color may have been. Her bare arms had a yellowish discoloring that matched the blotches all over her cheeks and chin.

Johnny's fingers slipped off Rico's shirt. He walked to the bars. The girl looked up at his face, showing no sign of intimidation whatsoever. Her narrowed brown eyes had a detached coldness to them.

"What are you doing in here, Sweetheart?" Johnny's gruff tone gave off a veiled threat. "What are you, one of the guard's kids or something?"

Rico swallowed the saliva that had built up in his throat. It had an eerie coldness to it. Johnny's guess didn't make much sense. What guard would ever bring their kid to work at a maximum-security prison, then let them roam free? "Yo, Johnny, something's not right about this girl, man. I don't like this—"

"*Would you shut up?*" Johnny snapped. "What are you afraid of, some puny little girl on the other side of the bars?"

A devious grin crossed the girl's lips. Rico widened his eyes. With the discolored patches and faded skin, she looked more scary than sweet. The kid was definitely a stranger to Rico, but from the way she looked at Johnny with a familiar twinkle in her eye, it was as if she knew him. That, of course, was impossible, considering he'd been in this prison probably longer than she had been alive.

Without a word, the girl strolled and passed

through the metal bars. Johnny leapt back, taken by surprise. "What the hell?" he screamed.

"Yo, how did she get into the cell?" Rico pressed his back against the wall. "Should we call for help? There's got be a guard somewhere out there, right?"

Rico looked to the hallway outside the bars. With all the noise and scuttling around, a team of prison guards should have run over with flashlights to make sure everything was okay. There were around two-dozen cells in this block alone. How did their screams and shouting not wake everyone up?

"How old are you, kid?" Johnny hunched to get a good look at the girl's scarred face. "You look about twelve."

"Nah," Rico called out. "She's skinny and all, but look at her cheekbones. They're older. She's gotta be a teenager, at least."

Now, with a closer look, he thought the scars on her face and arms could have been burn marks. But they were old, like they had been there a long time. Somehow, they looked much older than the girl who sported them. Did she somehow survive a fire when she was a baby?

"You know what? Either way, it's been real long and lonely in here." Johnny pushed a knuckle under the girl's chin. He reached for his waistband. "Any age will do."

"Johnny, man, are you serious?" Rico gasped. "You're thinking like that, *now*?"

The girl's grin grew into a full smile. She raised a hand and held out her palm. She whispered something under her breath. Her fingers violently closed into a white-knuckled fist. Johnny's pants suddenly ignited on fire. Smoke and flame shot out from the hem to the waistband.

Rico gasped. "Holy sh—"

Johnny scampered around the cell, slapping at his pants. He let out a loud howl when the flame caught onto his hands and wrists. Still no reaction outside the cell from the guards or other inmates. The flame from Johnny's lower body grew, filling the cell with black smoke.

"What the hell's going on?" Rico screamed. He tried to lunge without a destination in mind, but the girl threw out an arm, fingers spread wide. In response, Rico's flailing body flew onto the bottom bunk's thin mattress.

Another loud shriek nearly shook the entire cell. From his knees, Johnny, who was now covered in fire up to his chest, reached for the bars and pulled on them, but there was no escape. Two of the bars stretched out just wide enough for Johnny to stick his head through, which he did in a desperate attempt to escape. Without a sound the bars closed around his throat. Johnny's screams grew louder and higher pitched. So did the flames. They had now engulfed Johnny's entire upper body and arms. His skin sizzled and smelled like burned sausage. The girl, meanwhile, looked on with a deadpan expression. A slight grin formed along her lips. She waved a hand through the smoke which filled the air.

The fire covered Johnny from the back of his neck to his legs. His body fluttered with his head trapped, unable to escape. Johnny should have been dead by now. But, somehow, he was still alive, suffering under all that scorched flesh covered in a blanket of red and yellow fire. Soon, there was no movement, and no more screams.

Rico couldn't lift his body from the bed. It was as if a force held him in place. He could do nothing but watch the fire eat his roommate's body while praying he wouldn't be next.

Chapter One

The next day…

After saving the world, The Witches of Vegas chose to take permanent residence in New Salem, where they lived happily ever after…

Until one morning, six weeks ago, Zack's late uncle's phone rang for the first time in over a year. Zack answered the call out of morbid curiosity. It was the general manager of The Sapphire Resort who wanted them to come back to the theater for an eight-week reunion run. Zack was reluctant to take him up on the offer. The Wiccan members of their coven, however, were intrigued, then excited for the opportunity.

Tonight, they were about to practice their witchcraft on stage in front of a sold-out Vegas audience. They even checked into their Sapphire suites one week early so they could prepare and enjoy some time on the strip. Their mini-vacation and preparation for the show went by quickly. It was time for the opening performance in their reunion tour. Lucky for Zack, he kept up on his learned magic skills during his free time, much as Isis and her family had been doing with their natural Wiccan abilities.

At the moment, the Sapphire Theater's curtain was closed. The witches weren't the focus. It was Zack at the card table set up in front of the stage. As always, he was the opening act for the show. The excitement in the air radiating throughout the theater brought a huge smile to his face. It made him wonder why he hesitated to agree to this in the first place.

"Ladies and gentlemen, my volunteer selected a random card from this deck." Zack held up a deck of cards in his right hand for the dozen or more audience members surrounding the table in a semicircle. He waved it to the camera above him so the rest of the audience flocking in could see it on the big screen.

With his left hand, Zack waved to the young girl with blonde pigtails standing on his left. Her hair was two shades lighter than his. "Then, she placed that freely selected card in the middle of the pack, and the gentleman behind her shuffled it."

Of course, the word "freely" was part of Zack's patter. In truth, it was never a free choice, although he made sure it looked like one. It was good to see his skills hadn't diminished too much since his last performance. There wasn't much opportunity to handle playing cards, or to entertain with them in his new home. He recently handled cards more in the last few weeks than he had all year because he needed to reacquaint himself for the show. Even then, much of his practice took place in front of a mirror.

"After that, four of you each chose a card, none of which were the selected card." Zack waved a hand over four cards that lay across the table facedown. "So far, so good, right?"

The audience members in front of him all nodded in agreement. Zack was ready to move on to the big reveal. Yeah, he was definitely in his element. The screen high above flashed his name Zack Galloway: Card Master. Zack missed using his last name, something he couldn't use in New Salem due to their first-names-only policy.

Zack waved the little girl who originally selected the card to move closer to the table. Her parents, a few feet behind, snapped photographs with their phones of the big screen high above where the girl could be seen.

"Would you please choose one of the four cards on the table?" Zack asked her. "Any card. It's your choice."

The girl pointed at the card on the far right. Zack picked up that card and pressed the face against the pocket of his red vest. "Can you now tell us all which card you selected?"

The girl answered, "King of clubs."

"That's right, the king of clubs." Zack slowly turned the card around and held it high up so the audience, and the overhead camera, could see the face. Sure enough, it was the king of clubs. The entire audience cheered at the "miracle" they had just witnessed. It didn't matter which card the girl chose. Zack had swapped all four random choices with identical king of clubs cards, which he had hidden at the bottom of the deck. Listening to the cheers reminded Zack how much he had missed this.

"I see my time is about up." Zack scooped the remaining three cards on the table and added them to the top of the deck. "I now ask you to return to your seats and prepare to be amazed. The Witches of Vegas will return to the stage for the first time in almost a year, and it will happen in exactly fifteen minutes!"

The audience applauded. Zack plucked the

microphone from his white button-down shirt collar underneath the vest. As he walked up the stage steps, he was unable to wipe away the huge smile across his face. The Witches of Vegas' reunion tour had just started, but so far it had been all Zack could have imagined. For the last nine months, he had been an ordinary teenage boy who lived in a village where half the population was witches. But in front of this audience, Zack felt like the one with Wiccan powers.

"Hey, Zack Galloway, card master," called a sweet voice with a west coast accent.

It stopped Zack in his tracks. He peeked over his shoulder.

A girl around his age waved to him. She had long, straight black hair that hung down to her midsection. The tight pink tank-top and cut-up blue jean shorts showed off every tan line her body had to offer. To say she was in amazing shape would be an understatement.

"You were really awesome," she said through a coquettish grin. "You're also really cute. Do you have a girlfriend?"

Zack's cheeks suddenly felt warm, meaning they were turning red. He had been hit on twice behind that table during their previous run. Both times were by pretty girls who, if they ever passed him on the street or in a school hallway, wouldn't look at him twice. Amazing how standing behind a microphone and a camera could change people's perceptions.

"Thanks, and yes, I do," he answered with pride. "Sorry."

Zack took one last look at the disappointment in the girl's face, then stepped behind the curtain. He did have a girlfriend, and she was the only girl he'd ever want in his life. Together, they'd been through more than any other teenage couple on Earth. Maybe more than most, if not all, adult couples as well. An embarrassed excitement filled him upon seeing Isis waiting for him once he pulled the curtain closed. She wore the same outfit from their last performance almost a year ago, a mint-green blouse and black slacks. They were still a perfect fit.

"That was awesome, Zack," Isis said through her usual nervous grin. She walked up to Zack and gave him a quick peck on the lips. "I know you loved it out there. Admit it."

"Well, maybe a little." That was all Zack would confess, but Isis knew him far better than anyone else. Maybe even more than he knew himself. In truth, his adrenaline pumped the moment he stepped in front of an audience, and then even more so when he received his first cheer.

Isis ran her fingers over the side of his head. "But your hair got so messed up, as usual." She held her thumb and forefinger close together. "You know, with just a little bit of the gel my dad uses—"

"Nah, I'm good." Zack pulled back his head and laughed. "Messed up is kind of my style."

Isis sighed and shook her head. "I'm going to run to the bathroom. Then it's time." She took Zack's hands and gave them a squeeze. "Wish me luck out there?"

"Good luck out there," he said with a smile that matched the one on her face.

Zack kept an eye on Isis as she ran down the side hallway and into the dressing room. Wow, between her exotic olive skin and those deep brown eyes and hair… Isis was so unassuming, especially with that thin frame a strong wind could knock over. No one would ever guess she was perhaps the most powerful witch in the world. Or Zack's girlfriend. After everything she had been through—and then what they had been through together—her sweet demeanor never hardened. Zack had been debating his next move for a while, but now he knew for sure.

The adults of the coven all faced the black curtain that covered the back wall. Sebastian and Selena looked on while Sacha's raised hands glowed. Black wires rose and placed themselves against the curtain. Selena and Sacha's long red hair glistened underneath the spotlights, as did their sparkling blue blouses and white tights. Sebastian's short brown hair did the same, but with him, it was more likely due to all the gel he used on it. Their appointed coven leader wore a look of frustration as he kept straightening the bowtie on his black tuxedo.

"I still don't see the point of hanging these things," Sacha called out in her sardonic way. "They just blend into the curtain, and it's not like we use them, anyway."

"That's the idea, Little Sis," Selena replied, helping Sebastian with his bowtie. "But you already know that."

The strings were one of Zack's many ideas for red herrings hidden throughout the stage. He knew magicians in the audience would pick up on them, which, as Selena said, was the point. Protecting their secret was his primary job. There was nothing in their show that he had overlooked despite his mind being preoccupied. It was time to do what he was ready to do.

"Um, Sebastian, Selena." Zack stepped in between the couple. "Can I speak with the two of you in private, please?"

"Now?" Sebastian asked. "We're about to begin."

"It's important."

"Private?" Sacha scoffed. "I'm the only other one here."

"Sure, Zack." Selena tapped her husband on the arm, then waved a hand to the hallway. Zack took the lead with both Selena and Sebastian following.

"Sach, we'll be right back," Sebastian said on the way.

"Oh, sure, I'll just finish up all by myself while you all talk in private." The annoyance in Sacha's voice did not go unnoticed.

Once in the hallway, Zack peeked around to make sure they were alone, no eavesdroppers. He faced his coven leaders. He still couldn't believe he was in a coven, especially considering he wasn't a witch. Wow, Zack felt the sweat dripping from his hands. He wasn't nearly this nervous in front of the audience, but he had also performed on stage more times than he could count. This was a conversation he expected to have only once, so he sure didn't want to mess it up.

"Let's make this quick," Sebastian said, with a peek at his watch. "What's up?"

"Right." Zack wiped his sweaty hands against his pants, then took a deep breath. He looked up at Sebastian and Selena. If he was going to do this, now was the time. "The two of you always talk about destiny. Well, I believe mine is to someday marry Isis. I want to make my intentions clear to her, and since she is your adopted daughter, I thought it would be appropriate to ask for your blessing before I do."

Sebastian and Selena exchanged a glance. Both sets of eyebrows rose. There was a long and awkward silence, although it was possible they were discussing it in some sort of Wiccan way. Sebastian finally spoke up. "Zack, you just turned seventeen. Isis is still a few months away. I know you both share memories of that other timeline, but in this one, you've only been together a little more than a year. It's bad enough you've had…relations. Now you're looking to propose to her?"

Whoa, talk about embarrassing. Zack was sure he and Isis had been careful with their sneaking around. He should have realized her folks, as witches, kept good tabs on her. Plus, Isis was open about everything with them. Of course, she'd confide in them what they had been up to.

Sebastian did have a point about their ages and the amount of time they spent together. But for Zack and Isis, they'd been a couple a lot longer than just over a year. In that other reality, as vampires, they were married for over a century, and they lived together for a long time before that. But this wasn't the original timeline. "It-it's not a proposal," Zack stammered. "It's more of…a promise. For the future."

Selena placed her hands on both Zack and Sebastian's elbows. "Perhaps the two of you should discuss this man to man," she said with a slanted grin. "I'm going to help Sach finish setting up." She rubbed Sebastian's watch-wearing hand. "Just keep an eye on the time, okay? Our audience awaits."

Selena strolled off leaving Zack with two blue eyes peering his way. They were eyes he couldn't get a read on. Zack's relationship with Sebastian had grown over the last year. Sebastian put in huge efforts to be a father figure to Zack and make him feel like part of the coven—his family—which was appreciated. But despite his kindness and acceptance of Zack, Sebastian Santell was still Isis' overprotective father.

"A promise for the future. Interesting." Sebastian walked forward, bringing his chest up to Zack's face. "How about we take a quick road trip?"

"A road trip?" Zack squinted his eyes. He wanted to take a step back but thought it best to stand his ground. "To where? You're on in a few minutes."

"We'll be back fast." Sebastian shut his eyes and looked up. "Besides, it wouldn't be a Vegas show if it started on time, right?" He chanted, "Teleport."

Everything around Zack blurred. It was as if they were inside of a soap bubble. Soon, everything faded completely. When it cleared, he was looking up at the stars in the sky. They were off the Strip, but not too far off since Zack could see the skyline a few blocks away. They were standing in front of a small two-story house with a bright brown roof and a decent-sized front yard. The house looked lonely compared to the congested high-rise apartment buildings and store fronts on either end.

"Whose house is this?" Zack asked.

"The really cute young lady who expressed her interest in you after your performance. This is where she lives."

"You saw that?"

"I did. I even sensed your momentary temptation." Sebastian's hand pressed against Zack's upper back.

"Temptation? I told her no." Zack's confusion was dialed up to eleven. "Why are we here?"

"You are part of my coven, Zack, so I'm introducing you to an old Wiccan custom." Sebastian's hand moved to Zack's shoulder and forced him to face the oak front door with an oversized gold-plated knocker. "Before a coven member pledges his loyalty to a fellow member, he receives one chance to sow his oats and flush the idea of infidelity out of his system."

"I've never heard of that custom." And Zack knew more about Wiccan customs than perhaps any other non-witch, or actual witch, on Earth. That included Sebastian.

"Right now, her entire family is at our show in the Sapphire." Sebastian spun Zack around bringing them face-to-face. "This is your one opportunity before you pledge yourself to Isis. You stay here. I'll return to the theater and give the girl a hypnotic suggestion to go home. Then I'll teleport her here. You'll have about an hour to get it out of your system. Enjoy it while you can."

Zack did a double take from the house to Sebastian. He couldn't believe this was real, or that it was coming from a man who constantly preached about morals and loyalty. He was actually giving Zack permission, and the means, to be disloyal to Isis. Something had to be amiss. But whether that was the case or not, it didn't matter.

"I can't do that to Isis," Zack said. "Wiccan tradition or not, she wouldn't be okay with it."

"Isis is about to go on stage. She'll be focused on her lessons in witchcraft." Sebastian gave Zack a slight shove toward the house. "It will be our secret, and I won't think less of you. Isis never has to know. Same with Selena and Sacha. There's nothing to stop you."

Zack spun around and faced Sebastian. "I won't do that to her. Isis is the only girl I want to be with for the rest of my life. I could never look her in the eye again if I spent even a moment with someone else. I'm sorry to spurn your tradition, but no."

"I see." Sebastian looked down into Zack's eyes. He smacked him against the arm. "That was the right answer. Consider Selena's and my blessing granted. And thank you for coming to us about this first."

Zack dropped his jaw. "Wait. So this was all a test? For what purpose? You already know I'm loyal to Isis."

"Yes, I do know. But it wasn't too long ago a witch put you under a disloyalty spell." Sebastian tapped a finger against the top of Zack's head. "We had to make sure there were no lingering traces in there."

"I'm sure there's not. In fact, I've never been surer of anything in my entire life."

"In that case, let's head back and not keep our audience, or the ladies, waiting." Sebastian placed an arm over Zack's shoulders and walked them away from the house.

He shut his eyes, ready to teleport them once again. "Hold up." Zack stopped in place. Sebastian did the same. "You knew I was going to come to you with this, didn't you? You didn't seem surprised. Neither did Selena."

"We did suspect, yes," Sebastian answered. "And I had this test ready to go."

"How did you both know? Your Wiccan senses?"

Sebastian chuckled. "No, our parental ones."

Zack turned his body and looked back at the house. "That girl doesn't really live here, does she?"

Sebastian shrugged. "I have no idea who is in this house, or where that girl lives." His eyes shut again. "Teleport."

Everything blurred.

Chapter Two

Isis peeked through the backstage curtain at Sebastian who brought the microphone in his left hand up to his mouth. She gave a quiet golf-clap while watching her dad face the Sapphire Theater's audience with Selena on his left and Sacha on his right. The two sisters each had highball glasses raised in front of their faces. Selena's was filled to the top with red juice while Sacha's had purple grape juice. The sisters held the glasses high up in their right hands with twelve-inch checkered silks in their left hands. There were also two empty glasses standing front-and-center on the stage. Isis patted Zack's hand, which was at her side with his arm around her waist.

"As you can see," Sebastian said into the microphone, "the beautiful Quinn sisters are showing off their favorite afternoon beverages. But what happens when they get bored with their drinks and want to try the other juice?"

Sebastian held out his hand and closed his eyes. "Spotlight," he said away from the microphone. In response, the energy crackled and lit up the stage.

"Well, that didn't come off like witchcraft at all." Zack sighed. Isis covered her mouth and giggled.

Selena and Sacha wiped the silks across the sides of the glasses that faced the audience. After a quick spell, they whipped away the hands holding the silks.

Now the liquid in Selena's glass was purple and Sacha's was red. The audience applauded, as did Isis. It had been a while since the last time The Witches of Vegas practiced witchcraft on a stage—nine months, to be exact. Unlike the last time, they all felt ready for their return. This was the first act of their first show, but so far, neither Mom, nor Sacha, had missed a beat.

With each move, Isis kept a close eye on her three family members on stage. Zack was doing the same, although they were both watching for different reasons. Zack was eyeing their technique and stage presence. Isis was more interested in how they were able to sneak in their Wiccan spells without the audience noticing.

"Of course," Sebastian went on, "tonight, these ladies will need their sleep, so they may prefer a nice, tall glass of milk before bed."

Selena and Sacha once again wiped their silks across the front of their glasses. After both whispered chants, they pulled away the silks. Selena's glass was filled with white milk. Sacha's liquid, meanwhile, had turned into chocolate milk. Both sisters sipped from their glasses.

"You're the next act," Zack said to Isis. "Are you ready?"

"I guess," Isis answered. "I just hope I don't choke."

"You were great during practice."

"Yeah, but that was practice, although I guess technically, this is still practice. You know how hard it is for me to control the energy when I'm nervous." Isis swung her head to Zack. Her face scrunched. "Hey, where did you and my dad go before?"

Zack's eyes went wide. "Um, nowhere. Just some

guy talk."

Isis shook her head. Amazing how for a magician with some of the most unique experiences in his life, Zack was a pretty bad liar. Or maybe she was just good at seeing through him. She was so familiar with both this version of Zack and the one from a whole other reality that neither of them had lived. "Stay in the now, Isis," she mumbled under her breath. She was getting better at putting all those memories behind her, but she wasn't quite there yet.

"Now, what happens if the Quinn sisters wish to save their drinks for later?" Sebastian asked the audience.

Selena and Sacha covered their glasses with the silks for a third time, then pulled the cloths away. The glasses were now empty. Sebastian and the sisters motioned to the glasses in the front of the stage. Where both had been empty, now the one on the left was filled with white milk and the one on the right was filled with chocolate milk. "Then that's exactly what they do." Sebastian pointed to a small boy in the front row. "Young man, why don't you come up, choose a glass, and give it a taste? Remember, milk will help you grow."

With the encouragement of his parents who sat on either side of him, the boy ran from his seat to the edge of the stage. He chose the glass with chocolate milk, brought it to his lips, and took a sip. His eyes opened wide. He held it up for the audience and nodded his head up and down. The audience exploded in cheers.

"I knew they were going to pick that boy," Isis whispered to Zack. "I saw him watching your opener from his seat. He is so cute."

Sebastian's voice boomed through the speakers. "Let's give another hand, ladies and gentlemen, for the Quinn sisters! While we're at it, let's also have a round of applause for our young taste tester!"

Selena and Sacha took big bows, then skipped to the backstage. Sacha was the first to run past Isis and Zack, making a beeline for the dressing room. No doubt she'd want to change her makeup for their next routine. Selena stopped in front of Isis. With both hands, she gave Isis' cheeks a loving squeeze.

"Nice job, Mom," Isis said through a genuine smile.

"Thanks, Sweetie." Selena took Isis' hands. "How are you feeling?"

"I'm okay. Just a little nervous."

"I'm sure you'll be fine. Just remember to stay focused on the energy. We'll all be right here if you need us." Selena rushed to the dressing room to prepare for her next act. Isis' attention returned to the stage.

"And now for something really special," Sebastian announced on the stage. The excitement in his voice resonated throughout the theater. "The youngest member of The Witches of Vegas is about to come out here and amaze you as she shows off two skills at the same time. Please put your hands together for the future goddess of magic, *Isis!*"

A light melody played throughout the theater. Isis took a step toward the audience's view. She felt Zack's hand on her lower back. "Have a nice flight," he whispered.

"Funny." Isis looked back at Zack who looked at her through wide eyes. "What is it?" she asked.

"I'll tell you later." Wow. He definitely had

something on his mind. At least it wasn't anything dangerous. If it were, his eyes would have been even wider.

Isis strolled out onto the stage to a smattering of applause. She passed Sebastian who was strolling offstage. They made eye contact as he gave her a quick smile and a nod. Isis took her place center stage. She couldn't see the crowd due to the bright stage lights, but maybe that was a good thing. It was hard to focus while seeing thousands of faces all staring her way. That would be especially the case tonight for a reason the audience would never know.

It was Sebastian's idea for Isis to use this practice of her witchcraft to conquer a fear from the past. More than once, enemies used fire in an attempt to harm or kill Isis. The first time was when she was nine years old and she first discovered her Wiccan connection. It freaked out her foster family and, thinking she was possessed by the devil, wanted to burn the evil out of her. Then the wicked Wiccan vampire Valeria used fire as a weapon. In the other reality, Isis had faced Valeria's flame a few times. Most recently it was Valeria's follower, Erisa Cross, who tried to take Isis' life by pitching a fireball at her face.

All those experiences left Isis irrationally uneasy even when she smelled smoke. She had created illusions of fire on stage before, but they were always just an illusion, and those never bothered her. They didn't have the acrid odor that caused her eyes to sting. Tonight, she would stand in front of the audience and create the real thing. Could she make actual fire and be its master without freaking out? Easier said than done. But what's life without mystery? Time to find out. The audience was waiting.

"Lighter than air," Isis whispered to the energy crackling around her. "Lighter than air."

She no longer felt the ground beneath the soles of her sneakers. The audience was now looking up at her. Isis was floating like a balloon. It was a spell she had mastered. The hard part was in splitting her attention on two spells at once. Especially the one she was about to create. Isis held out her arms in front of her and focused.

"Lighter than air. Create fire," she chanted while forming the picture of what she wanted in her head. She mumbled the chant again and again.

Three fireballs appeared in front of her. They were each the size of baseballs and sizzled with snake-like hisses. The crowd's "ooh" meant they could see them, and maybe smell them too. Isis stretched out her arms and pointed her palms up underneath the three fireballs. She then concentrated on having the flames rotate in a circular motion. To the audience, it looked like she was juggling the fire. All the while, she kept part of her attention focused on her levitation spell.

Isis had been worried she'd freeze up, yet so far, it was going well. She peeked at Zack. After all of his encouragement, he had to be thrilled to see her handling the fire so easily. To her surprise, his attention was on the theater's floor. He was past the backstage curtain and in sight of the audience, a complete "no-no" during a performance. Zack understood that better than anyone, yet he was too distracted to even notice where he was standing. Someone was there in front of the stage, but Isis couldn't make out the person.

Sacha had mentioned something about a girl hitting

on Zack, but she also said he rejected her advances. That couldn't have been who had his attention. Could it? No, it definitely wasn't that, not when he was waving the others over. Isis didn't have any need to feel suspicious of Zack. He had proven his love for her many times. But Sebastian and Selena stepping onto the stage did raise her concerns.

"Concentrate, Isis," she mumbled. "You're almost done."

To quote her dad, *time to bring it home*. Isis willed the three fireballs to merge into one large sphere. She made it rise above her head. Isis spread her arms. The heat from the flame caused her to sweat. In her mind, she visualized the fireball exploding into hundreds of sparks like fireworks. A loud bang was followed by cheers from the crowd below. So far, so good. Her use of the energy proved successful, as did her personal confrontation with her fear.

Isis focused on slowly lowering herself to the stage floor. Seconds later, her feet touched. She raised her arms to the loud cheers that rocked the theater. She peeked over to the end of the stage to Zack. Whoever he was looking at now had the full attention of Selena and Sacha as well. Selena was squatted and speaking to whoever was in the darkness in front of the stage. The apprehension on their faces did not escape Isis' notice.

Sebastian rushed to her side with the mic in-hand like a man on a mission. "Let's have another hand for Isis!" he announced.

The crowd applauded. Isis took a bow, then eyed Sebastian. Something wasn't right; she could sense it. Sebastian always smiled when addressing the audience, but not this time.

"Ladies and gentlemen," he continued, "The Witches of Vegas are not just a show made up of talented magicians. We are also a family. Right now, a family situation has come up, so we must cut the show short." The audience groaned and booed. Understandable after less than fifteen minutes of "magic." But, damn, this may have been Isis' best use of the energy on the stage, and instead of a buzz in the air, all she heard were boos.

The lights in the theater came on. Isis could now see who was standing near the stage holding the family's attention. The older and well-built man with the blond ponytail made her gasp.

"Paul!" Isis exclaimed.

The vice president and head of the task force for New Salem. He had traveled all the way to Vegas to see their show once before, and he did it in support of a family under his charge. This time, he wore a far more serious and official look to him.

"Please accept our apologies," Sebastian said to the audience. "You will receive a full refund for tonight's show. We hope to make this up to you soon. Meanwhile, we ask that you make your way out of the theater in an orderly fashion. Thank you for your understanding."

"Dad," Isis whispered to him. "What's going on?"

Sebastian eyed Paul from the distance. "I have no idea, but for Paul to come all this way, and ask us to stop the show, something major must have happened in New Salem."

"Is he here by himself?"

"He says he's not."

Sebastian and Isis joined the rest of the family. Isis

exchanged a confused glance with Zack. Paul walked up the stage steps, watching the disappointed audience leave through the exit doors in the back and on each side.

Selena looked up into the almost six-foot-tall man's face. "Okay, Paul, we just ended the show and sent everyone home. Now you have our attention. Can you please tell us what this is about?"

"Is everything okay back in New Salem?" Isis asked.

"Isis." Paul straightened his back. His unblinking eyes fixed on her. "The president is here and needs to meet with you immediately. You are to accompany me to the hotel's conference room where she is awaiting your arrival. Your guardians may join us as your advocates."

"The president wants to meet with *me*?" Isis looked to the others, then back at Paul while biting down on her bottom lip. Her hand grabbed onto Zack's. "Do you need my help, or did I do something wrong?"

"Isis." Paul's eyes narrowed. "This will all go much smoother if you come to the conference room without any trouble."

"Well, damn, this sounds serious," Sacha said through a smirk. "Can we at least get changed first?"

"Take all the time you need," Paul replied. "You aren't invited. Neither is Zack."

Zack's head darted. "Why not?"

"What in the world is this about?" Sebastian's usual friendly tone had disappeared.

Paul stepped to the side, exposing the aisleway and the backdoor. The theater was near empty. "Please," he said in what was clearly not a request.

Selena wrapped her arm around Isis' shoulders as they, and Sebastian, followed Paul down the steps and up the aisle. Isis peeked back at Zack and Sacha. Neither of them had moved. The confused looks on their faces matched the butterflies she felt in her stomach.

Chapter Three

"*Sacha!*" Zack shouted at the dressing room door. "We have a problem!"

The door swung open. Sacha ran out. Zack pointed at the Sapphire general manager, Jerry Blanco, storming down the hallway. A red vein protruded across where his hairline once existed. The disheveled black three-piece suit did little to cover the extra pounds he put on since The Witches of Vegas last worked for him.

"Good evening, Mister Blanco," Sacha sang, clearly expecting an explosion.

"Where's Sebastian?" Blanco said between deep huffs.

"Sebastian and my sister have been called away," Sacha responded. "Is there anything we can help you with?"

"You can answer one real simple question." Blanco's pace came to a screeching halt in front of Sacha. He jabbed a hairy finger just inches from her face. "*Are you freakin' kidding me?*" His volume nearly shook the entire hallway. "You ended the show soon after it started and then gave away the entire gate? What the hell are you people thinking?"

Zack moved to the side, trying to escape the smell of beer and salmon on the general manager's breath. "We had an, um, unexpected emergency."

"As I recall, this troupe always had a lot of those, but I've never seen one come up in the middle of a performance." He flicked the back of his hand against Zack's chest. "You, of all people, should understand that. You were practically brought up on the stage."

"I...I do understand, but the situation really couldn't be helped."

"And what situation is that?"

Blanco shot his evil stink-eye yet again at Zack, waiting for a response. But Zack had none to offer. He could have told the truth, but it was doubtful that "the vice president of a hidden village in the swamp forests of Sweden that housed witches from all over the world just demanded an immediate meeting" would fly. Instead, he just shrugged.

The general manager's face whipped to Sacha. After a moment of thought, she shook her head. "Nah, I have nothing."

"I can't believe I took another chance on the goddamned Witches of Vegas after you burned me before. More than once, in fact."

"Whoa, hold on one sec! Took a chance on us?" Sacha stormed closer to the general manager, invading his personal space. "No, sir, you created a mini golf course attraction based on The Witches of Vegas. You did that without our permission, by the way, and it ended up becoming super popular!"

Sacha waved a hand toward the stage. "This isn't you taking a chance on us. This is you trying to cash in on our name being out there again! Go ahead. Tell me I'm wrong."

Zack's eyebrows rose while he took a step back. He had no idea Sacha had it in her to be so serious, and forceful. From Harry Blanco's stunned face, he didn't expect it either. She was right about the themed mini-golf course being popular. Zack and Isis were finally able to get in and play after their fourth day in the hotel. That was only because it was twenty minutes before the mini-golf course's closing time. They were both surprised to see no depictions of their coven, only cardboard cutouts of generic cartoon witches on each hole.

Blanco rubbed a hand across his forehead. "Am I right in betting you'll be canceling the rest of your run? Again?"

"That is probably the case," Sacha replied. "Would it help if I said we're genuinely sorry?"

Blanco's glance at Sacha's flippant sarcasm would have struck her dead if it could.

Zack wanted to say something reassuring, but what? He understood the stress the man dealt with as the general manager, especially if bringing The Witches of Vegas back to the stage was his idea. Their actions tonight would probably have a negative impact on the themed mini-golf crowd as well.

But Sacha was right on both fronts. Vice President Paul and even President Tia came all the way to Vegas to see them. Since neither of them were witches, it had to be a long trip, which meant this was probably something huge. They had to find out what, and as soon as possible. It was now the top priority, even more than the show.

Paul said they were here to talk to Isis. What in the world could that be about? The memories in Isis' head did include intimate knowledge of possible events in the future. Was there something they needed to run by

Isis to see how it played out in that other reality? It was the only possibility Zack could think of, but if that were the case, why was he left out of the conversation? He had the same set of memories running through his brain, and they knew that.

Blanco shook his head, about-faced, and marched up the hallway. "My next stop should be to speak with our corporate lawyer, but it's not like I have a clue where you people live outside this hotel. Needless to say, whether I still have a job by the end of the day or not, you won't be hearing from me ever again."

"Jerry..." Zack called to him, but he still didn't have any idea how to make this right. An apology wouldn't mean a thing to a man forced to refund six weeks' worth of show tickets to sold-out audiences.

The general manager stopped in his tracks. "Just clear all your stuff from the theater and check out of the hotel by the end of the day." Blanco turned a corner. His shadow followed him down another hallway that led to the lobby.

A pang of guilt slapped Zack's heart at the trouble they had caused for the poor guy.

Sacha snatched Zack's hand. "I think you and I could use some air, don't you?"

She didn't wait for an answer. The hallway suddenly blurred, then faded. The silence was replaced by the sound of engines and beeping horns. Zack inhaled the fresh air through his nose. He glanced up at the huge skyscrapers and neon signs. They were outside The Sapphire and looking down the strip at all the various resort hotels.

"So, where are we going—"

Zack let out a gasp, taken by surprise by who he

saw on the sidewalk across the busy street. Five teens, which included three boys that were all the size of linebackers, strolled along laughing and joking without a care in the world. Zack recognized one boy's jet-black mullet hairstyle. It belonged to Glen Dobbs. Glen was the bane of his existence during middle school and the year and a half he spent in Las Vegas' high school. He singlehandedly made Zack the joke of the entire school with names such as "Nerdini" and "Magic Dork" despite being in the audience with his family for "The Amazing Herb Galloway Show" several times.

Zack turned his body, hoping Glen would be far down the block without ever noticing him. His nervous behavior caused a sideways glance from Sacha. "Everything all right?"

Despite all he had been through against *real* world-changing threats, seeing Glen Dobbs still made him anxious. It helped that Zack spent over a year across the world. Luckily, there were no Glenn Dobbs in New Salem to worry about.

He had seen Glenn one time walking into the theater during their first series of return shows nine months ago. It caused all of his anxieties to resume. Zack asked Sebastian and Selena if he could not open the show that day and just work behind the curtain. He claimed a stomachache. Despite their confusion, his request was granted. He promised himself he would not do such a thing again.

"Yeah, I'm good." Zack peeked over his shoulder. Glen had disappeared into the crowd of people across the street. He asked his question again. "Where are we going?"

Sacha shrugged. "I guess for a walk. We need

something to distract us from some all-important meeting with our coven that we were left out of yet again."

"Can you—" Zack couldn't believe he was even suggesting such an idea, not after Paul chastised them the last time he talked Sacha into this. "—do your witch thing to listen in on them?"

"You don't think I tried in the dressing room?" Sacha flashed Zack a devious smirk as they strolled. "I couldn't see or hear them, which means they brought along a witch, or maybe a few, who cast a privacy spell. I'll bet they're using enchanted crystals."

"Damn. What could it possibly be about?" Besides his concern for Isis, Zack's curiosity was at an all-time high.

Sacha stopped in her tracks and looked at a large electronic billboard displayed high up on the wall of a nearby hotel and casino. The adults in their coven never spent as much time walking the strip as Zack and Isis, which meant this may have been the first time Sacha had seen this particular billboard.

The rectangular image featured a plump man seated on a stool with a microphone in his hand. He wore ruby red glasses and a huge smile that showed off his teeth, which had started to corrode. The longhaired black wig and white cape spoke volumes to his eccentricity. Scrolled across the bottom of the screen was the text, "Simon the Vampire, exclusively at The Sky King Lounge." The words faded and were replaced by new text that read, "Listen to the history and world views of an undead vampire with an alternative lifestyle."

"So, this is why Simon stayed behind when we

returned to New Salem?" Sacha asked through a sarcastic grin. "To sit on a stool and talk about being a gay vampire?"

"He does a full hour, six nights a week," Zack replied. "Forty minutes talking about it, twenty minutes taking questions from the audience."

Sacha's eyes squinted. "And people actually pay to see this?"

"Isis and I wanted to get tickets while we're in town so we could surprise him."

"Why didn't you?"

"We tried, but the show is sold out for months."

"Oh. In that case, I'm happy for him." Sacha dropped her head and shook it. "Hopefully, he moves on before anyone realizes he doesn't age and it's not just him playing a lame character with a flaming big mouth."

"You're poking fun at him for talking about being gay?" Zack eyed at the back of Sacha's head with surprise. "That's a bit hypocritical considering who *you're* dating in New Salem."

"With me it's different." Sacha threw out her arms as if she were being showered with applause on stage. Her gaze never left the billboard. "I go wherever the wind takes me. And in New Salem, it takes me to Carolyn's amazingly firm thighs."

Wow, that was more information than Zack needed to know. Best to change the subject before his pseudo primary caretaker went into more detail on where else the wind took her. "Should we head back? I'd really like to know what's going on."

A fog suddenly rolled in out of nowhere. Within seconds it had become thick to the point Zack couldn't see anything up the block. He had seen fogs engulf the strip, but not like this. This one was rapid and looked like the ones caused by rainstorms. Yet, there wasn't a single cloud in the sky.

"Yeah, I'm up for that. Let's go find out why they came all this way just to talk to my sixteen-year-old niece, and why we couldn't be there."

Zack tilted his head. Sacha's voice had echoed as if she were miles away. Sacha was still staring up at Simon's billboard. The abrupt weather change must have escaped her notice. If he didn't know better, he'd think she used her Wiccan connection to create it. "Sacha, any idea what's up with this fog?" he asked.

Sacha turned around to face him. "Zack?" Her head spun from far left to far right. "Zack, where did you go? Are you playing magician games with me or something?"

Zack waved his hands. "Sacha, what are you talking about? I'm right here."

He could barely make her out from only inches away due to the thickness of the fog. Zack tried to reach for her, but his arms wouldn't move. Neither would his legs. "What the hell's going on?" Zack's heartbeat achieved a staccato rhythm. Sweat poured down his forehead, but he couldn't move his hands to wipe it. "Sacha, what is this? What's happening?"

Sacha's face was wide with panic. She spun in every direction. Her mouth moved, but Zack couldn't make out a word she was saying. He screamed her name, but he couldn't hear his own voice either.

Sacha shut her eyes. Her mouth moved in what had to be a chant. She was tapping into the energy. Good. Hopefully it would bring answers to whatever was happening here—

A moment later, Zack could no longer see Sacha, or anything, in front of his face. Only thick, white fog.

Then, almost as quickly as it came, it dissipated.

Zack was able to wiggle his fingers and toes, which was a relief. But a glance around revealed he was no longer on the strip. He was in a small and empty room with white walls, a white floor, and what looked like a clear glass ceiling. Past that ceiling was the same fog, but it held a green hue. There was no furniture in the room. Also, no windows or even a door. An odor much like fresh paint filled the room. It made Zack's nostrils itch.

This was the ultimate escape room worthy of a magician such as himself. Except when Zack looked along every crevice along the walls and floor, he couldn't find a single trace of a starting point. All he saw were clear surfaces. He had no idea what to do. None of this made a lick of sense.

Chapter Four

Paul led Isis and her folks from the theater and through the entire first floor of The Sapphire Resort. It was a slow and awkward walk until they finally reached the conference rooms. The vice president never uttered a word the entire time. Isis' anxiety had hit an all-time high. What could this possibly be about? Whenever the president had called for Isis in the past, it was to probe for information about the other reality's future. But this felt different. This time, maybe because of Paul's intentional silence, Isis had a sense like she was being escorted to the principal's office, or the interrogation room of a police station.

The Sapphire's conference center had a large circular hallway, off which six sets of double doors led to conference rooms. Paul knocked on the double door under the placard which read "Conference Room A." He pulled open one of the two doors and held it for Isis and her folks to enter. President Tia—perhaps the only twenty-year-old in the world in charge of an entire land—was seated behind a long rectangular table facing the door. All other tables were folded up and leaned against the back wall of this banquet-sized room. A small open laptop faced Tia.

"Good afternoon, Madam President," Sebastian said firmly. "Can you please tell us what this is about?"

"Of course." Tia motioned to the three chairs

facing her from the opposite end of the table. "Please have a seat." Her usual presidential smile was absent from her greeting.

Once in the room, Isis felt a slight hum on all sides. She sensed the vibration around the entire family. It meant the Earth's energy surrounded them and was in use. She peeked down at the beige carpeting and noticed a tiny round bauble in the corner, which had a shine from the overhead fluorescent lights. It was an enchanted crystal. To work, it had to be one of five in the room each placed at an equal distance from one another. Isis' head spun to every corner. Wherever those crystals sat, they also had to be under the control of a witch.

Standing several feet behind Tia was the twenty-something witch who'd emigrated as a child from Russia to New Salem. She was one of the village's most powerful witches just behind Isis, her family, and of course, the resident doctor, Mac. She was also a member of Paul's New Salem Task Force charged with looking after the village's safety. Yet, despite being the most powerful member of his team, instead of watching over their people, she was here in Las Vegas. Not a good sign at all.

"Hey, Natasha," Isis said.

"Hello," the woman responded in her thick accent. "Please sit."

Natasha always had a friendly and informal relationship with Isis and her family. But not today. Isis took another step farther, as did her folks. She sensed the concerns in each of them that mirrored her own.

Isis sat in the end seat on the left from the other two. She focused on the energy, just in case, but she could barely feel it. It was a good chance Natasha was using the crystals to dampen everyone else's connection. Selena sat on the middle chair and clutched Isis' hand under the table. Sebastian stayed on his feet behind the chairs which held his wife and daughter.

Paul marched to the opposite side of the table and stood to Tia's right. "Have a seat," he said to Sebastian.

"If it's all the same, I'd rather stand," came the reply. Her dad was definitely on guard, and on edge. Isis felt the same way.

Paul's grimace tightened. Before he could respond or react, Tia grabbed his wrist. "Paul, it's okay," she said. "He may stand if he wishes." The vice president nodded and stepped back.

Selena let go of Isis' hand and sat up straight. "Okay, we are here. What is going on?"

Tia smacked her palm against the table, then leaned their way. "First, let me make clear that you are all residents of New Salem in good standing. Therefore, we are pledged to help you in any way we can. We are on your side." Her eyes panned onto Isis. "But to do so, we will need complete and open honesty. Understand that only by knowing everything can we determine the best course of action moving forward."

"In other words," Paul added, "no lies and no games."

"We're still not understanding what this is about," Sebastian replied. "You told us it has something to do with Isis?"

"It does," Paul abruptly responded. "Isis, can you tell us your whereabouts last night at approximately…" Paul shut his eyes in thought, then reopened them. "It would have been around nine p.m. your time."

"My whereabouts?" Isis sat as far back as the chair would allow. A moment of confusion and anxiety left her blank. She had to dig into her mind to recall the events of last night.

"Nine o'clock. That was after our practice for today's show. We all had dinner at the hotel restaurant, then Zack and I went out for frozen yogurt. After that, we hung out in his hotel room." Her gaze swung to her folks. "We just talked and cuddled, nothing else."

"Were you ever out of Zack's sight?" Paul asked in an accusatory manner.

"I may have gone to the bathroom once or twice, why?"

"At what time?"

"What time did I go to the bathroom?" Isis thought about it. "I don't remember."

Tia and Paul exchanged a glance. As did Selena and Sebastian. Tia eyed the screen in front of her and tapped her fingernails against the table.

"With all due respect," Sebastian said, "are you going to tell us what this conversation is about? Other than Isis' bathroom habits, that is."

"If you're accusing Isis of something," Selena jumped in, "I think we have a right to know."

Tia exchanged another glance with Paul before speaking up. "Let's try another approach. Isis, do you know the name, John Horace?"

"John…" A coldness ran through Isis' body. She never expected to hear that name ever again, especially out of the mouths of people from New Salem. "Yes…I know who he is."

"John Horace?" Selena's head tilted toward Isis. "Who is he?"

41

Isis' brain flooded with memories she had pushed aside, never thinking she'd need, or want, to access again. "They called him Johnny. That was...Nikki's brother."

"Nikki?" Sebastian asked. "Wasn't she—"

"My-my foster mother before you saved me from them." Isis took three deep breaths to calm herself down. It was a technique she learned from Doctor Mac in New Salem, but it was barely working. Her left hand balled up into a fist while her right foot tapped the floor at a rhythmic pace. "He was in jail for life. I never knew for what, but I heard a little bit when they talked about him. He did some really bad stuff to women...to everyone."

Paul placed his hands on the table and peered toward Isis. His face was scrunched, filled with suspicion. "Have you met him, Isis?"

Isis shut her eyes tight. She wrapped her arms around her midsection. "Oh my God..."

"Isis?" Sebastian said in a low and concerned tone. "It's okay. You can answer the question."

"Yes, I met him when I was eight." Her jaw shook as she spoke. "Their sister died, so he got a day pass for the funeral and wake. The wake was at Nikki's place. It was a long day, so I went to my room. He followed me in there and shut the door. He asked me my age." Isis pushed her chair away from the table. Her voice cracked. "When I told him, he said it had been a long time in there and any age would do."

An arm wrapped across the back of Isis' shoulders. It was Selena's. "Isis..." The words trembled out of her mouth. "Did he...did he rape you?"

Isis' head suddenly felt as if it were being squeezed

in a vise. Keeping her composure was becoming more difficult by the moment. "He covered my mouth with one hand and stuck the other one in my pants. The way he touched me down there, I remember it hurt so much. He told me to stay quiet, and then he took his hand off my mouth and reached for his belt buckle. But then their mom called for him to hear the reverend speak."

"What happened then?" Selena whispered in her ear, her voice filled with dread.

"Nothing. He just left the room. I stayed in there, standing against the wall, crying. I-I didn't know what else to do."

"Of course not. You were only eight years old." Sebastian walked to Isis' left side and dropped to his knees next to her. He clutched her hands and looked up into her face. "My God, why didn't you ever tell us about this?"

"I never told anyone." Isis finally opened her eyes. "That's not true. After the wake, I saw Nikki alone in the kitchen. I told her."

Seeing the look on her dad's face as if he had just been punched in the breadbasket nearly brought her to tears. She didn't dare look at Mom, who wrapped her arms around her and leaned her forehead against Isis' temple.

"What did she do when you told her?" Selena's squeeze tightened as if she didn't want to hear the answer.

"She slapped me so hard, I fell to the floor. She told me if I ever said anything about it to anyone, she'd toss me out and I'd be living on the street. A few months later, after I turned nine, my connection manifested, and they noticed. That's when, with their neighbors, they tried to set me on fire…in the middle of the street. Then you guys rescued me and took me in. It was all over."

"Oh, Isis." Selena sniffled. She placed her hand against the side of Isis' face and kissed the opposite cheek.

For Isis, she didn't know what was worse, hearing Mom's sobs or Dad's eerie silence. "You gave me a new life and a loving family." She tried hard to form a smile for their sakes. "So, I put the old one behind me. I never thought about it again."

"Isis," Tia called out. Isis looked her way, as did her folks. "I am so sorry you went through this, and at such a young age. I can only imagine what that experience must have done to you."

"It is horrifying," Paul replied with far less compassion.

Damn, Isis was so caught up in telling her mom and dad the story, she almost forgot she was in the middle of an interrogation. Why was Johnny brought up in the first place? What did he have to do with anything now?

Paul exhaled deeply. "However, it is also motive. Isis, you need to compose yourself and prepare to answer some hard questions."

"First, how about you answer one for us?" Sebastian stood from Isis' side and faced the New Salem administration. "What the hell is this all about? Motive for what?"

Paul eyed Sebastian straight in the face, making his intentions not to back down well known. He may not have been a witch, but his deadpan expression was far more intimidating than Sebastian's. Isis was relieved there was a table between them since both men looked ready to come to blows.

"Sebastian, stay calm." Selena rose from her chair. Her hand never left Isis' shoulder, even as she faced the New Salem administration. "Could one of you please explain to us what is going on? Why is this all coming up today?"

"Very well." Tia stood and straightened her back. "Last night, John Horace was killed in prison. The way his cellmate described it, a teenage girl of Hispanic descent stepped through the bars and set Mister Horace on fire. He insisted that the girl did it with her mind."

"Are we taking his cellmate's word for it?" Sebastian asked. "Is he a reliable source?"

"Perhaps, perhaps not," Paul replied. "What we do know is that Horace was found burned to death with his head trapped between the cell's steel bars. The cellmate claims he was pinned to his bed by an invisible force but, otherwise, was left unharmed. That's enough to suspect a Wiccan attack, wouldn't you agree?"

Isis' jaw popped open. Being honest, she wasn't sorry to hear the news at all. She never wanted anything bad to happen to anyone, but she wouldn't shed a single tear for a monster like John Horace. The only problem was that now she fully understood why New Salem administration had come all this way to see her. It wasn't to ask for her help.

"You think I did it." She gasped.

"I don't understand." Selena removed her hand from Isis' shoulder. "How could you possibly think Isis would do such a horrible thing?"

"She has reason, and the ability to do so," Paul answered. "John Horace was housed in one of the most populated maximum-security prisons in this country. It just so happens we set up a former resident of New Salem with a guard position in that facility. Part of his agenda is keeping an eye out for any Wiccan activity and preventing exposure of your kind. We have that sort of placement in several locations deemed high risk throughout the world."

"Unfortunately, this particular incident happened in the middle of the night," Tia added. "Our operative was not on the premises at that time. Perhaps, he could have stopped it from happening, Isis, or talked you out of it. That aside, he could have cleaned the area and erased evidence left behind—"

Isis felt her blood boiling. She wanted to jump across the table and grab them both by their throats. But she knew it wouldn't help the situation or prove her innocence. First, she needed to know why she was a suspect—no, not just a suspect—the prime suspect. They sounded sure, like they had already made up their minds. She tried to take another deep breath, but it wasn't helping.

"Why do you think I did this?" Isis screeched. "My God, am I the only Hispanic teenage girl out there? I'm sure Johnny did much worse to others. Maybe some of them are witches, too."

"Really," Sebastian growled.

"Isis, it's time to come clean." Paul shot her an aggressive glare. "I can hear the anger and rage in your tone. So let me ask one more time, did you enter that prison cell last night and kill John Horace?"

"No, I did not!" Isis screamed. She'd never felt so offended, or accused, in her entire life. This time it was by people who should have known her better. These were supposed to be her friends, her allies, and the protectors of her new home.

"I admit, I never really got over what that monster did to me. Even now, there are nights when I'm trying to sleep, but I can't, because in my head, I still see that smug look he gave me as he walked out of my bedroom. It was like I just didn't matter." Isis closed her eyes and shook her head. A tear squeezed its way from between her left eyelids. "I admit, I've thought about finding and confronting him over what he did to me. Sometimes, I've even thought about how, as a witch, it would be so easy to confront him. Make him feel the same fear and helplessness that he made me feel."

Isis wiped her face, then looked up at Paul. "But I won't do that. Not to myself and not to my family. I'm not a killer, and I decided long ago that it's best to move on with the life I have now. I'm not sorry about what happened, but whoever killed him, it wasn't me."

Paul's eyes narrowed. His lips scrunched with what Isis took as disappointment. "Perhaps we need to begin again."

"I can see it on both of your faces," Selena screeched. "This isn't an investigation. You're looking for a confession. What *is* going on? What do you think you know?"

"Madam President?" Paul said.

Tia tapped a fingernail against the top of the laptop's screen. "There is a camera in the cell block hallway," she explained. "It caught the intruder as she left. Our operative was able to send us a screenshot from the camera *before* it went into evidence."

The president turned the laptop around so the

screen would face their three guests. Isis leaned in, then widened her eyes to where they were ready to pop out of her head. The image was black and white. It was also pixilated. But it was clear enough to make out the face.

It was Isis.

Chapter Five

Zack walked along the walls rubbing his hand against the surface, trying to feel for something, anything. If there was a way to escape, he was determined to find it. How long had he been in this room, anyway? Minutes? Hours? The phone from his back pocket offered nothing but a blank screen. So much for reaching out for help. To make things worse, Zack was sure that cloud covering high above was watching him. It seemed to move in whichever direction he went.

"Is this a test?" Zack shouted. "Why don't you come down here and tell me what you want?"

Damn, he felt like a rat in a maze. He tapped his foot against the floor. The sound echoed, which was strange because his voice did not. If only there was a door somewhere. Even if it had a lock, Zack knew how to pick those. He even kept the set of lock picks his uncle gave him in his wallet. It wasn't due to paranoia; they were simply a memento from the man who raised him, then gave his life to save the world. Not that they'd do him any good getting him out of this trap.

"Okay, I know you're not looking to kill me." This time, his voice bounced off every wall in the room. He gazed up at the cloud covering. "If you wanted to, you would have already, right?"

Still no answer. Zack's only hope was to appeal to

his captor. He needed information so he could figure out his next move. Like it or not, he was at the mercy of whoever brought him here.

"Hey, I know you're a witch. You must be!" Hopefully the person or people were listening. "You must have teleported me here for a reason, and I'd like to know why!"

Damn, still no answer. But he did see a circular movement in the clouds. His captors had to be on the other side. "Listen, there's nothing I can do, so I'm clearly not a threat! I just want to know what you want! Why have you taken me prisoner?"

"You are not a prisoner."

The anxious tone in the voice nearly caused Zack to jump through that cloud covering high above. He spun around to see a short, rotund girl who wasn't there a moment ago. She was close to Zack's age and, although he had never seen her before in his life, she gave him a sense of déjà vu. The wide eyes, dark skin, and braided black hair hanging over her shoulders…Zack knew this girl, but from where?

"You are not a prisoner," she repeated. "But we shall speak with you. Yes, that is what we must do."

A memory from the other timeline shot through Zack's brain like a bullet. He suddenly remembered how the first Zack and Isis interacted with this girl and her Wiccan ability to see into the future. It was that ability which helped the first Isis fix Valeria's perversion of the timeline. Zack knew exactly who this was even though she wouldn't be born for another two hundred years.

"You're Domina, aren't you?"

Another voice spun Zack around for the second

time. "That's not exactly right," it said.

This was someone else Zack's age, or maybe a bit younger. This face Zack was sure he didn't know. His bright green eyes put Zack's to shame. His dark brown hair was uncombed, and his green button-down shirt looked like it had never felt an iron. His light olive skin tone glistened as if he were standing under a bright sun after a long swim.

"Who are you?" Zack barked.

"I'm Harry," the boy said through a smirk similar to Sacha's. "And Domina over there, she's actually a manifestation, or at least that's how it was explained to me."

"A manifestation…" Zack refocused on Domina. "You're *not* the Domina I saw in Isis' memories? The one we knew in the far future?"

"I was she and she is me," Domina answered. "Over two hundred years from now, I am eighty and still spry. My Wiccan senses knew a change to reality from the past was about to catch up. There were only moments to spare before all life would end abruptly. That is when the energy absorbed her into me upon death. We are here to offer a unique individual perspective within the energy."

Zack's face shot up to the cloud covering. He knew enough about the energy surrounding the Earth that gave witches their power. But nothing about this room felt like Earth. Was he inside the energy, if that was even possible? He reached out for Domina, but his hand went straight through her. Because she wasn't actually here.

"I am here," Domina answered the question Zack hadn't asked. "I am also everywhere else at this time."

Zack's tilted his head. "Did you just read my mind?"

"I did not."

"But I didn't ask that question."

"You were about to."

Right, the Domina who Zack knew—or the Zack from the original timeline knew—used her connection to see into the future. If this truly was the energy's manifestation of the original person, it made sense that she would see through time as well.

"It's crazy, right?" Harry said. "She answers my questions before I ask them all the time. As I recall, I also put my hand through her the first time we met."

Okay, Domina he knew. Sort of. But this guy... Zack reached out and touched Harry's chest. He was solid, meaning he was an actual person, not—whatever Domina was supposed to be.

"Who exactly are you?" Zack asked.

"I told you, I'm—"

"Yeah, Harry, I know. I mean, like, where are you from?"

Harry's smirk turned into a full grin. "I'm from New Salem, like you. Although, at this time, I'm not born yet."

"You're from the future?" Zack's gave the comment a moment's thought, then shook his head. "That's not possible. I know everyone who lives in New Salem, both now, and in the future."

"Untrue." Domina shook a finger. "You have memories from a timeline that no longer exists. Things are different now. Some people will be the same, others will be different."

Zack opened his eyes wide and snapped his fingers.

Domina was a manifestation of the original, absorbed into the energy before her death. She mentioned others, a select few. Zack thought back to the girl who warned him of an impending danger almost a year ago. She must have been one of those others. It was the only explanation that made sense.

He ran to the center of the room and looked up at the clouds. "Let me see you!" Zack yelled as loud as he could. "I know you're the one who brought me here!"

"Which one are you talking to?" Harry asked.

"You told me there is a threat coming, that we would have to make a great sacrifice to win!" For the first time, Zack realized there was no clear ceiling. It was just the clouds overhead. "Is that what this is about? If it is, I want to hear it all directly from you!"

A cloud peeled from the covering and slowly descended to the floor. Once it landed, the cloud faded away leaving a familiar girl in its place. It was Isis, but it wasn't Zack's Isis. This one's skin was smooth, but pale. Her brown eyes were filled with experience. This was the Isis who spent two hundred years as a vampire with Zack until she sacrificed herself saving history from the far more experienced Wiccan vampire, Valeria. This Isis shouldn't exist, except for the memories she put into her past self's head, yet this was the second time Zack had met her.

"Whoa!" Harry screeched at the top of his lungs. "You already know her?"

"He does," Domina answered from behind Harry. "This manifestation revealed itself to him nine months, thirteen days, and eight hours ago."

Harry threw up his hands. "Well, damn, and I thought I was special."

"Hello again, Zack." Her tone made her sound like a much older adult than what her body and face showed. "I'm sorry we had to bring you here this way, but it is important that we have your attention. We needed to speak with you first before the others."

"Wait, let me see if I'm getting this." Zack waved his hands in front of his face. "The energy is like a hive mind except for the two of you?"

"Nah, I don't think the energy has any kind of mind at all." Harry gawked at the clouds above. "And it's not just these two. There's a few others."

"How many others?"

"Zack, please stay focused!" Isis demanded.

"Right, right." That definitely sounded more like the Isis he knew. "The last time we spoke, you told me there was a major threat to the world that Isis and I would have to face. You said we had time before it arrived." Zack smacked his hand on top of his head. "That threat is here, isn't it?"

"The situation has arrived," she answered. "The threat to the future of this timeline is here."

"Then why are you first addressing it now?"

"Because our role is to allow reality to continue on, we don't intervene. But we are now at the time where this reality diverges due to an unnatural interference." She shot a finger at Harry. "He can attest to this. He will live through it all."

"I did live through it." The smile melted from Harry's lips. "She wanted to kill Valeria, so she tore open a hole between the dimensions, this one and the Other World. Then she left it open so she could get back."

"She?" Zack asked. "Who are we talking about?"

Harry went on, ignoring Zack's question. "The hole was unstable, and it forced the Earth to stop spinning. Half the world burned, then the other half froze. I believe every witch on Earth tried, but none of them had the power to close that stupid wormhole."

"You're here," Zack pointed out. "People must have survived."

"The people of New Salem—at least those who were left—relocated to an island on the equator which was one of the few areas on Earth that was still habitable." Harry bit his bottom lip as he spoke. "I was just born when we went to that island. We had a good situation, all things considered, but then things changed again. The war in the Other World was over, and the victor came through the hole to claim her prize."

"Wait!" Zack held up a hand. "Which one came through? Was it Valeria?"

Harry shrugged. "We were pretty isolated, and whichever one came out left us alone. The rest of the world…not so lucky. Those who were alive and trying to endure the elements, they were hunted by that Wiccan vampire for their blood. Very few survived. It wasn't long after the air went bad, we were the only ones left, then she came for us." He jabbed a thumb over his shoulder. "That was when they brought me here."

Wow, Zack felt like he had just been slapped across the face. His lunch wanted to shoot up his throat and out of his mouth. After everything he and Isis had gone through, could it really have been all for nothing? The immortal vampire Isis sacrificed her own reality to save the world, and it was doomed anyway. Zack was never a crier, but right now he felt like bawling. Harry may not have known which demon escaped, but Zack had a feeling it was Valeria. Hunting people for blood was her style. It turned out all of humanity would inevitably be destroyed by her after all. But what if it's the other witch who destroys the world? Could nature truly create two such corrupt monsters—

"No," Domina snapped. She walked up to Zack and looked him in the eyes. "What you are about to say is not true. What will happen is not a natural occurrence. It is caused by the timeline being invaded by someone who should not exist, not anymore."

"Another witch who invaded the timeline." Zack's brain went into overdrive. Another witch on Valeria's level, he didn't think that was possible... "Who is it? Where does this witch come from? Someone, please tell me!"

"Zack," the former Isis said. "Focus on all you've seen from my memories. You know exactly who it is."

Zack dug through the second set of memories trapped inside his head. Her clue was specific. She'd said, *someone who should not exist, not anymore.* That meant whoever created the hole, besides having an abnormally strong connection, was also from the previous reality. Zack couldn't think of anyone with a connection that strong except for the immortal Isis herself. It certainly wasn't her. She may have had the strength, but not the lack of heart to be so brutal. Not to mention, she was in the room—sort of—trying to stop the threat.

But Isis was forced into a third reality, the one Valeria created when she went back in time. They had come to refer to it as "The Queen Valeria timeline." It couldn't have been the queen. Sloth and complacency had taken her over. So that left only one other possibility. One witch with a connection strong enough to break barriers. The idea of her existing was perhaps even scarier than Valeria herself.

"Oh no," Zack exclaimed. "It can't be…there's just no way—"

"It is who you believe it to be," Domina replied.

"I don't…I don't understand." Zack pressed a hand against his chest feeling the rapid heartbeat under his skin. "Who I believe it to be can't exist. Her entire timeline was wiped out. How could she be, let alone exist, in *this* reality?"

"She saved herself and fled here before the change could catch up to her." The original Isis walked up to Zack. "Remember, she is as powerful as I was before I ceased to exist."

Zack's head spun from Domina to Isis. This was far more dire than he expected. "Wait, if you *are* the energy, certainly you have the power to stop this from happening, don't you?"

"The energy does not act directly," Isis explained. "Witches are our conduits. They have been chosen by chance to use their connections freely. That is why we brought you here, Zack. You need to let Isis, the family, and all of New Salem know so they can stop her."

Zack eyed the original Isis. "You told me that Isis…my Isis…would be needed to stop a major threat. Will she succeed?"

"We can only hope so." She shrugged. "The Apprentice is from outside this timeline. That means we can't be sure how these events will play out now that we have interfered. However, we have heard echoes. Isis can win, but only with great sacrifice."

"You've mentioned this before, but what does it mean? What sacrifice?" Zack waited, but neither manifestation answered. Harry kept quiet as well. "You said there were others like you. Do they know I'm here? Do they know that you're telling me?"

"This was the only way for us to act," Domina answered, without actually answering. "The time to stop future events is now. Otherwise, for most of humanity, there will be no tomorrow."

Isis gave a look at Harry, one that raised Zack's suspicions. It was a similar look that his Isis had shared both with him and with her family whenever they had an unspoken concern. They shared a lot of information—devastating information, and it terrified him—but they weren't sharing everything. Whatever it was, Zack needed to find out, and fast. As far as he was concerned, this wasn't the time for secrets.

"More will come clear to you," Domina said, answering Zack's thoughts. "But, for now, you must act. The powerful people around you must act. It is time."

"Rally the troops," Isis said.

"I think it would help if I knew more—"

"Enough talking about it!" Harry shouted. He raised a finger in the air. "Time to go to the past and save the future!"

Everything once again turned pure white. Both manifestations were gone. Zack held his hands up in front of his face. They were glowing along with his entire body. So was Harry's.

Chapter Six

Isis stared at the laptop's screen. It displayed a still shot of her face surrounded by a place she had never been to in her entire life, much less last night. Yet, although it wasn't a perfect image, it sure looked like the face and body that stared back at her every single day in the mirror.

"I don't understand." Isis' gaze never left the screen. "This can't be me. I wasn't there. I was here in The Sapphire. I was in Zack's room the entire night."

"We want to believe you," Tia responded. "But the resemblance is hard to dispute."

Isis looked up at her folks. "You know I'd never kill anyone, or expose witchcraft. That's not me. I don't break into prisons. You believe me, don't you?"

"Of course, we do," Selena assured her. "There has to be a reasonable explanation."

"Maybe we could bring Zack here to verify?" Sebastian asked.

"I don't see the point," Paul responded. "I'd expect him to back her up whether it is true or not."

Isis stomped the floor. "*Of course, it's true!*"

Sebastian walked to the long table. He moved in front of Isis as if he was trying to block any accusations from hitting her. "Madam President, Mister Vice President, if I may?" he said in a formal manner. "We have raised Isis since she was nine, so we know her well. When Isis breaks even a minor rule, she becomes distracted, unfocused, and anxious from guilt. Those symptoms linger and progress until she finally breaks and confesses to what she had done. Isis is not a sociopath; she'd never be able to hide the guilt of an actual murder. We've been with her all day, and we saw none of those signs."

"Understood. We've known Isis long enough to judge her strong character as well." Paul swiped his hand over the laptop. "But how do you explain this image?"

"I…can't." Sebastian's eyes locked on the screen. His fingers scratched against the side of his head, which meant he was trying to deduce the riddle. So far, he had nothing.

"Wait! I got it!" Isis waved a forefinger from each hand at her folks. "You're always tracking me whenever you're not around. You'd know if I teleported across the country, right?"

Selena let out a deep sigh. "Isis, we stopped keeping tabs on your location when you turned sixteen. We felt you earned the trust and the freedom. Besides, we were living in New Salem for the last year. There's not that far you could go."

Isis' arms slowly dropped to her side. Her face dropped along with them. God, she wanted to scream so badly, except she needed to show everyone in the room that she was in control of her emotions. That she was not some sort of psycho witch who would break into a prison and kill someone out of a seven-year revenge plot.

"We need to get ahead of this," Tia said. "I'm not saying it was right, but if you did do this, there is justification here. Psychological trauma for the pain this man had caused you—"

"I *swear* I was with my family, then Zack the whole night!" Isis placed a hand over her eyes. Her fingers spread out so she could take another peek at the screen. "I know that looks like me, but it's not. I swear to you it's not me. It couldn't be."

"Whatever is truly going on here, Isis," Paul spoke with authority, "your image is now out there. Authorities are looking for you. With the recognition software this country has, and the fact that you have performed in a public venue, it is a matter of time before they track you down as the prime suspect of a murder. If that happens, they will ask difficult questions that could lead to the discovery of the Wiccan world. We cannot allow that to happen."

"What do you suggest?" Sebastian asked.

Paul eyed Isis like an interrogator in a police station. Even if Sebastian and Selena believed her, Isis was sure Paul did not. "For starters, we need to get you back to New Salem immediately. Within our borders, you will not be found. From there, we can conduct our own investigation into the matter—"

"Madam President, Mister Vice," Natasha screeched, pulling everyone's attention to her. "I sense a burst of the Wiccan energy nearby. A witch has teleported in front of this conference room."

Damn, Isis wanted to know what Paul meant by "an investigation." New Salem didn't have a prison. They used a house arrest system, or banishment, whenever necessary. A loud pounding came from the other side of the double doors. Paul reached for the pistol in his holster. Tia nodded to Natasha who waved a hand. The doors swung open. Sacha ran into the room as if she was being chased. Her breathing was heavy and erratic.

"Sacha, what is it? What's going on?" Selena asked her sister in a huff.

"We have a serious situation!" Sacha jabbed a thumb over her shoulder. "Real serious."

"We are dealing with a serious situation in here!" Paul ran around the conference table and stepped in Sacha's way. There was little patience in his tone. "How did you know which conference room we are in? Natasha masked our presence."

"It's the only one with the doors closed, duh!" Sacha waved Paul off. "Whatever this is, put it on hold. Zack is gone!"

"Gone?" Isis dove between Sacha and Paul. "What do you mean gone?"

Sacha let out a deep exhale trying to regain her composure. "One second, he was standing there." Sacha held out two fists as if they were Zack and herself. "The next second…" She placed her left hand behind her back. "Poof, gone! I tried, but I couldn't sense him anywhere. It was like the boy just vanished into thin air."

Everyone looked at Sacha through an aura of disbelief that filled the room. Sebastian broke the silence. "Zack is not a witch. He couldn't just teleport away."

Isis closed her eyes and focused on Zack's thoughts. Thanks to their strong connection she could always sense where he was. But not this time. "Nothing!" she screamed. "I can't sense him anywhere. This happened before, in the other timeline…when

Valeria went back…she erased his existence…"

Isis' body shook. She couldn't feel her legs. She could barely make out Selena screaming her name as she fell forward into Sebastian's arms. The table rattled, which forced Tia to push herself away with her chair. "Sweetie, you need to breathe," Selena said with a hand against the back of her head.

"Isis, try to calm down." Sebastian lowered them both to their knees. "And stop panicking. Zack has not been erased from existence."

Selena took her hand. "He's right. Zack is somewhere out there, and we will find him."

Isis opened her eyes to see her parents' faces. Her breathing slowed which meant one of them was using a spell on her. Probably Mom. The table stopped rattling. "How…how do you know this isn't time travel again and Zack wasn't erased?" Isis whispered. "How could you know?"

Sebastian answered loudly. "Because we all still remember him!"

Isis' head rotated around the room. Tia and Natasha were behind the table eyeing her with concern. Sacha stood to the left of Isis' folks with Paul on their right. Dad had a great point. After Valeria removed Zack from their history, no one had ever heard of him. "What do we do?" she asked.

"Don't worry, Kiddo," Sacha said, "we're not leaving here without Zack."

"I beg to differ." Paul's commanding voice filled the room. "Perhaps not all of you, but Isis needs to return to New Salem immediately."

"No!" Isis roared in a way she had never heard herself before. "I'm not leaving until we find him."

"Isis, listen to me." Tia leaned over the table. "I promise you, we will do everything in our power to find Zack. But, right now, it is not safe for you to be here."

"She's not wrong," Sebastian said. "We do need to get you to the safety of New Salem before it's too late."

"But we can't just…I can't abandon him." Isis gasped at a sudden thought that had snuck into her head. It couldn't be coincidence that the one and only alibi to her whereabouts last night was missing. Whoever set her up, if that's what happened, must have also abducted Zack. But who…and why?

"We're not abandoning Zack," Sacha snapped. "Selena and I can stay here and find him. Right, Sis?"

"I'll stick with Isis." Sebastian gave Paul a suspicious glance. "To keep an eye on her once we return."

Selena nodded with a face filled with determination. "Isis, get everyone back to New Salem now. Sacha and I can teleport ourselves—and Zack—once we locate him. It is the best plan right now, all things considered."

Isis stared at the frozen image on the laptop's screen. She'd never seen such cold eyes in a reflection, or in a picture of herself. To Isis, that was proof this girl couldn't have been her, but it wasn't enough proof, not when the figure was so exact. She didn't want to leave without Zack. She had no idea where he was, but it was a good bet he was in trouble. Wiccan trouble. She didn't have much of a choice, though. Not unless she was willing to blatantly defy all the authority figures in her life.

She shut her eyes and focused one more time on Zack. "Please feel me," she mumbled. "Where are you?"

A voice popped into her head. "I'm here!"

Isis opened her eyes wide. "Zack!"

"Zack?" Sebastian's head spun her way. "You hear him? Where is he?"

"There!" Natasha pointed to the door.

A white circle that looked like a hole filled with smoke appeared. It then faded just as quickly. Two boys appeared in its place. One of them, Isis didn't recognize, but the other she knew well. "Oh my God, Zack!" she screamed.

She ran with her arms stretched out, ready to envelop him and never let go. Zack snatched her wrists before she could. "Isis, wait!" His voice shook. "Please listen to me."

Her mouth popped open. After living through two realities, Zack had to know her well enough to understand how much their physical touch meant to her. That was especially the case now after he had just disappeared. She couldn't imagine what revelation he could offer that was more important than knowing he was safe, and she needed to embrace him for it.

"Zack," she muttered. "What is it—"

"It's *you*, Isis!" he gasped. "You did it…or you're going to do it."

"What do you mean?" Isis took a step back. How could he have even known what happened at the prison? "You were with me all last night—"

"No, not you, the other you!" His jaw trembled. "*That* you."

"Zack," Selena interrupted. "What are you trying to say?"

"Oh, jeeze," the other boy snorted. "He's trying to

say that The Apprentice is *here!*"

"Yeah, that," Zack said through deep breaths. "The Apprentice is in our reality. She's the threat I was warned about."

Isis let her arms drop to her sides. Nothing he could have said would be more important than knowing he was safe. Nothing, except for that. "The…the…" God, she couldn't even say the name. "How is that possible?"

Isis flipped around and flashed another glance at the screen. The facial expression on the girl was so cold and detached with eyes that were blank. The image was gray, so she couldn't tell that the skin tone was far more faded than her own, the side effect of being a two-hundred-year-old vampire. But it suddenly made sense. She looked exactly like Isis because she was Isis, but a different Isis who should never have existed in the first place.

"The Apprentice?" Selena gave a curious gasp. Her attention also turned to the screen. "Isis, you told us about her. She was from the timeline Valeria created, the one where she was queen."

"You also told us she was a vampire," Sebastian added. "And, more importantly, wiped out along with her entire reality."

"People, please. That is her." Harry walked up to the laptop and smacked a knuckle against the screen. "She escaped by coming here before she evaporated into nothing."

"Excuse me," Paul barked. "Who, exactly, are you?"

"I'm Harry," he answered, looking directly into Paul's narrowed eyes, unfazed by the intimidating tone or the hand nearing his sidearm.

"Paul, be warned." Natasha's hands suddenly glowed yellow. "He is a witch. His connection is strong, just like theirs."

"Whoa, hold up!" Zack ran in front of Paul, waving his hands. "Harry is, um, from the future. He's here to help...I think."

Sacha's eyebrows rose. "I'm sorry, but did you just say he's from the future?"

"It's true. I come from a bunch of years ahead of today," Harry answered. "And, yes, I'm totally here to help." He walked to Isis, staring her up and down as if he was seeing an old acquaintance for the first time in a long while. "Um, hi there," he said.

"Do we...will we know each other?" Isis asked. Harry nodded. "You're from which timeline? The one with The Apprentice?"

"Those events never existed, thanks to you. Remember?" Harry glanced around at all the confused faces in the room. He rolled his eyes. "I am from this timeline. Obviously."

"I have so many questions right now," Sacha said, shaking her head.

"I think we all do," Tia said in her presidential tone. "But we need to pull it together. Selena and Sacha, if you would please use the energy and return us to my office in New Salem?"

"Will do," Selena nodded in response.

Tia walked around the table and up to Harry. "Once there, we would very much like to hear your story."

"Great," he replied. "Because I would very much like to tell it."

Chapter Seven

"So, you claim to be from our future." Tia, seated in her oversized cushioned chair, folded her hands across the executive desk. "Exactly how far in the future?"

"I don't really know." Harry waved a hand to the window. "All this was gone by the time I was born."

Tia had plenty of witches, and non-witches, sitting across from her in the few years she had been president. Many had strange and unusual stories to share. But none were as strange and unusual as this one. On the outside, she kept her presidential posture. Having Paul standing to the left, and her future husband, the tall, muscular, and amazingly handsome Jasper on the right, did help give off that presence. But on the inside, an anxiety ran down Tia's spine like a waterfall after a storm. This boy from the future had just assured everyone in the room, which included the powerful Witches of Vegas standing behind him, that the world was about to be destroyed. She had no reason to doubt him.

The Witches of Vegas. It had been Tia's idea to invite them all to immigrate into New Salem. That was in spite of Paul's misgivings on the idea. It turned out to be the right move. They endeared themselves quickly to the residents, and each contributed much to the village. They also made life in New Salem far more interesting.

This group had been through a lot, particularly the two youngest members. Their past, and even their future, tended to show up unexpectedly and create worldwide consequences. It was amazing that Zack, the one non-witch among them, was the most composed. That was the case even with his Wiccan girlfriend's arms tightly wrapped around his waist.

"The Apprentice," Tia said. "As I understand it, she is a two-hundred-year-old vampire version of Isis, correct?"

Harry nodded. "The Apprentice is from a timeline created when Valeria went into the past to make herself queen. Before Isis fixed time, she was tortured, then trained to be Valeria's apprentice. That's how she earned the name."

"Isis met her!" Zack chimed in. "Well, not this Isis, but her in the original reality, the one who gave her the memories, which she also gave to me."

"The Apprentice helped me, um…her." Isis' grip around Zack tightened. "She did it so everything could be fixed and Queen Valeria would never exist."

"And now she is here." Paul rubbed his temples. His usual calm and cocky demeanor had disappeared.

Tia looked over her left shoulder at New Salem's resident soothsayer. "Jasper?"

"I have had no dreams depicting upcoming events related to this moment," Jasper folded his arms across his chest. Jasper's deep voice and African accent radiated. "But we are dealing with time travel. That is far beyond what I can foresee."

"Regardless—" Paul looked to Harry. "—if you are truly from New Salem's future, members of your family must be here now. Who are they?"

"I'm not sure if I should answer that," Harry responded. "That sort of question could change history."

"Isn't that why you're here?" Sacha asked, leaning against the back wall. "To change history?"

"Well, yeah, obviously. But not such a huge change where I won't be born." Harry sank into his seat. "What I can tell you is that I was really young when the last members of the village relocated. I don't remember this land at all."

"Last members?" Paul asked.

Harry flipped a finger toward Paul, acknowledging his question. "My dad died when I was really young. I think I was three. Death hit a lot of people in New Salem. My mom and sister found habitable land and led the survivors there. I was six when we were attacked. No one survived except for me, and only because my sister hid me when it all went down so I wouldn't be discovered." Harry looked up and smacked his lips. "There's a good chance I would have been found and sucked dry anyway if the energy's avatars hadn't brought me to that room and kept me there."

"Hold on!" Zack broke from Isis' grip and walked to the right of Harry's chair. "How old are you now?"

Harry eyed Zack from his slumped position in the chair. "I'm fourteen."

"You were in that room, all alone, for *eight years*?"

"It may have been eight years." Harry cupped his hands behind his head. "It could have also been a few hours, a few months, or an eternity. Time works so different outside the fabrics of reality, so who knows?"

"I'm afraid we don't," Tia answered.

"Young man," Paul growled. "Would you kindly

sit up?"

"Sorry, guy." Harry pushed himself up in the chair and straightened his back. "Better?"

Wow, this kid was the textbook definition of obnoxious, but it didn't mean his warnings should be ignored. At least that was Tia's take, which she'd have to make clear soon enough. She felt the eyes of Jasper, Natasha, and even Paul, aimed her way. They were waiting for her to make an executive decision on how to proceed.

It wasn't like she had any historical reference for a world devastation-sized threat from an alternate future to fall back on. There was really no telling how far ahead Harry came from, but she suspected it was within their lifetimes. Harry was trying to play it off, but it was clear he recognized them all. It was a good chance Tia would still be president during Harry's childhood. Which meant whatever decision she made in that moment would fail.

Now, however, was not the time for self-doubt. In situations that were alien to her, Tia had a mindset. She'd ask herself what her grandfather would have done during his presidency if presented with the same conundrum. The answer was always the same; he'd put the safety of New Salem and its residents first. Tia placed her palms on the desk and stood from her chair.

"Wherever or whenever she may be from, we need to stop this Wiccan vampire from opening that hole," Tia said to everyone. "We know this won't be an easy task, but we have been forewarned. Hopefully we have enough power and experience in this village to tip the scales."

"It would help to know exactly how long we have."

Paul stood over Harry with his hands on his hips. "Do we know when she opens this wormhole between dimensions?"

"Domina had an idea on it," Harry replied. "She said sometime after overmorrow."

"Overmorrow?" Sacha's face squished. "What does that mean?"

Tia responded. "It's the day after tomorrow, which means we don't have a lot of time. We need to enact a plan now before she attempts to cross over."

Tia peeked past everyone to the front of the office near the door where Sebastian and Selena stood. They were quiet throughout this meeting. It was uncharacteristic for the couple, both of whom were natural take-charge people. She suddenly realized why. Although neither of them spoke, their eye contact meant they were holding a long and deep conversation.

"Sebastian, Selena, please share your thoughts."

After exchanging a nod, Sebastian stepped Tia's way. "We're in agreement. We need to take action and keep The Apprentice from opening that portal." He pointed a thumb at his chest. "However, this is our responsibility. It's our mess to clean up."

Tia had to admit, this family was impressive. But they weren't big on receiving help. In this case, however, they'd have to learn to accept it. "The Apprentice is a danger to us all. That's you, New Salem, and the entire world. We cannot and will not abandon you to face this crisis alone."

"Agreed," Paul added. "The New Salem Task Force stands with you."

"No vote?" Sacha called with a hint of sarcasm. "I thought the village voted on everything."

"This is not the time for a vote," Tia answered. "If The Apprentice succeeds, every life will be forfeited. This is a Wiccan threat. Therefore, it is our role to keep the world safe."

"Thank you," Selena said. "We accept, and appreciate, your assistance."

"Knowing who will confront this threat is not enough." Paul peered down at Harry. "When and where did she open the hole?"

After several silent moments, Harry lifted his head. His eyes popped open, as if he hadn't realized Paul's question was directed at him. "I have no idea," he answered.

"Do you know where she is now?"

Harry shrugged. "No clue."

Tia caught the red vein popping out of her vice president's neck. "First of all, please stand up from that chair while you are being addressed," Paul snarled. He waited until Harry did as was asked. "Now, how do you not know? Isn't this the reason you came from the future?"

"Hey, I wasn't even born when all this started." Harry shrugged again. "It's not like I had anyone in the energy to talk to about it. No history teachers in there, or anything else."

"We may have an idea where to find her," Sebastian chimed in. "The fact that she killed John Horace means she had the exact same childhood experiences as Isis, and that she's on a revenge spree toward those who hurt her before she opens that hole. My guess is she'll be going after her former foster family in the Bronx."

"That's if she hasn't killed them already," Selena

added.

"It's as good of a place to start as any." Paul grimaced at Harry. "I don't suppose you have a plan on how to stop this vampire, do you?"

A sly grin flashed across Harry's face. Tia had a hunch he had been waiting for someone to ask the question.

"That I do have." Harry raised a finger in the air. He eyed every face in the room that was staring his way like a performer about to show off his act. "Vampires have very few weaknesses. But one of those weaknesses, besides really long memories, is that they are just as emotional as the living. So, all we need is something to trigger an emotional memory that'll work as a distraction. Then, in the second we'll have, we sneak enchanted crystals around her and cut her connection."

"Do you know what will distract her?" Paul asked.

"Probably not." Harry turned his back on Paul. He leaned his head toward Isis and her family. "But I'll bet *they* can come up with something. Am I right?"

Isis, who had been quiet throughout most of the meeting, opened her mouth to speak. She was quickly cut off by Sebastian. "We do!" He took Selena by the hand. "We're going to be the distraction."

Wow, no hesitation at all. "Are you sure?" Tia asked.

Isis' head spun toward her parents. "Wait—"

"Yes, it's our best plan," Selena answered, also cutting Isis off. "What Harry is saying about vampires coincides with what we learned from our old mentor, Luther. The Apprentice was Isis until the age of fifteen, which means she will have an emotional connection to us."

Sacha tossed up her arms. "Yeah, okay, I guess I'm in, too."

"No!" Isis stormed between Sebastian and Selena. With her back straight, hands against her chest, and determination on her face, this usually meek girl was angry. It was a new look for her, one that suggested growth. "I would be a better distraction."

"That's a really bad idea," Harry called. "You should stay here."

Isis' nasty glare sent Harry a message. It told him to "butt out."

"I'm the best choice and guaranteed to work as a distraction." She looked around the room with her right hand pressed against her chest. "I'm her. Of course, she'll hesitate if she sees me."

"No chance in hell," Sebastian lashed out. "Harry's right. You need to remain here. You and Zack."

Isis' head shot back. She turned her body to face Selena. "Mom?"

"Sorry, Sweetie," Selena responded. "But all things considered, I am in full agreement. It's better if you stay in New Salem."

"Why?" Isis snapped. "I'm the strongest witch here. You've told me that all my life. Let me prove it!"

From behind, Zack clasped a hand on her shoulder. "Isis, chill out," he whispered. "It's not worth the fight."

"Not worth the fight?" Isis gasped with bulged eyes.

"Isis." Paul stepped toward Isis. "As a reminder, you are a prime suspect in a murder. If she is in the United States, that is the last place on the planet you should go."

"But I didn't do it. We all know that."

Paul raised a hand as a clear warning. "We do. But if you were spotted and apprehended by the FBI, they will interrogate you. And what would you tell them? That a two-hundred-year-old vampire version of yourself from another timeline committed the crime?"

"This is my responsibility! I have to face her again."

"Technically, you never faced her the first time," Harry replied.

From the red cheeks and body twitches, it was clear Isis was getting flustered. As president, Tia needed to say something before this dispute escalated to where this young but powerful witch lost control of her connection. It had happened in the past during moments of emotional stress.

Jasper cleared his throat. His fists were clenched. He must have had the same concern. "Tia," he whispered. "My dream about Isis on fire…I did not know what it meant, but it could be this moment."

"Okay, Isis, let's talk," Tia said in her friendliest presidential tone. "Why do you believe this is your responsibility?"

Isis cupped a hand across her forehead. "I didn't make sure Valeria was dead when I had the chance. That's why she escaped into the past. That's where she changed things, and that's why The Apprentice exists in the first place. Now she's here in our timeline. It was all because I was careless and let my guard down for two seconds—"

"That wasn't you, Isis. It was the other you," Zack explained. He looked up at Tia, trying to ignore Isis' wide-eyed glare. "But it was the other her who told me it would be Isis who would have to face The Apprentice."

Harry raised a hand like a student in class. "She also said she would need to make a huge sacrifice if she did."

"A huge sacrifice," Sebastian repeated. "I'm sorry, but having you as the bait could end badly. I won't take that risk—"

"*I won't screw up!*"

"You don't know that for sure!" Paul shouted. "Maybe you already did screw up. Our best hope for success is to change the plans." The vice president removed the walkie-talkie clipped to his right hip and brought it up to his mouth. "Natasha, Carolyn, could you please come in?"

The office door swung open. Natasha entered, followed by a muscular woman in a green camouflage tank top. She wore a baseball cap of the same design, and a holster on her belt. A handgun rested in that holster. She exchanged a familiar glance with Sacha then marched to the center of the room. Zack jumped out of her way.

"Carolyn," Paul said like a commander addressing his soldier. "Please escort Isis and Zack to Doctor Mac's medical center so they can follow village protocol of a virus check once reentering New Salem's grounds."

"Virus check?" Zack asked. "Since when is that a protocol?"

Carolyn stepped in front of Isis and Zack. She waved a hand to the door.

"No! You can't keep me from following you! Or

force me to go get a checkup just to keep me busy." Isis raised her voice in a way Tia had never seen or heard from this usually timid and somewhat awkward teen. Her bravado, however, to Tia's trained ear, sounded more like desperation.

"Isis…" Sebastian gave the stern warning from under his breath.

Tia felt for the girl. She knew Paul was dismissing them from the conversation even though she probably belonged here. But it was better that both Isis and Zack stayed behind, and this was the best way to make it happen. Technically, New Salem did have a protocol for residents after their visits to other countries, but it was rarely ever enforced. No one knew village protocols—and the best times to use them—better than Paul.

"You may be right, Isis," Paul replied while motioning her adopted parents to stand down and let him handle the situation. "But it is my hope that you will respect the authority of New Salem, as you pledged to do, and comply with what is being asked of you."

Zack suddenly jumped in front of Isis and touched her face. "Hey, why don't we get out of here and let the adults handle this? Okay?"

"For real?" Isis' wide eyes shifted from Zack to her parents. Both stood firm. She then looked to Sacha who simply shrugged. Her head dropped. "Not for nothing, The Apprentice is a two-hundred-year-old immortal version of me. I would think you would want as much power as you can get."

"Even with you, we'd be outgunned," Harry replied. "Power isn't going to win this. They tried that with a whole land of witches."

"More than power, we need a plan," Paul said. "Once in place, we have plenty of ammunition. Sebastian, Selena, and Sacha, you will provide the distraction. Natasha will place the crystals. We can also bring along a few other witches from the village. I will be there to coordinate the efforts."

"Count me in, too," Harry called out. "It's why I'm here."

"Very well, we can use your perspective and your Wiccan power on this mission." Paul paused, then turned to Tia. "If this plan has your approval, Madam President."

"It does." Tia let a slight grin sneak out. Paul was a military strategist long before he moved his wife and daughter—both of whom had a Wiccan connection—to New Salem. As vice president, he formed the New Salem Task Force in order to keep the village safe. But Tia always suspected it was to keep his military wits fresh. In this moment, planning a strategy for a world saving mission, he looked more vibrant than he had in years.

"*His* Wiccan powers?" Isis' hands let off a slight glow. "We haven't seen a single shred of evidence that he even has a connection."

"Isis, be careful," Zack whispered to her, eyeing the glowing hands.

"I sense the energy within him," Natasha said. "I am sure we all do, including you, Isis."

Harry faced his accuser and clapped his hands together. "To the medical center!" he chanted.

A puff of purple smoke formed where Zack, Isis, and Carolyn stood. It cleared as fast as it had come leaving one of the three behind. Carolyn spun her head in every direction and then looked back to the president's desk with her pistol in hand. Tia stepped back. Jasper, being his usual protective self, jumped in front of Tia.

As far as she knew, the crystals in place around her office were active. Natasha used them to form a pentagon of energy that cut off every witch's connection except her own. This was a safety measure used during Tia and Mac's meetings with resident witches. Only Doctor Mac and Isis, the two most powerful witches Tia had ever known, were able to still access their connections within the crystals. Apparently, this boy from the future could be added to the list.

"Whoa!" Sacha screamed.

"Where the hell did you send them?" Sebastian roared. His face had turned red with rage.

"As I said, to the medical center." Harry twirled around and faced the presidential desk where Tia, Paul, and Jasper stood. "So, are we doing this or what?"

Tia responded with a nod. This boy was confident, and maybe a bit brash. He was definitely a product of New Salem.

Chapter Eight

Purple smoke surrounded Zack. He reached for Isis' hand but couldn't find it. This was the second time this morning he was teleported without consent. The smoke cleared as the smell of ammonia filled his nostrils. He and Isis were facing Doctor Mac who had his white lab coat on and a stethoscope around his neck. At the moment, he was scrubbing the metal table in the middle of his medical room with a sanitary wipe. He had a spray bottle in his other hand.

Doctor Mac picked up his head. His dark brown eyes met theirs. "Welcome. I've been expecting the two of you." He strolled around the table and approached his visitors.

"Hey, Doctor Mac," Isis said with a smile. It never mattered how upset or stressed she was, she always dropped the attitude around the doctor. She had even used the word "impressive" to describe him on more than one occasion. The guy may have been tall and had the thickest black curly hair Zack had ever seen on a human head, but he still didn't find him any more impressive than any other witch in the village.

The doctor waved a hand toward the medical table. "Zack, why don't we start with you? I promise, I'll make it quick. I know how uncomfortable you are in here."

Zack walked to the table, although he doubted this

checkup would be quick. Among his many medical degrees, Doctor Mac had one in child psychology. He liked to utilize it to get his patients—particularly the younger generation—to talk about their problems and feelings. Isis appreciated it; she liked talking to him about her life. Zack, not so much.

"Doctor Mac, could you also check to make sure he's not under a witch's spell?" Isis' angered glare at Zack spoke volumes. "It's happened before."

"Under a spell?" Zack stopped mid-step and shot around to Isis. "Why would you think that?"

"Not worth it? Let the adults handle it?" Her voice growled. "You're supposed to be on my side."

"I'm always on your side, Isis."

"My side isn't sending my family into danger." She let out an angry sigh. "I need to get myself over there. I'll back them up whether they want my help or not."

Zack pressed his back against the medical table. Doctor Mac held his right hand in front of him. It let off a white glow.

"Oh, I'm sure they'll be just fine," Doctor Mac said, running his hand a few inches from Zack's body. "Especially with Paul and the task force leading the charge. They have pulled off the impossible before."

Zack's eyebrows rose. "You're all caught up on the situation, aren't you?"

"Doctor Mac, you said you were expecting us," Isis said. "But we were just teleported here. Who contacted you? When?"

"President Tia did just before the vice president and his team left."

"They left already?" Isis glanced at Zack, then back to Doctor Mac.

"Yes, about thirty minutes ago."

Isis' head tipped back. "Thirty minutes ago?"

Zack's brain spun like a hamster's wheel. There was one possibility, but as far as he knew, it was beyond a human witch's ability. He was almost embarrassed to bring it up. "Is it possible Harry sent us forward in time?"

"No." Isis' eyes scrunched. "Could he?"

"Hmm, a witch that can control time. Interesting." Doctor Mac stepped back. "Zack, you are virus free. Isis, please take his place."

Zack moved away from the table. He jumped in Isis' path. "Anyway, they're not in danger at all. The Apprentice is not going to the Bronx. She's not looking for vengeance against your old foster family."

"How could you know that for sure?" Isis slid around him.

Zack snatched her hand, forcing her to look his way. "I know you better than anyone else," he said, pulling her closer. "I also remember many conversations about your former foster family. You don't resent them. You don't think they deserve to die."

"Of course not. They were just scared about what I could do." Isis gave Zack a curious look. "I barely even think about them anymore."

"The Apprentice is you, Isis." Zack released his grip of Isis' hand so she could back herself against the table. "If there's nothing deep inside of you seeking vengeance, then she's not going after them either. Right now, it's probably the safest place to be."

"That does make sense." Isis' tone was a little less antagonistic. She straightened her back and waited as Doctor Mac's hand glowed across her entire body.

"Okay, clean bill of health for both of you." The glow around Mac's hand faded. "You do realize...if Zack is right and The Apprentice is not in the Bronx, then this is only a reprieve. Your family and the task force will need to track her down and hope they're not too late."

"According to Harry, we have a few days," Zack pointed out. "Fact is, as an immortal vampire, she's not in a rush. The Apprentice could open the hole in a hundred years if she wanted to."

"She won't wait that long. I don't have that kind of patience," Isis replied. "Doctor Mac, your connection is strong. You could probably be a huge help against her, couldn't you?"

"Against a witch with two centuries of experience? Probably not. Besides, I'm not a soldier like Paul. I'm a doctor." He looked around the medical room. "This is what my Wiccan connection is for, keeping my people healthy and safe. I don't fight in wars."

A cold chill ran down Zack's spine. If they did find The Apprentice, and she was determined to rip open that hole in reality, they were in for a war.

"The two of you are free to go," Doctor Mac said. "Provided you remain here in New Salem."

Zack didn't wait. He made a beeline for the door. He never stayed in the medical center, or around Doctor Mac, any longer than he had to.

"Thank you, Doctor Mac." Isis waved with a friendly smile. She caught up to Zack and followed him out of the examination room.

****

"Wow, you had me worried for a minute, Zack," Isis said as they walked through the medical center's hallway toward the front double doors. "You really believe The Apprentice won't be in my old neighborhood?"

"What do *you* think?" Zack replied, tossing the ball back into her court. "You should have more of an idea on what she could be thinking."

"I know. She's supposed to be me."

Isis reached for the knob to exit the building. The double doors led to the Quad, a large grass area that made up the center of New Salem, titled due to the four buildings—which included the medical center—one on each side. Isis suddenly gasped. She grabbed Zack's arm and moved them away from the door. She pressed him against the wall.

"Isis, what is it?" Zack tried to look through the glass doors, but he was too far away. Her grip around his wrist was tight. "What's the matter?"

"It's her!"

Zack's heart dropped into his stomach. Did she mean The Apprentice? He pushed past her and ran to the door. It wasn't The Apprentice. It was Amelia strolling through the quad toward the marketplace. It had been nearly a year since she put Zack under that spell in Vegas and then tried to kill Isis. Now, she lived here under new guardianship.

The pink dye had faded from her hair revealing that she was a brunette. The cockiness, however, was still in her step. Amelia already earned a reputation of being a handful, but so far she had lasted a lot longer than either Zack or Isis thought she would in New Salem without getting exiled, or worse.

Amelia checked the market door's handle. It was locked as expected two hours before their official opening time. A circular portal formed in front of her. Amelia walked through it, disappearing. The portal closed behind her.

"What do you think she's up to?" Isis whispered to Zack even though they were the only two in the hallway.

"It looks to me like she's heading to her job in the marketplace." Zack didn't share the same contempt for Amelia that Isis had, but he certainly understood it. "I'm betting you want to check on her to make sure that's all she's up to, right?"

"It's not where I really want to go, but if we're grounded, we might as well, right?"

"We're not really grounded, just—"

Isis grabbed a hold of Zack's wrists. She shut her eyes and chanted, "Teleport outside the marketplace."

The hallway blurred. Then everything came back into focus. Zack and Isis were now facing the rear of the marketplace with the circular rows of cottages behind them. Isis dropped to her knees, ducking underneath one of the building's first floor windows. Zack did the same. They stretched their backs and necks so they could peek through the window without revealing more than just their foreheads and eyes.

The marketplace was made up of long rectangular tables that stretched from one side of the building to the other. They usually held supplies such as books, clothes, toys, home goods, and other items for the taking. At the far end was a counter with two commercial-style ovens behind it. There they made and displayed sandwiches, baked goods, and various types of foods along the counter. At this time of the morning, however, the counter was as uncharacteristically empty as the tables.

Amelia stood behind one of the tables, staring at an open door across the way. It led to the storage room. Her guardians and the managers of the marketplace, Milo and Hanna, walked out wearing white aprons wrapped around their wide girths. Each held a cardboard box. They placed the boxes at Amelia's feet. Hanna spoke to Amelia and tapped a hand against the table's surface. Her lips moved fast, and Zack couldn't hear her through the window. Amelia, however, nodded her acknowledgment.

Milo and Hanna returned to the storage room. Amelia, after a huge eye roll, reached down into one of the boxes and removed a gray shirt. She examined the tag attached to the collar, then folded the shirt and placed it at the end of the table. She pulled out another shirt and did the same.

"What do you think she's up to?" Isis whispered.

"Nothing mysterious or devious," Zack replied. "She's just sorting the shirts in size order."

"I guess. I just don't trust her. Not after everything she did to us back in Vegas—"

A hand clasped Isis' shoulder from behind. She peeked back, but there was nothing there, just empty space. "What the hell?" Isis screamed and whirled around. Zack did the same. The loud set of cackles were suddenly joined by two teens their age who materialized out of thin air. Jeb held two Styrofoam cups in his hands.

"Maya! Jeb!" Zack screeched. "What the hell?"

"Sorry about that." Maya rubbed a long fingernail across Jeb's buzzcut. "We saw you two over here spying, and we couldn't resist."

Jeb stared down at one cup and said the word, "cold." He held out the cup for Zack to take. "Cola?" he asked.

"Sure, thanks." Zack took the cup. It was three quarters filled with soda. The cup took a moment to grip since it felt like pure ice.

"Anytime, bud." Jeb smacked Zack across the back, which almost caused him to drop the cup. "It's cool, just like you."

Both of their like-minded senses of humor were sometimes taxing, but they were Zack and Isis' best friends in the entire village...and maybe their only friends. They were both a few inches taller than Zack and Isis. Jeb's shoulders were also far wider. But no one Zack's age had ever referred to him as cool. Well, not until Jeb. Coming from a city like Las Vegas probably made Zack and Isis seem that way, especially to Jeb who was born in New Salem, and Maya who had lived here for most of her life.

"Are you two still watching that girl?" Maya drooped an arm around Isis' shoulders. The fact that her long blonde hair always stayed straight, even in this humidity, was the sign of a modern-day miracle. Or witchcraft. Most likely witchcraft.

"There's a lot of reason not to trust her," Zack replied after a quick sip. He handed the cup to Isis who also took a mouthful. "She may not be up to anything now, but there's a good chance she'll try something eventually."

Jeb tapped Maya's shoulder. "She's got a lot of history with these two. My folks were talking about it just last night."

Isis looked at Zack with an eyeroll. Neither of them

liked the idea that they were gossip among the residents, even when they were home having dinner with their families. Zack thought they'd get used to that by now. Guess not, but gossip was the grandest form of family entertainment in New Salem.

Maya pointed a hand at the window. "Is that really the witch you should be worried about?" Her finger then shot at Isis. "Not the vampire you?"

"Oh my God." Isis gasped. "How…how do you know about that? Does everyone know?"

"Nah, just us." Jeb took another swig from his cup. "Because Maya breaks the rules."

Zack and Isis eyed Maya, who rolled her eyes at Jeb, then sighed. "Fine, all right." She tossed up her arms in defeat. "I can see through my dad's eyes, and since he's the vice president, I get a lot of info I'm not supposed to know."

Maya looked to the group, then shrugged. "Hey, if I'm going to be president someday, I need to stay caught up on all relevant information, right?"

"Yeah, but your dad will still kill you if he ever finds out you can do that," Jeb said with a smirk.

"That's why we're going to keep our big mouths shut and not tell him, Hon." Maya aimed a narrowed stink-eye at Jeb. "When I heard you two were brought back early, I peeked. That's when I saw that boy teleport the two of you out of President Tia's office."

"Can you check on them now and make sure they're all okay?" Isis grabbed Maya's hand like a beggar desperate for loose change.

"They're such a far distance from here. That's something I've never tried before." Maya straightened her back and shut her eyes. "But let me see if I can do it."

Her eyelids moved back and forth. The lines on her forehead tensed as she mumbled what had to be a spell under her breath. The idea that she could do this impressed Zack, but it also scared him. If she could see through her father's eyes, could she do the same with anyone else at any given time? Responsibility and restraint, none of those were Maya's strongest qualities.

After several moments, a grin formed across her lips. "Yes, I see them, but I can't really hear them. The voices are muffled, maybe because of the distance?" She leaned in as if she was watching a program on a screen. "They're all in front of a big, ugly brownstone. Natasha's head is up, looking at one of the higher floor windows. Your dad's talking to my dad while pointing at his watch. So far, no evil vampire."

"I told you she wouldn't be there," Zack whispered to Isis.

"You were right." Isis shrugged. "But, like Doctor Mac said, they won't quit looking for her."

Maya opened her eyes. Her face lit up. "Hey, why don't *we* find her?"

"That's not a good idea!" Jeb's head snapped Maya's way. "Isn't she, like, super connected?"

"Yeah, real connected." Her wide eyes shot at Isis. "But so is she. And, we have a game plan."

"What plan?" Zack asked.

"Their plan!" Maya clapped her hands together. "I can get my mom's crystals. I know where she keeps them. And, as far as a distraction goes..." Maya wrapped an arm around Isis' back and gave her a playful shake. "I'd think you're right about being better than the adopted family she hasn't seen in two centuries, right?"

"They really should have brought me," Isis mumbled with her head down.

Maya walked around Isis to face her. A huge grin crossed her lips. "So, what do you think? Are you in? We nab her before they do? We show our parents that we don't need to be protected? Let them see we are old enough to get the job done, too? While they're all hanging around in the Bronx, we come back to New Salem with The Apprentice in an enchanted crystal cage."

"Even if we all agree to this," Jeb said, rubbing his temples, "we don't know where she is, either."

"Let's go with best guess." Maya clutched Isis' shoulders. "If you were a two-hundred-year-old vampire who traveled through time to now, where would you hide?"

Zack wandered away from the group, needing to clear his head. Through the window, he watched a few residents of New Salem entering the market. Apparently, the place had opened early. Amelia greeted them with an unfriendly wave, then motioned to the T-shirts on the table in front of her. Behind him, the conversation went on. Somehow, Maya was selling Isis and Jeb on the idea.

Maya's excitement was contagious, but was this really a good idea? Confronting a corrupt version of Isis with two hundred years of experience as a witch—even with a plan—was dangerous. Maybe even suicidal. But one of the groups, whether the adults or them, had to face her. If The Apprentice succeeded in opening that hole between dimensions—and without interference, she inevitably would—then everyone dies. Everyone.

"I...honestly don't know where I would go," Isis said to Maya. "I don't know how to find her."

"But isn't she you?" Maya asked. "Wouldn't she go wherever you'd go?"

"Maybe, but maybe not," Isis replied. "All I know is I'd never go to a prison and kill someone, no matter who it was."

Jeb spit out a mouthful of soda. "Who did what now?"

Zack's eyes fixated on Amelia, another threat to the world, but maybe no longer without the influence of her mother, the corrupt Erisa Cross. Now, she seemed very much into her work, placing the shirts along the table until she turned over the empty box and placed it at her feet. She then raised her hands up high. A circular blur opened above her. Moments later, a second cardboard box dropped from the portal and landed into her outstretched arms. From the way Amelia staggered, the box must have been heavy with a lot more T-shirts.

Amelia's Wiccan connection, which focused on making portals, was still strong. At least now she was putting it to good use... Wait! Portals. Zack raised his eyebrows, then spun from the window and faced the group. "If we're really going to do this, I know how we can find The Apprentice!" He looked directly at Isis. "But you're not going to like it."

"How?" Isis stepped back with widened eyes. She had accused Zack in the past that whenever he uttered that phrase, "you're not going to like it," he rarely disappointed. This was about to be one of those times.

Zack's head spun to the window. "We can find her through Amelia, if she's willing to help us."

Isis' head shook back and forth. "No way!" she

exclaimed. "That's a really bad idea."

"Amelia?" Jeb asked. "How can she know where to look when the two of you don't?"

"When she messed with us in Vegas, she always found us." Zack's hands moved in several directions as he spoke. "Wherever we were, Amelia would pop out of a portal. She showed up when I was in a store early morning, and then again when I was alone in my bedroom. She ambushed Isis in the hotel's elevator when she dragged her to the desert so they could fight."

"You two fought?" Maya clutched Isis' arm. "Who won?"

"My point is"—Zack's voice rose to keep everyone's attention—"finding us all those times didn't happen by coincidence. Maybe her portals are more than just wormholes from one location to another. Maybe she can use them to locate people as well."

"Ooh, that would be super if she could," Maya exclaimed.

The three fixed on Isis whose bottom lip shook. "Come on, Isis," Maya said, through an anxious grin. "The entire world is counting on us, not to mention our people here in New Salem."

"You don't understand—"

"Sure, we do!" Maya shrugged. "But we don't have much time before The Apprentice ruins the world, right? What if she decides to cross over early? That's far more important than a simple grudge, isn't it?"

Isis shut her eyes and cringed. Zack knew that upset reaction; he'd seen it many times. Once or twice, it was even aimed at him. It was Isis' way of clearing her head and trying to get past her own stubbornness. Sometimes, it helped her come to the right decision, even if it was one she didn't like. She let out a deep exhale, then punched her right fist into her left palm.

"Damn it, all right," Isis growled. "Let's go talk to her."

Chapter Nine

Isis paced several feet from the dumpster near the marketplace. Zack was nearby, as always, with Maya and Jeb behind him. Soon, Amelia would step through the back door and Isis would have to face her. Being honest with herself, this confrontation stressed her out just as much as facing The Apprentice. Amelia was the witch who tried to manipulate Zack with her mother's love spell. Not to mention, she tried to kill Isis. Twice.

The idea that they'd have to interact with her was the last thing Isis ever wanted to do. She was content with living out her life in New Salem and avoiding Amelia as if she were the plague. But Isis couldn't get past the thought that Amelia would eventually try to screw over this peaceful village. Seeing her every single day did play a role in Isis' vote for the family to return to Vegas for their show's latest run. If they never spoke again, it wouldn't be long enough.

Now, Isis had to initiate contact. She had to ask her mortal enemy for help with a far worse threat. The thought made her want to throw up. But it was the only way.

Might as well get it over with, but first, they'd need Amelia to leave the marketplace.

"Are you sure she's coming out here?" Maya asked.

"Of course, they're sure," Jeb scoffed. "They spy

on that girl all the time. I'm sure they know her schedule as well as they know their own."

Zack peeked at his watch. "She'll be here soon enough. It's her job to take the morning trash to the dumpster, always around this time."

"She should put herself in that dumpster," Isis mumbled.

"I don't get all this sneaking around," Maya said. "Why don't we just walk in there, sit her down, and talk to her—"

The back door swung open which immediately stifled the conversation. Amelia stormed out dragging a huge, overstuffed garbage bag across the dirt and grass. The bag was tied in a knot at the top. Amelia's eyes rolled. "Don't teleport the garbage. Take it out there yourself." She waved her free hand in the air as she spoke in a mid-southern drawl clearly meant to mimic her guardians. "Better to learn to work without your gifts. It will make you appreciate what you can do." In her own snarky voice, she said, "Whatever."

A hand pushed against Isis' back. "Go," Maya whispered into her ear. Isis took a step toward Amelia. Zack did the same.

Amelia looked back and forth, from the garbage bag to the dumpster. A portal suddenly opened underneath the bag, causing it to fall through and disappear. It then fell out of another portal which had formed above the dumpster. "Garbage dumped," Amelia said.

It was now or never. Isis walked to the dumpster one step ahead of Zack. Amelia's face shot her way. A moment of surprise made way for her slanted-eyed smirk. "Well, well, long time, no talk," she hissed like a snake. "Did you get bored of watching me through the window and decided to take a closer look?"

"You knew they did that?" Jeb's voice made Isis jump. She was so focused on Amelia she hadn't noticed the two witches following her and Zack.

"They're not exactly subtle about it," Amelia answered, without looking Jeb's way. "Neither of them could ever become private investigators. That's for damn sure."

Amelia strolled past Isis and walked up to Zack. She flashed a devious smile. "Hi."

Zack stood tall, but the discomfort was written all over his face. God, Isis wanted to shoot a huge hole straight through her heart, and one that would rival even Amelia's portals. But Isis knew how fast Amelia could be. It was the reason their battles rarely went her way. Maybe with Maya and Jeb as backup they'd be able to pin her down. There would be more of an advantage, but that wasn't why they were here.

"So, to what do I owe the pleasure?" Amelia asked in a mocking tone.

Isis took a deep breath. She really didn't want to say it. She didn't have to. Zack took the initiative and said it for them. "Amelia, we need your help."

Amelia's eyebrows rose. That was clearly not what she expected. "You need *my* help? Really? For what?"

"Zack believes you can find people with your portals," Isis replied. "Is that true?"

"Why? Did you lose someone?"

"Just tell us," Isis snapped. She placed a hand on her heart and took a deep breath. She needed to stay calm. "Is that how your connection works?"

Amelia snorted. "What exactly is this? Now that

you need my help, you're willing to let bygones be bygones? Is that it?"

"Bygones be bygones?" Zack's voice rose. "After everything you did to us in Vegas? You're lucky they gave you this new life and second chance!" Isis snatched Zack's wrist to calm him down. She had never seen him so agitated, although this was with good reason. Amelia was clearly taunting him.

"Whoa, it's been almost a whole year since all that went down, and you still feel some kind of way about it? Get lives!" Amelia's smile faded. She motioned an angry finger at Isis. "Besides, you killed my mother, so maybe *I* should still be mad at *you*!"

"Hold on, is that what you think happened?" Maya stepped between Isis and Zack. "Newsflash, honey, my father executed your mother. He saw her as a threat, and that was his job, eliminating threats."

"Your father, the vice president guy?" Maya's head tipped to the side. "I'm not sure I believe that."

"Maya doesn't lie," Jeb replied.

"It's true." Maya cupped her hands together and pointed them forward. "He did it for the good of the world, and the good of New Salem, which now includes you. Now, an even bigger threat to both is on our heels, and we need to stop it, which we can do with your amazing connection. You can help us save everybody on the entire planet."

Isis stepped back and let Maya take control of the situation. The girl was impressive, both in her persuasion and in taking responsibility for her father's decision. Maya had grown up to become president of New Salem in the other timeline. If this interaction was any indication, she was destined to do the same here.

But how would Amelia react to Maya's sudden revelation?

Isis clenched her fists and focused on the energy in case they needed it. She wouldn't put it past Amelia to explode and go on the offensive. Could this confrontation turn into a preliminary fight before the main event? Amelia spun away from Maya and locked eyes with Isis.

"Well, that's one hell of a surprise," she said. "But it doesn't mean we're friends now, or that I'd be inclined to want to help you find anyone. Frankly, if I was going to open a portal for you to walk through, I'd rather connect the other side to outer space."

Isis' eyes narrowed. Her fists tightened. "Outer space?"

Zack stepped in front of Isis, facing Amelia. "What if we were to tell you it's a two-hundred-year-old Wiccan vampire version of Isis from another timeline? And she will probably kill us when we confront her?"

Amelia looked back and forth at the four. It was the first time Isis had ever seen this overly confident girl speechless. "So, there's two of you around?" Her face scrunched. "Oh, come on, do I have the word sucker written across my forehead?"

"It's true," Isis said. "Yeah, it sounds insane, but Valeria changed time. A future version of me, who became a vampire then created a whole other timeline—it's the one we live in now. Those other timelines no longer exist, but somehow, another version of me, the one from Valeria's change—she's also a vampire—is here. She's going to destroy the whole planet if we don't stop her."

"That's a hell of a story." Amelia's tongue rolled

across her bottom lip. "You know, Doctor Mac fancies himself a shrink. Maybe you should go see him."

Jeb chimed in. "They're not making this up—"

"Oh, please, how would *you* know?" Amelia's scream cut him off. "This crazy story could totally be in their heads, or maybe they're scamming us. That whole coven is full of manipulators."

"Manipulators?" Isis scoffed. "You're the one who put a love spell on Zack and tried to kill me!"

"Really?" Jeb's head tilted. "You really put a love spell on Zack?"

"Well, technically, my mother did it on my behalf," Amelia explained through a smirk. "But she had her reasons."

"Like what?"

"Back to the subject!" Zack waved his hands in the air to get everyone's attention. "Amelia, you're right, the story is crazy. But is it any crazier than us living in a village of witches in the swamp jungles of Sweden? There are actual vampires out there. You create portals that can go anywhere on the planet. Isn't that just as ridiculous? Now, maybe we're making it up and this is all crap. But, if that is the case, what do you have to lose? Your portal won't find her; we don't go anywhere. We can go back to avoiding each other. But, if the threat is real, then we need to get to wherever she is right away."

"Get to wherever *who* is right away?" The adult voice spun Isis and the others to the marketplace's back door. Carolyn stood perfectly straight with her chiseled arms folded across her camouflage-color tank top. Her baseball cap was turned around.

"Carolyn," Maya said, through a nervous grin.

"What are you doing here? Aren't you on village patrol?"

"I was just inside breaking up a verbal altercation between Farmer John and Hanna when I noticed this little get-together from behind the window." Carolyn marched their way. Wow, even her walk was intimidating, like a champion fighter storming across the ring. Everyone in the village was on edge around Carolyn. Everyone except for Sacha, of course. "You look like you're up to something, I hope nothing stupid."

"Not at all," Isis answered. She peeked at Amelia, hoping she wouldn't turn them in.

"We're just worried about our parents," Maya said.

Carolyn faced Isis and peered down into her eyes. She had several inches over her. "I promised your aunt I'd keep an eye on the two of you while your family is away on assignment." She looked back and forth from Isis to Zack. "I told her I'd keep you here and safe. Do not make a liar out of me."

"Yes, ma'am." Isis saluted. Her gesture wasn't reciprocated or appreciated.

"She warned me you might try to join them. I'm telling you now, don't. I have to inform the president of what happened in the marketplace. After that, I will be checking up on you." Carolyn looked at each of them, her deadpan face radiating a definite threat. She turned and reentered the marketplace after throwing a last glance to assure her words were received loud and clear. But it was one order Isis didn't feel they could follow.

A loud cackle broke Isis from her thoughts. It came from Amelia. "Well, I'll be damned." Her head shook.

"The Boy Scout and Little Miss Perfect are actually sneaking around and breaking the rules. Isn't that a shocker?"

Isis shrugged. "We have no choice. We need to find her before they do."

"That's true," Zack added. His eyes went wide. "For what it's worth, even if we survive the Wiccan vampire, Isis' folks will probably kill us."

"Okay, now you're actually tempting me." She eyed the dumpster while tapping a fingernail against her cheek.

Isis was sure the answer would be yes. Hopefully Amelia was just toying with them by feigning indecisiveness.

She finally responded. "You still have one issue."

"What's that?" Zack asked.

Amelia peeked over her shoulder at the marketplace's window. Inside, Carolyn marched from one side to the other, her head turning in every direction. While taking a sandwich from the display table, she eyed the group intently through the window.

"We still need to get rid of your tail," Amelia said. "Isis, how about you send her away?"

"Me?" Isis gasped. "How am I supposed to do that?"

"Send a message into her walkie. Say there's a commotion somewhere else and she's needed." She looked at Isis with a sly grin. "Or do you want to just stand here and wait until she gets bored of watching us?"

"No. I'll do it." Isis shut her eyes and focused. She hated the fact that Amelia was manipulating her just as she did back in Vegas where she made Zack act in ways that were out of character for him. Manipulating anybody, including Carolyn, was certainly out of character for Isis. But, right now, they needed Amelia, and they did need Carolyn off their trail. She'd let her have this victory.

"Muffled voice," Isis chanted. "Muffled voice." Her thoughts were on what she wanted that voice to say and where she wanted it to come from.

Carolyn snatched her walkie-talkie and brought to her ear. "There's a situation in the medical center," Isis whispered. "We need assistance immediately." It was the best place to send her since the medical center had a walkie-talkie in case of an emergency. That meant she wouldn't have reason to doubt the communication came from them.

Carolyn spoke into the walkie, gave the group one last hard glance filled with warning, and then ran for the marketplace's front door.

"Okay, she's gone," Isis said to Amelia. "Now, will you help us?"

"Help you? That I won't do, but I will take you to this other you." Amelia jabbed a finger Isis' way. "Once there, I'm not part of your little hit squad, got it?"

"I got it," Isis replied through grinding teeth. "Are we all ready to go?"

"First, Jeb and I need to run back to my place for a second," Maya replied. "I know where my mom keeps her crystals. That's part of the plan, right?"

"Well, okay then. Let me put my hair up." Amelia reached behind her head with both hands and made quick work with a scrunchie. "And then let's go find us a vampire."

Chapter Ten

New Salem had around seventy residents, and just over half were witches. Some had less of a connection than others, but enough supernatural ability to qualify as witches. A few such as Doctor Mac, Natasha, and The Witches of Vegas—especially Isis—had strong connections. The rest of the residents had no connection at all.

Of the five about to enter Amelia's portal, Zack was the only one who fell in the "no connection at all" group. Even worse, no one knew where the portal would lead, not even Amelia. The Apprentice could be anywhere on Earth, from an active volcano to a high mountain in frigid Tibet, and they were confronting her with no idea what to expect. Maybe this was a mistake.

"Come on, let's go!" Amelia yelled, sounding more than a little annoyed. "I'm not keeping this thing open all day."

Realization suddenly hit, and everyone, including Isis, froze in place. That portal led to a confrontation with an all-powerful Wiccan vampire on the other side. This may have been far too dangerous for them, but it was a necessary confrontation. Plus, Zack was convinced that they had a better chance of the adults' plan succeeding with them implementing it, especially with Isis as the distraction.

So far, no one made a move for the portal.

Someone had to take the lead. Zack put down his head and walked straight through to wherever it led. Unlike teleportation, Amelia's portals didn't cause blurriness or slight vertigo. It felt more like walking straight through a door. Time to find out what was on the other side.

Once through, Zack's sneakers tapped on concrete. Engines roared, horns honked, and hordes of people passed by, either staring at their phones or holding conversations with each other. The others exited the portal, coming into view beside him. The portal faded away behind Amelia. All eyes went up toward the skyscrapers on either side of the street.

"Oh, wow," Maya exclaimed. "Is this…"

"Vegas," Amelia answered. "And we're in front of The Sapphire. How appropriate."

Isis spun around and gave Amelia an accusatory glance. "I thought you were taking us to The Apprentice?"

"Who? Oh, you mean the other, slightly cooler version of you?" Amelia pointed to the long alleyway between The Sapphire's hotel and theater. They were attached by a bridge several stories up. "That's where we are. When the portal opened, I sensed her somewhere over there."

"You know, Amelia," Zack said, taking a huge chance, "we really could use your help. With your amazing portals and skills, we'd get her back to New Salem quickly and you'd be a hero."

"Oh, Zack, you're such a flatterer." Amelia patted his cheek. "But I said I'd get you here, and that's what I did. I'll even bring you back, but I'm not engaging. This isn't my fight. Besides, I have someplace else I'd rather be when this all goes down."

Jeb tapped her shoulder. "Where's that?"

"There's a real awesome restaurant not far from here that serves everything supersized. Their waffles cover the entire plate." Amelia waved a hand. A portal opened behind her. "I'm going to head there and grab a bite. I'll come back when I'm done. Good luck."

With that, Amelia jumped back into the portal, which then faded away. Damn, deep down, Zack was sure she'd stick around and help them out. Working together could have even mended some fences. Guess that would have to wait for another time.

Isis faced the group. She held out her hand, revealing the five enchanted crystals they had taken from Maya's cottage. "Let's take these and go scope the area." The bravado in her voice was weak.

"Okay, little miss distraction." Maya held out her hand. "Pass them along."

Isis picked up two of the crystals and placed them on Maya's palm. She handed one to Zack and one to Jeb. Her fingers wrapped around the last one. Zack stared at the crystal in his hand. The sunlight above made it glisten. For this to work, he'd have to be extra sneaky and rely on his magician's instincts. He had a bond with Isis, but would that extend to The Apprentice if she caught him? Thanks to Valeria, that version of Isis had never met the Zack Galloway of her timeline.

"Holy crow!" Jeb's scream made Zack nearly jump out of his sneakers. The two girls jumped as well. Jeb waved a hand at an electronic billboard in the distance. "Check that out!"

Isis pressed a hand against her chest, then let out a sigh of relief. After a collective deep breath, they all looked where Jeb was pointing.

"It's Simon on that screen!" Jeb shouted.

"Was that really worth such a scream, Babe?" Maya slapped Jeb across the shoulder.

"But it's Simon, and he's on a huge movie screen. Is he a star now or something?"

"His show is popular here in Vegas," Zack explained.

"That's why he didn't come back home with you and stayed here?" Jeb asked, still eyeing the video. "Does he do anything besides sit on a stool and talk about himself?"

"That's pretty much what he did back home, anyway," Maya scoffed.

"Guys," Isis pleaded. "Can we please focus?"

Maya eyed Isis and Zack. "Maybe we should ask Simon for help. It wouldn't hurt to have a vampire to catch a vampire, right?"

"He can't help us." Isis walked toward the alleyway. "We have to do this and stick to the plan. It's the only way."

Isis disappeared around the corner. Zack ran to catch up to her. Maya and Jeb followed them into the long alleyway. With each step, Zack felt a growing feeling of dread. He gripped the crystal in his hand tight.

"Damn, it smells back here," Maya said, as they tiptoed through the alleyway. "I'm not sure of what."

"It smells like death." Jeb cupped a hand over his nose. "Hey, if she is back here, won't she sense us coming?"

"I'm hiding us," Isis answered. "If my spell is working, we're invisible to her."

"That's a smart move— Yikes!" Maya stopped short and stumbled back. Jeb caught her from falling on her backside. A middle-aged man lay face-up wearing nothing but beige slacks and black dress shoes. His lips were an awkward shade of purple, and his skin had the texture of a deflated balloon. His eyes were open, but they were empty.

Jeb leaned past Maya for a closer look. "Whoa, that guy didn't die of natural causes, did he?"

"No, he did not," Zack said, keeping his distance from the body. "He was feasted on."

Zack stared at the body, unable to avert his eyes. It was the same with the others. After several tense moments, Isis spoke up. "We need to keep going."

She maneuvered around the corpse. The others did the same until they were midway through the alleyway when all four froze in place. "Oh my..." Maya shrieked.

Zack ran to Isis' side. She quickly grabbed his hand. Several feet ahead, a skinny teenage girl with brown hair that looked brittle and unkempt sat on her knees. Her head was down with her mouth pressed against the stomach of an elderly woman's body. Like the man, the woman's upper body was naked and lifeless. Loud slurps filled the alleyway. The girl lifted her head and swallowed. Her face, like her exposed arms in her tank-top, were covered in what looked like ages-old burn marks. Her eyes were pure black.

The hair, the scars, the blood across her mouth; it was like nothing Zack had ever seen. But he knew that body and jaw structure. He knew that face under the distorted skin and darkened eyes better than he knew his own.

It was the same exact face as the one to Zack's left.

Chapter Eleven

The vampire finished her feast by rolling her tongue across her mouth and lapping up the excess blood. Isis' stomach turned. She wanted to throw up. She could never so callously kill people, even to preserve her own existence. Then again, she was also never ripped from the love of her adopted family and tortured by a psycho for two centuries.

"Man, my folks are going to kill me for being here," Jeb whispered. "Maybe we should get the adults, let them deal with this mess."

The Apprentice's head lifted from her lunch. She looked directly at the group.

"Oh, crap," Jeb exclaimed. "Isis, I thought you're masking us."

"I am," Isis answered. She took a step back, as did the others.

"She's a two-hundred-year-old vampire," Zack said. "Her connection and control of the energy is beyond anything you've ever seen."

"Go now," Isis whispered.

Maya nodded, then placed her closed fists on each of the boys' shoulders. They all faded away.

Isis moved ahead, careful to keep a distance. The Apprentice rose to her feet and stepped over the carcass. She looked Isis up and down, from her head to her feet. Two fangs protruded from underneath her upper lip. Her eyes were still dark, but at least she wasn't attacking. That may have been out of morbid curiosity. At least The Apprentice was distracted as they had hoped.

"I'm not here to hurt you," Isis said in a calm voice. "I couldn't even if I wanted to."

Despite her shaking knees, Isis wasn't as nervous as she expected she would be. Even with the differing events that made up their lives, The Apprentice was her. If anyone knew how to talk to her…

The Wiccan vampire took another step. Isis put a hand out, a request for her other self to stay back. "I know you've been through so much," she said. "It's changed how you see things, from how I see things. But I know there's still a piece of me inside of you."

The darkness in the vampire's eyes faded, revealing angry brown eyes. Zack slid out from behind the dumpster on the right. The Apprentice's head swung his way. Zack waved his left hand out as if to say hello. It was a ploy; his right hand, which hung to his side, opened and dropped the crystal in place. Jeb, meanwhile, on the opposite side of the alley, placed his palm on the ground. The asphalt in front of him turned icy. He slid his crystal so it landed across from Zack's.

"Apprentice, look at me," Isis said. The vampire's head slowly turned her way. "I know you want to do the right thing. But what you're planning isn't it."

Maya appeared a few meters behind The Apprentice. She held out both her hands, palms up. The crystals resting in her hands floated and then landed equal distances from the other two around The Apprentice.

"Mom, Dad, and Sacha—they can help you," Isis

said. "Just like they always have."

The curiosity on The Apprentice's face turned to rage, which meant Isis must have said the wrong thing. She then did something Isis had never done. She snarled like a rabid wolverine. She hunched over, ready to pounce. The eyes once again went dark.

"Okay, I get it. You're mad at them." Once again, Isis stepped back. "Maybe it's because they weren't there to save you when you needed them the most. But you must remember how much they loved us. If they could have, they would—"

"Now!" Zack shouted.

Isis dropped the last crystal. The five formed a perfect pentagon around The Apprentice. Isis raised her hand and took control of the energy within. A pyramid-shaped dome formed from energy shooting from the crystals. The Apprentice eyed the shield on all sides, realizing she was trapped. Her hand thrust forward. The invisible barrier sparked.

"Yes! We got her!" Maya skipped over and joined Isis at her side. She grabbed Isis' arm and raised it high. "Now we know who the better Isis is. With a little help from her friends, of course."

Isis sure didn't feel like the better version at the moment. She meant every word she said to The Apprentice, but all the while knowing she was using them as a distraction to trick her. Within the dome, she watched a tortured soul who looked exactly like her drop to her knees like a caged animal. Isis had to put her guilt aside and maintain control. The Apprentice had enough experience to easily overpower her use of the crystals and murder them all.

Zack's head spun from The Apprentice to Isis.

"Okay, we have her. Now what?" He faced Maya. "What was the adults' plan from this point?"

"No clue," she replied. "I think our best bet is to get her back to New Salem while keeping her within those crystals. They should all be back by now, so they can implement whatever they had in mind. Agreed?"

From her kneeling position, The Apprentice's eyes fixed on Jeb's. She leaned toward him, the energy crackling throughout the dome. She was up to something…

"Guys, be careful—"

Before Isis could finish her warning, Jeb's eyes went blank, as if he was suddenly not there. He charged ahead like a zombie being led by the call of flesh.

"What are you doing?" Maya reached out, as did Zack, but it was too late. Jeb kicked the front crystal aside. The energy dome disappeared. Then The Apprentice did as well.

"No!" Isis shrieked. She spun her head in every direction. "Where did she go?"

"This is not good," Zack muttered.

"Babe!" Maya screamed at Jeb. "What happened?"

"I-I…" Jeb grabbed his head, then rubbed his temples. "I don't know…"

"Wow, she teleported so fast." Maya waved from one building to the other. "Do you think she went far? Maybe she's in one of these buildings—"

The Apprentice reappeared in the air in front of Maya. As she dropped to her feet, her right hand chopped through Maya's, severing it from the wrist. The hand sank to the ground. They all screamed as The Apprentice once again teleported away.

Maya held out her wrist, the end covered in blood

which dripped down her arm. Her eyes rolled to the back of her head. Her body collapsed, falling into Jeb's massive arms. He slowly lowered her to the ground. "Holy crap! What...what do we do?" the huge teen sobbed.

"Isis!" Zack shouted.

"Yeah, I-I can heal her."

Isis dropped to Maya's side and grabbed the severed hand. She had healed a near-death injury before—most notably Zack's last year in Vegas—but could she reattach an actual body part? It wasn't like she had knowledge of human anatomy, or any medical training. She wasn't Doctor Mac, or even her adopted mom. But if she stayed calm and trusted the energy...that may have been Maya's only hope.

"Isis, you have to stop the bleeding," Zack said. "If not, she could die before you can reattach her hand."

Isis nodded then held her hands over Maya's limp wrist. "Stop the bleeding," she chanted. "Stop the bleeding..."

Energy crackled around Maya's arm. The river of blood flow slowed. It was working, but how would she reattach the hand? Stop worrying, stop doubting, she told herself. Right now, she had to trust the energy to guide her—

"Isis!" Zack gasped.

From behind, an arm wrapped around Isis' throat. A body pressed against her back. A hand, which looked like her own, shot past Isis' face and held its palm straight out. The crystals flew to it as if they were being sucked in by a vacuum. Then everything blurred.

****

"What...what do we do?" Jeb stuttered from

Maya's side. His body shook.

Zack's breathing was so heavy he thought he might have been hyperventilating. The reaction was understandable; his girlfriend had just been abducted by a two-hundred-year-old Wiccan vampire, and that had to be a second priority. Maya, their friend, was still bleeding from the wrist, although it was less than before. Her hand lay inches away. Unfortunately, Isis didn't have a chance to finish her healing spell. They had to help now, or Maya would die.

"Jeb! Can you heal?" There was no response. Jeb just gaped at his girlfriend's severed hand through wide eyes. Zack kneeled and yanked Jeb's arm, shaking him from his fog. "Jeb!" he shouted as loudly as he could.

Jeb's head shook. "N-no, I'm not…I'm not strong enough. I don't know how."

Damn, they had to do something. An idea popped into his head. It was a long shot, but it was a use of the energy Jeb was most comfortable showing off. "Jeb, you create cold. Freeze the hand and the wrist!"

"Freeze?"

"Yes, freezing the hand will preserve it. Freezing the wound should stop the bleeding." Zack sure hoped he was right about all of that. Maya's life depended on it.

Jeb held his hands over Maya's hand and wrist. Nothing happened. He was scared for her, and the fear cut him off from the energy. "I-I can't…"

"Jeb, listen to me." Zack crawled around Maya's body so he could look Jeb in the eyes. "I know you're freaked out, but you need to put that aside. Just focus on the energy. Focus on your freeze spell. Let the energy flow through you and let it create what you need it to."

Zack wasn't a witch, but he had memories from another timeline of training witches for two centuries. Those may not have been his personal experiences, but they were still memories of events he could utilize now…if Jeb was listening.

Jeb nodded. He refocused on Maya. "Freeze," he chanted over and over. After several moments, a frost formed around the severed hand. Maya's wrist froze as well. The bleeding stopped while her hand's skin formed an arctic blue tint. The hand, frozen over, looked solid from the ice, like it had been preserved.

"Did…did we do it?" Jeb muttered.

"*You* did it, Jeb," Zack answered through a deep exhale. "You saved her." But for how long? Jeb's actions were a temporary band aid at best, but at least Maya looked stable to Zack's untrained eye.

The sound of a heavy wind forced Zack to look up. His fists instinctively clenched. Amelia stepped out of a portal licking her lips and with a napkin hanging from her collar like a bib. Syrup stains covered the napkin. The portal closed behind her.

"So…" She wiped her mouth with the makeshift bib. "How'd it go?"

Chapter Twelve

Isis was slammed against the ground hard. It wasn't solid ground like a street or a sidewalk as she expected to hit. It was all dry sand, accompanied by the sounds of waves hitting a shore. Isis pushed against the sand to lift her upper body and look around. The Apprentice had taken her to a small island just like the one Zack's late Uncle Herb was buried—

The tombstone her family had made for Herb Galloway stood not ten feet away under one of several green-tinted trees with round pink fruits hanging from the branches. This was the exact island where Valeria had trapped Isis' family along with Zack and his uncle. She convinced them they were prisoners in the Other World. They believed her, but Zack, using his phone—something Valeria hadn't taken into account—figured out they were still on Earth. Once they realized the scam, they escaped and rescued Isis from the old witch's clutches.

The Apprentice walked up to Herb Galloway's grave and glared down on it. She turned and looked over her shoulder at Isis with disdain. It was a look Isis had seen aimed her way many times before, but never from her own face. Isis jumped to her feet. Instinct told her to run, teleport back to New Salem, and seek help. But she couldn't feel the energy. Sparks from an invisible pyramid surrounded her. She was trapped within the crystals, and with her connection cut off. It was the exact same trap they had set for The Apprentice back in Vegas.

The only option left for Isis was to get into The Apprentice's head. She would just have to use arguments that would persuade herself. After all, they were technically the same person. If Isis couldn't convince her to listen, at least she could keep her busy. The others had to be looking for her. Eventually, they would come.

"I know you and I lived through very different histories," Isis said in a slow and calm tone. "In your timeline, Valeria made sure you never met Zack. He wasn't on the island with our family. Because of that, they all died right here. Then, you were tortured by Valeria."

There was no response. The Apprentice kept her back to Isis, staring out into the miles of water surrounding the island. Was she listening? "I can't even imagine what you must have gone through. I'm sure it was horrible..."

The Apprentice twisted around with a scowl. She stormed through the energy dome. Her eyes turned black as night. Isis dropped to her knees and raised her hands, hoping that this version of her would accept a sign of surrender. "What are you going to do?" she asked.

With lightning speed, The Apprentice's hand shot out and clutched Isis' forehead. Her vision went dark. Isis could no longer feel her body. Opening and closing her eyelids didn't make a difference. The Apprentice's hand no longer had a grip of her, but the throbbing in her forehead felt like the inside of her skull was being used for a drum. Her stomach suddenly turned into one huge cramp. Isis tried to throw up, but nothing came from her mouth except for dry heaves. She wanted to ask what was happening to her, but she couldn't move her bottom jaw.

Everything was dark. She could barely make out anything, but the stink of body odor made her nostrils burn. Isis grabbed at her body. Her clothes were shredded and dirty. Where in the world was she? And why did it feel like she had been in this darkness for a long time…

A metal door creaked open. A bright light shot in from a doorway. It blinded Isis, but she couldn't turn away. She could finally make out that she was in a small room, like a dungeon or a prison. High-heeled footsteps tapped her way. Isis forced her eyes to open. A huge woman with long brown hair and wearing a red dress stared down at her. It was Valeria.

"It has been over twenty-four hours since your last meal. I am sure you must be famished, my dear." Valeria's cackle echoed throughout the dark. "Lucky you have me as your new master to see to your continued existence. It is only through my tender mercies that you may survive."

Valeria stretched out her arms. "*Corpus adducer*," she chanted.

A man with long gray hair that was as dirt-covered as his skin appeared in front of Isis. His hands were tied behind his back by thick rope. His bare feet and mouth were bound as well. His wide eyes looked up at Isis, begging for his life.

"This man has a wife and two young children," Valeria explained. "But that does not matter, only that he can satisfy your need for his blood. Now, end your agony and placate your hunger. If not, your existence will come to a slow and meaningless end."

The man's widened and defeated eyes looked up at Isis. He muffled one word, which Isis couldn't make out, but she knew what he was trying to say. The word was "please."

"I leave you with your meal." Valeria backed toward the bright doorway. "Then we can resume your training tomorrow. I am sure as the decades pass, you will be more open to the education I have planned for you."

The door creaked closed, leaving Isis on her knees in front of this poor soul who muffled pleas through his gag. Vampire or not, Isis did not want to hurt him, or anyone, but she smelled his blood. It was like being in a bakery right after all the cake, cookies, and pies had just come out of the oven. The pain in her stomach stretched to her throat. She could barely focus her vision as the headache increased. It felt like her brain was in a vise.

Isis stared at the man. His blood would save her. It would take away all the pain, but how could she ever intentionally drink someone's blood, killing them in the process? She didn't want to, but it smelled so tasty. She needed it to end the craving...

The man, and the dark, faded. The pain stopped. Isis was back on the island, her body and clothes now covered in sweat. The Apprentice stood up and glared down at Isis, who pressed hands against her head and stomach. The cravings were gone, because they weren't her cravings to begin with. Reality had changed so that experience never happened. But to The Apprentice, it was real; it was her existence.

"Oh, wow!" Isis looked up at her other self. "I knew she tortured you, but I had no idea it was like that."

The Apprentice's stare never wavered. Her eyes fluctuated from brown irises to pure black ones.

"What you went through was horrible," Isis said, still trying to communicate. "But, the first Isis, she stopped Valeria from creating your timeline. You shouldn't even exist—"

The Apprentice grabbed a handful of Isis' hair and yanked her off the sand. She then leapt in the air, taking Isis with her. Isis' eardrums popped. Once in the sky, they came to a sudden halt. The island looked at least a half-mile away. But that was far outside the pyramid formed by the crystals. Isis felt her connection to the energy return; she was whole once again. Even better, this was her chance. Isis reached with her hand and gestured at The Apprentice.

"Lightning—"

Isis' body propelled toward the island as if she had been thrown out of an airplane without a parachute. Both witches plummeted to the sandy ground. The Apprentice landed on her feet. Isis landed on all fours and rolled. But she was free, at least for the moment.

The Apprentice charged.

"Sandstorm!" Isis chanted with a hand steered downward. In response, sand exploded into The Apprentice's face, forcing her to throw her hands in front of her eyes. It stopped her, but only for a moment. She flashed her fangs and snarled like a wild animal ready for a fight.

Clearly, this was a battle Isis could not win. The Apprentice was too powerful. Isis needed to run, to return to New Salem where the witches could mount an offensive front. Even her future self couldn't handle all of them at once. Could she? Isis focused on New Salem. "Teleport," she yelled.

Everything blurred, but then the teleporting stopped. Isis hadn't gone anywhere. She looked up at The Apprentice who held her glowing right hand in a fist. Somehow, she interrupted Isis' teleportation spell. The Apprentice was so powerful, but Isis had caught her by surprise once. Could she do it again? Only one way to find out. Isis aimed her hands. She focused on the energy around her. "Force blast!"

A burst of white energy shot at The Apprentice. It may have been the strongest blast Isis had ever created. But it went straight through. Somehow, she knew it was coming and turned her body intangible. Instead, the blast hit the tree behind her. It rocked, then toppled over, crashing into another nearby tree.

The Apprentice, with a snarl, swung her arm. Isis' feet yanked out from under her as if they were lassoed by a cowboy's rope. Isis fell back-first on the sand. The Apprentice disappeared. Isis looked around, in every direction, but her other self was gone.

A moment later, The Apprentice reappeared, seated on Isis' stomach. Even though they both had the same thin frames, Isis couldn't budge her off. It was like having a linebacker sitting on her, holding her in place. The Apprentice stretched her clawed fingers and clutched Isis' throat, cutting off her air. Her eyes turned black as she squeezed with a determined grin. Isis had a hunch she knew what her other self was looking to do. She wanted to kill her and then bring her back, make Isis just like her. A vampire.

Isis grabbed The Apprentice's thumb and pulled. But it wouldn't budge; the grip was too tight. "Push, push," Isis chanted to the energy, but to no avail. That same energy was being used against her by a far stronger conduit.

"Please, don't," Isis pleaded with whatever sound she could get through The Apprentice's throat grip. "You know we hate being a vampire."

The Apprentice's head tilted. She ripped her hand from Isis' throat. After several coughs, Isis looked up at the charred face glaring down at her. This time, she didn't struggle. "Wha-what do you want? Why are we here?" Her voice croaked as she took in heavy breaths of air.

The Apprentice leaned in close. Her voice was low and raspy, the result of barely speaking over the centuries. She did, however, get one raw word out of her throat. "Revenge." Breath that smelled like rotten onions slapped Isis in the face.

The Apprentice rose from her chest. Isis let out a deep exhale. "I-I know what you want to do. The portal between dimensions you want to create, it'll destroy this world. We met someone from the future. He says *everyone* dies. I know that's not something we would ever do, no matter what we've been through."

Isis' body dragged across the sand. She dug her fingers to stop, but it was like being pulled by an invisible rope. Never had she ever felt so helpless. The Apprentice could literally do anything to her. Maybe that was the message she was trying to send.

The dragging stopped once Isis was again between the five crystals. Isis sat up. The Apprentice dropped to a knee so they'd be face-to-face. She lifted Isis' head by the chin and said in the same raspy voice, "Screw the world."

The Apprentice turned around and stormed across the sandy island. Sparks formed once again around Isis, keeping her trapped like a scared animal in a cage.

Chapter Thirteen

Zack was back in New Salem, and in lots of trouble. He was seated on one of three chairs in the middle of Sebastian and Selena's living room with Jeb pressed against the seat to his left and Amelia on his right. The angry eyes of Sebastian peered down at all of them as he paced back and forth. Zack turned his chair to the left where Selena and Sacha sat on the floor with their legs crossed and eyes closed, facing each other. Both sisters chanted "Find Isis" over and over.

"Any luck?" Zack asked anxiously.

Harry was leaned against the dining room table across the room with his arms folded. His eyes rolled. "Obviously not yet." His lips smacked. "If they found her, they would have said something, don't you think?"

Amelia let out a snort. Zack wanted to tear into Harry and his sarcastic wit. *Why are you even here, you snot-nosed punk? You've been less than useless!* Zack wanted to shout it at the top of his lungs—maybe throw in a "Mister Future boy." But right now, it was best he kept his mouth shut.

Zack's chair suddenly shifted and skidded across the floor. It moved a few feet, stopping in front of Sebastian. Zack looked into the glowing eyes that faced him like an angry judge ready to announce sentencing. His Adam's apple felt heavy like it was about to drop into his stomach. Zack had never pissed off his new guardians like this, never defied their orders so blatantly. He also never screwed up so badly. Damn, he should have thought better of the plan and talked them all out of it.

"Zack, what the hell were you thinking?" The glow in Sebastian's eyes faded. His tone was surprisingly calm, all things considered. "What were any of you thinking? What was your plan if you did capture The Apprentice? Did you even have one?"

A peek over at Jeb let Zack know he was in this alone. Jeb's eyes were wide, and his knees were shaking. He had never been through such a traumatic experience in his entire life. He had to be as worried about Maya as Zack was about Isis. Jeb was so lost in that worry he was oblivious to the interrogation. But Sebastian had asked the one question Zack could counter and maybe ease some of the heat so they could focus on finding Isis.

"We were following *your* plan!" Zack sat up and pointed at Sebastian. "Did you adults have a plan once you captured The Apprentice?"

"Yes, we did!" Sebastian's voice rose. He waved a hand at Selena and Sacha. "The sisters can open a portal to The Other World, which they were going to do. Then we were going to send The Apprentice through and close it up. Get her the hell off this planet and stop her impending destruction!"

Zack's shoulders slumped. His head dropped. "That's actually a really good plan," he mumbled.

"And you!" Sebastian shot an accusatory glare at Amelia. "Vice President Paul gave you a second chance at a life here. Now his daughter is in critical condition. This is how you repay him?"

Amelia raised her hands, palms out. "Hey, don't look at me. This was all their idea. They recruited me for transportation."

"That's true. We brought her into this."

Wow, Zack hated having to defend Amelia. But that was the truth, and he needed everyone to refocus on finding Isis. Sebastian's anger was justified; he had to be worried sick. They all were. Hopefully they'd sense her location fast before The Apprentice did anything crazy...like kill her alternate timeline twin.

"Ugh!" Sacha stood, breaking her trance. "We can't find them. The Apprentice must be masking their location from us."

Selena looked at Sacha from her seated position. "Sit back down, Sis. We're not giving up. We must break through and find her."

Sebastian spun to Harry who now sat on the table with his hands cupped against the back of his head. The kid was really comfortable considering the crisis they had in front of them. "You say your connection is strong, and you're from the future. Can you help locate Isis?"

Harry tossed Sebastian a sideways glance. "If I could, don't you think I would?" His head swung toward the door. "By the way, someone just teleported outside—two someones, actually. One witch, one non."

Paul and Natasha suddenly materialized in the middle of the living room. Zack nearly jumped out of his seat. Sebastian's angry face could be intimidating, but it was put to shame by Paul's. Natasha didn't look particularly happy either.

Jeb, who had sat frozen in his chair from the moment they entered the cottage, jumped from his seat.

He ran to Paul in a frantic manner. "How is she?" Those were the first words he had uttered since Amelia brought them back to the village.

Paul's demeanor calmed, perhaps from seeing the anxiety on Jeb's face. He placed a hand on the huge teenage boy's shoulder. "Fortunately, Doctor Mac is a powerful witch. He was able to reattach Maya's hand. It will take time before she regains feeling, if that ever happens."

"But…but she's going to be okay?"

"I'm sure she will be." Paul offered a half smile. "Why don't you go see her? I'm sure she'd appreciate the company, and right now, I'd like time to speak with this coven alone."

Jeb nodded, then ran for the door. He pulled it open and rushed through. Once the door closed behind him, Paul's back and shoulders straightened. He moved in like a man on a mission. Sebastian stepped in front of him.

"Paul, on behalf of my coven, also my family, I apologize for what has happened."

"I respect the bravery. I do." Paul walked past Sebastian and stopped in front of Zack, who rose from his chair. The top of his head barely came to Paul's shoulders. "But you were foolish. You could have come to us and told us where to locate our target. Now, she has Isis, and we have no idea where they may be."

"I know, I'm sorry. We just thought we could—"

Paul raised a hand, stopping Zack mid-sentence. "We can only pray The Apprentice does not move up her plans to open a hole to the Other World. We could all be in a lot more trouble right now."

"Hold on a sec!" Amelia's head popped up. She

128

leaped out of her chair and eyed Zack with scrutiny. "The Other World…is that what this is about?"

Amelia's eyes opened wide. Her tirade broke Selena and Sacha from their spell. Amelia stormed to Zack. "That vampire Isis…she's going there for Valeria, isn't she?"

"Right now," Paul growled, "we need to stay focused on the main issue—"

"Zack, you and Isis held out on me, didn't you?"

"Amelia, if The Apprentice opens that portal, it will destroy this planet." Zack shot a finger at Harry. "He's from the future. He's seen the destruction firsthand."

Amelia's eyebrows rose. She eyed Harry. "Are you really from the future?" Harry gave her a thumbs-up.

"We don't have time for this," Sebastian shouted. "We need to find them, now."

Selena rubbed a hand against Sebastian's back. Her face was filled with distress. "This is going to be tough. The Apprentice is blocking our Wiccan senses. They could be anywhere on the planet. We need to come up with another way."

"If The Apprentice is strong enough to hide from Wiccan senses," Natasha said, "then there is no other way."

Zack felt the discouragement and panic throughout the room, especially from the family. Sebastian resumed his pacing.

"Hey!" Sacha reached for Selena's arm. "We're not just going to give up, are we? Between us, we have a pretty damned powerful connection. We also know how to use it better than most. So, let's break through whatever spell she has conjured."

129

"Sach, Isis is already on our level." Selena shook her head. "This version of her also has two hundred years of experience controlling the energy. If she doesn't want to be found—"

A light bulb suddenly went off in Zack's brain. "There is another way!" he shouted. "We can find them through Amelia!"

All eyes focused on Zack. "How?" Paul asked.

"It's how her portals work! They take her to whoever or whatever she wants to find." Zack flashed his hands at Amelia like a magician showing off a huge prop to the audience. "That's how we found The Apprentice in the first place. Amelia focused on her, and the portal opened near her."

"Amelia." Sebastian's arms folded across his chest. "Is this true? Is that how your connection works?"

"It is," Amelia answered. "I just think about a person or place, the portal opens, I step through, and, boom, I'm there."

"Then let's do this!" Selena said. "Sach, you still have your enchanted crystals?"

"Of course, I do," came the answer. "We're going with the same plan, I take it?"

Harry jumped off the table. "It's a good plan."

"Same plan." Paul removed his handgun from its holster. "Natasha and I will join you. We might not have the element of surprise anymore, so we will need to go in hard and fast."

"There's only one huge problem with this plan," Amelia announced.

"Problem?" Zack's head spun her way. "What problem?"

Amelia strolled to the end of the room. A distorted

circle of static formed behind her against the wall. "The problem is that I'm not taking you there." Amelia turned and ran through the portal. It closed behind her.

"Wait. What?" Sacha exclaimed.

"Well," Harry snickered. "I sure didn't see that coming."

Chapter Fourteen

Isis stood between the crystals, eyeing the energy surrounding her in a pyramid shape. It was her prison so long as The Apprentice kept control of it. The Apprentice circled the island, staring down at the sand, perhaps looking for a perfect spot to open her hole into the other dimension.

Wow, talk about blowing it. According to Harry, The Apprentice wasn't supposed to open that wormhole between dimensions for two more days. That was before Isis, Zack, and their friends decided to do something stupid. Really stupid, and that was in spite of Mom and Dad's orders to stay behind. She had always listened to them before. Why did she ever think defying them this time was a good idea? Maybe because she thought she had something to prove.

Way to prove herself. She was now The Apprentice's captive while Maya could be permanently crippled...or dead. The Apprentice rolled her foot across the sand, forming a big circle. That must have been the spot she had chosen to create her portal. Damn, she really was going to do it now despite Isis' warning of what it would cause.

"You don't have to go there," Isis shouted, but she was clearly being ignored. How demeaning that another version of Isis found her unworthy of a response. Maybe she just needed a different approach.

"Our histories went very different," Isis said, thinking back to all she had learned about The Apprentice's life from the implanted memories. "In your history, Valeria killed Luther. In this one, Luther taught Mom and Sacha how to open the portal to the Other World. He remembered the spell from when the witches of his time created it. Then he dragged her through. Here, Valeria never became queen, never tortured us. She and Luther have been in the Other World all this time together."

The Apprentice froze. She pulled her foot back from the circle it was digging in the sand and turned to face Isis.

"You remember Luther, the Witches of Vegas' vampire mentor?" Isis continued, hoping she was getting through. "He made us promise never to reopen a path to the Other World. He won't approve of you going there, especially if you try to kill her. Luther will try to stop you. You're not going to battle Luther, are you?"

The Apprentice's glare made her intentions clear. The face was filled with psychotic determination without a shred of care as to what consequences her actions would cause. At one time, Isis had the same anger toward Valeria, but could she ever become so detached from compassion? She never thought it possible, no matter what she had gone through. Yet, the proof to the contrary stood front and center. For The Apprentice to exist, Isis must have had the capacity to be so ferocious on some deeper level.

An oval-shaped distortion suddenly formed between Isis and The Apprentice, who jutted out her fangs and snarled at it. A momentary hope filled Isis that this was her family and friends from New Salem arriving to save her. That hope fizzled when Amelia stepped through. Talk about the last person Isis wanted for her hero. The portal closed behind Amelia, meaning she was alone. But why? What was she trying to accomplish coming here by herself?

Isis wanted to shout for her to get lost, and fast. Before she could get a word out, The Apprentice acted. Amelia levitated off the sand. She hovered in the air as if she was trapped in an invisible balloon. The Apprentice's fists glowed at her side. Her eyes darkened.

"Whoa, whoa. Hold up!" Amelia yanked off the white napkin, which hung from her collar, and waved it like a flag of surrender. "I didn't come here to fight you. I came here to help you."

Amelia's upper body and legs contorted. Her chest and knees pushed closer together. Amelia's face cringed. "Hey, wait!" Amelia cried out. "Hear me out, okay? You want to get to Valeria? I can make it super easy for you. That's my Wiccan power. I create portals that can go anywhere. Together, we can make one that goes to the Other World!"

"Amelia!" Isis gasped. "What are you doing?"

"Being a hero, just like you suggested." Amelia's eyes never left The Apprentice. "I can make a portal. All you would have to do is guide it to the Other World. Together, we can take you from this place to that one. Then you get exactly what you want, a face-to-face with the top badass witch."

The Apprentice's eyes squinted. Amelia's upper body and legs straightened meaning they were no longer being crushed by an invisible force. She lowered to the sandy ground. The Apprentice's fist stopped glowing while the darkness in her eyes faded.

"I take it we have a deal?" Amelia asked through a smirk.

Isis tried to spring forward, but The Apprentice's invisible force field kept her from moving more than a step. "Just so you know, she hates Valeria," Isis yelled to Amelia. "She wants to go there to kill your mother's hero!"

"Oh, I figured that out on my own." Amelia waved the napkin again to get The Apprentice's attention. "And I'm okay with that. Valeria has been my mother's obsession her entire life. That obsession made my life a living hell. It's what got her killed. I am happy to use my connection to help this vampire get a piece of that one." Amelia flashed a smile toward The Apprentice. "Does that sound good to you?"

"Amelia, you need to run!" Isis slammed both fists into the energy shield. Static formed then solidified where her fists connected. "Get out of here now while you still can!"

"I don't think that's necessary." Amelia rolled her eyes. "This Isis and I have come to an understanding, something you and I could never do—"

"No! You don't get it!" Isis' voice screeched. "She doesn't need *you*, just your connection! Witches can steal another's connection! It happens when a witch is set on *fire!*"

Amelia's eyebrows rose. "What are you talking about? I've never heard that." She looked at The Apprentice. "Is that true?"

"Yes!" Isis shouted. "It's true! Get out of here!"

The Apprentice closed the gap by two steps with

her fists clenched and her eyes narrowed. Amelia's cocky smirk left her face. A portal suddenly opened behind her. Amelia turned around and ran through, but she was quickly yanked out by what seemed like an invisible hand that wrapped around her waist which then slammed her down onto the sand. The portal faded away.

"What are you doing?" Amelia cried out. "I'm here to help you!"

"No! Don't do it!" Isis shrieked. "There's no reason!" But it was too late.

Fire shot out of Amelia's body, from her arms to her legs and torso. Isis averted her eyes. But she couldn't keep from hearing Amelia's high-pitched screams. Or keep from smelling the abrupt odor of cooked flesh. It smelled like meat on the barbecue. Isis' hands pressed harder against her face. She just couldn't bring herself to even peek, not until the screaming stopped. Even then, she only opened one eye.

There was nothing left of Amelia, no flesh, no bones, just a huge pile of black and red ash across the sand. A wind ruffled the sand around it. It whispered up and engulfed The Apprentice. "You actually did it," Isis gasped, her voice barely above a bird's squawk. "You killed her."

The Apprentice raised her head and shut her eyes. Her chest compressed, and a look of contentment filled her face as if she were slurping the remains of an ice cream sundae. Isis never really understood the process of taking in another witch's connection, not like she'd ever try it herself, but, right now, it made for a good distraction. The Apprentice's face pointed to the sky. Isis needed to take advantage of the moment. There was no telling how long it would last.

Isis ran past the crystals. This time, there was no invisible shield keeping her prisoner, not while its controller was too distracted to hold onto the spell. Isis focused on New Salem's quad. "Teleport!" she chanted. Everything blurred…but not before The Apprentice disappeared and then reappeared directly in front of her.

The Apprentice snatched Isis by the throat with one hand. The blurriness immediately cleared, meaning the two-hundred-year-old Wiccan vampire once again interrupted Isis' teleportation spell. The Apprentice snarled like a rabid dog. She tossed Isis back between the five enchanted crystals. Before Isis could react, the energy sparked around her.

The Apprentice's eyes were filled with anger. One word uttered through her raspy voice. "Stay."

Isis rolled to her knees, then held her hands out in surrender. "Okay, okay. I won't try to go anywhere. I promise."

The Apprentice nodded. She walked to the island's shore, looking out at the water smacking the shore. A portal—one of Amelia's portals—opened in front of her. Another opened inches from the crystal pyramid. The Apprentice walked into one and exited through the other. Both portals faded away.

Satisfied with her test run, The Apprentice strolled to the opposite end of the island just past Herb Galloway's grave. With a wave of her hand, the crystals around Isis leapt in the air and landed in a perfect pentagon in front of The Apprentice. She focused on the space between the crystals where another portal opened.

"That leads to the Other World, doesn't it?" Isis

asked, already knowing the answer. "You should know, Amelia's portals always close behind her. You won't be able to keep it open, and there's no Wiccan energy on the other side. Once you go through, you'll have no way to return."

The Apprentice looked back at Isis with a huge grin, which showed off her two-hundred-year-old corroded teeth. Isis knew that smile well. It was one she was guilty of displaying whenever she came up with what she believed to be a brilliant idea. Zack had mentioned it several times before, as had others who knew her well.

Isis suddenly lifted in the air and moved toward The Apprentice and the portal as if she were in a river flowing downstream. The vampire's plan was now clear; she wasn't going alone. Isis dropped on her backside next to The Apprentice, who watched her, giving her time. Isis knew what she was expected to do before they went through. Despite the instinct to defy her other self, she also knew there was no choice. She had to reach out and let her family know. If not, she'd be trapped on the other side for the rest of her life. They would have to come and get her while leaving a way back. A way back that The Apprentice could exploit.

Damn, it actually was a brilliant idea.

Chapter Fifteen

"I can't believe she bolted on us." Zack was sure he had the same befuddled look on his face as everyone else in the room. On second thought, he shouldn't have been so surprised. "Now what do we— *Whoa!*"

Zack clutched his head with both hands. He dropped to his knees. An image formed in his head of a circle of static on a beach, or an island. It was a familiar portal moving closer to him, or perhaps he was moving closer to it. He suddenly realized that he was seeing through someone else's eyes. "Oh, no," he gasped.

The static filled Zack's vision from all directions. He was inside the portal. Then the image was gone.

"Zack!" Natasha dropped to her knees next to him.

Sebastian, Selena, and Sacha came close and did the same. Paul stood over them while Harry hadn't budged a step.

Sacha grabbed Zack by his elbow and pulled him to his knees. "Talk to us, Zack. What the hell just happened to you?"

"It…it was Isis." Zack's head spun to the concerned faces that surrounded him. "The Apprentice just stole Amelia's connection and took Isis to the Other World. She used Amelia's portal power."

Selena placed her hand on Zack's back. "Calm down. Take deep breaths."

"What do you mean The Apprentice stole Amelia's

connection?" Paul asked. "How could a witch do that?"

"Through fire." Sebastian stood from Zack's side. "A witch can steal another's connection by—"

"Uh-oh!" Harry's usual sarcastic tone was replaced by one of dread. "If she took Isis to the Other World, then we failed. Everything is happening the same way."

"The same way?" Zack asked while Selena and Natasha helped him to his feet. "You mean the same way it happened in your timeline?"

Harry waved his hands in the air in a frantic manner. "I told you, this *is* my timeline! I was pulled by the energy and sent back to change it. But this is exactly how it went the first time around."

"It can't be the same, not the way you described it," Zack responded, dusting himself off. "I just saw through Isis' eyes. The Apprentice used Amelia's portal ability to take Isis to the Other World. Amelia's portals always close as soon as she steps through."

Harry rolled his eyes in frustration, a frustration neither Zack nor anyone else in the room understood.

"What are you trying to tell us, Harry?" Selena asked.

"The Apprentice doesn't freeze her own portal between the two dimensions," Harry explained in a slow and deliberate voice as if he was talking to children. "She freezes the one Sacha and Selena make when all of you try to rescue Isis from the Other World."

"That is what happens?" Paul leaned in with a scowl. "And you knew this all along but never shared it?"

Harry backed away from Paul, but after his first step, he bumped into Sebastian who moved behind him.

"Hold on." Sebastian grabbed Harry's arm and spun him around. "If you knew how things would play out, why did you say nothing when we went to the Bronx to watch over Isis' former family?"

"You even came with us," Sacha added.

Harry looked back and forth from Sebastian to Paul, and then to everyone else in the room. "I know the general idea of what happened, but I don't know all the details. I wasn't even born yet." Harry shrugged. "I thought it made sense that you'd face off with The Apprentice there and stop it all from happening in the first place. It turned out we were all wrong."

Sebastian's eyes went wide. "Harry, when we made those plans to look for her in the Bronx, my instincts went off telling me to leave Isis and Zack behind. That was you, wasn't it?"

"I had the same thought at the time," Selena said.

"As did I," Paul added.

Harry held a hand over his head to indicate himself. "Guilty. From what I knew, Isis and Zack were there during the initial confrontation with The Apprentice, and that's where she was captured. I figured them staying behind was the best way to keep the events from repeating themselves. Turns out, it didn't matter. She was taken anyway."

"She was taken because she did not come with us," Natasha said. "Isis and friends confront Apprentice alone. You, Harry, create future."

"Well, yeah, that might be right." Harry stepped back and smacked his chest. "But this time, it'll be different. I'll be there. It's time for Plan B where I stand guard at the open portal and protect it from any Wiccan vampire that may try to manipulate it. We'll make sure things go differently this time."

"Or they could go exactly the same way, just as they have thus far." Paul marched past Harry. He faced Sebastian and the sisters. "I am sorry, but as much as I want to see Isis safe and sound, we cannot risk the safety of everyone in New Salem, and the entire planet. I'm afraid I cannot allow you to open a portal to the Other World."

"What?" Sacha screeched.

Selena leaped at the vice president. "That is our daughter over there, Paul. She can't survive in the Other World, even if there weren't two vampires in battle."

"I understand, and this is not an easy decision for me to make. But, under the circumstances, do you think even Isis would want you risking billions of lives for her—"

"Do we really need his permission?" Harry shouted. "We could just go get her on our own."

Natasha held her hand out. Harry hovered an inch off the ground. From the struggle on his face, he was clearly trying to move his limbs, but with no luck. He suddenly floated until he was face-to-face with Paul who narrowed his eyes. "That would be inadvisable, young man," he growled.

"Paul, please listen to reason," Selena pleaded.

"I am all about reason right now. Each of you are residents of New Salem, whether that residency is today or someday in the future." Paul eyed Harry as he spoke. "Understand, this is not an easy decision, but I expect my executive orders to be followed." Paul's head rotated to face the others. "I don't think conflict with the New Salem Task Force is in anybody's best interests, agreed?"

"To leave her there is to kill her," Zack said, hoping he could get through to the vice president where everyone else failed.

"I do understand that," Paul responded as Harry dropped onto his feet. "And I hate to make this call, believe me, I do. But it is the only way. I am sure Isis would not want billions of lives lost because we attempted to free her."

The room turned into an eerie silence. Zack and Sacha looked across the room to Sebastian and Selena. It was Selena who spoke. "Paul, you cannot expect us to just accept this. We have to save our child—"

Sebastian stepped in front of Selena, cutting her off. He faced Paul and said the last three words Zack expected to hear him say. "We will comply."

"Um…Sebastian?" Sacha gasped.

"I am the leader of this coven, so it is my decision to make!" Sebastian turned to Selena and grabbed her by the shoulders. "Selena, on our love and our marriage, look at me and be with me on this."

Selena's eyes shut. Her head dropped. She pulled away from Sebastian, walked across the room until her forehead pressed against the wall.

"Sis?" Sacha asked in disbelief. The shock on her and Harry's faces were not a surprise. It mirrored exactly how Zack felt.

"Paul, as hard as this is for us, everything you're saying is true. You can trust us to follow your orders. Right now, you should be with Maya," Sebastian said, looking Paul directly in the eyes. "Please give me time to speak with my coven alone."

Paul nodded, then turned away. "Natasha, please

take me to see Maya. After that, I will meet with the president and fill her in on what has transpired." He looked back to the coven. "I am truly sorry about this."

"As am I," Natasha said. There was a hint of bitterness in her voice.

Natasha mumbled a word in Russian right before both she and Paul faded away. Zack wasted no time storming up to Sebastian. "What the hell just happened?" he shouted. "You can't possibly be willing to just leave Isis over there to rot, can you?"

"Not at all." Sebastian snapped. "But we weren't going to convince them and, frankly, we didn't have the time to try. We're on our own here."

"Nice," Harry said through a grin. "Then we are going to try to rescue her."

"Um…Sebastian." Sacha raised a finger. "I was sure I felt the energy surge. Did you just use an influence spell on the vice president of New Salem?"

"I did."

"How in the world did Natasha not notice?"

Selena looked back from the wall. "I blocked her senses so she wouldn't pick up on it. I can't be sure I succeeded. Natasha has a strong connection."

"Well done!" Harry gave a slow and deliberate clap. "He said *be with me on this*. Now I got it. Man, I love being part of this coven!" Zack squinted, wondering when Harry became part of "this coven."

"Either way, they'll figure it out soon enough." Sebastian walked to the front door. "Isis needs us, so let's not dawdle. Sacha, grab your enchanted crystals. You and Selena open the portal. I think it best we attempt this outside of New Salem's border—"

"We do it in the cemetery!" Sacha announced. "It

circles the village because that's where the Earth's ley lines were formed, and where the energy is most sensitive. Right, Zack?"

"That's true," Zack said, remembering all he had learned both here and in the other timeline. "It was also how the first vampire Isis was able to form a shield around New Salem during the war."

"Sacha, do you still remember the spell?" Selena asked.

Sacha responded with an affirming nod.

"Good," Sebastian said. "You open it. I'll go in, find Isis, and bring her back. Hopefully I can get her before we're noticed on either side of the portal."

"I'm coming with you!" Zack said as sternly as he had ever spoken before. "Don't try to force me to stay behind. I won't." He prepared himself for an argument he had every intention of winning.

After a moment's hesitation, Sebastian let out a deep sigh. "Okay, but we must be careful. Harry, you'll come through the portal as well and stand guard, as per your plan."

Wow, that went far better than Zack thought it would.

Harry's calm demeanor suddenly went cold. He looked lost in thought, like something was weighing on his brain.

"Harry, is there something else we need to know?" Zack asked.

Harry picked up his head. A huge smile crossed his lips. "Nah, I think we're good. Let's do this."

"Let's do this," Sebastian repeated.

"I'll meet you there," Sacha said, then chanted, "Teleport to my bedroom." She faded away.

The others surrounded Selena, who closed her eyes and mumbled a teleportation spell for the entire group.

Chapter Sixteen

Isis landed on all fours. The sand that covered her pants and shirt poured onto the grayish grass underneath her. The grass felt like weeds against her hands. She lifted her head in time to see sparks of the energy fizzle out where the portal once stood. A sense of loneliness filled her stomach. There was nothing around except for the grassland and thick trees with thin branches and thorns along the bark. There wasn't a leaf in sight, or sign of civilization. This was definitely not home.

"Zack, I hope you got the message," she mumbled to herself.

Isis had several ideas of what the Other World would look like. This didn't match any of them. There was no sunlight or clouds, just a light gray sky. Isis took a deep breath. The air tasted foreign, like trying to suck oxygen inside of a paper bag. Where Earth was alive and vibrant, this place felt listless and lonely. Except she wasn't alone. A vampire with her face and pure black eyes stood over her.

"Okay, we're here," Isis said. "Now what?"

The Apprentice leaped in the air and grabbed onto one of the nearby tree's thin branches. She slammed a hand down, breaking off the end. She dropped to the ground, landing on the soles of her bare feet. The tip of the branch was sharp like a foot-long stake made of bark. The other end was the size of a baseball bat. The Apprentice held the sharp edge in front of her face, then nodded her approval. Although Isis wasn't a vampire, that edge could still do great damage to her body. Hopefully, it wasn't meant for her, but it wasn't a chance she wanted to take.

Isis propelled herself to her feet and ran. The Apprentice landed in front of her with the stake pointed out. It forced Isis to stop short, causing her to lose her balance. The Apprentice grabbed Isis by the belt, preventing her from toppling backward. Then, with one hand, she lifted Isis in the air and thrust her over her shoulder. She about-faced and took off at what had to be a record pace. Isis grabbed onto the back of The Apprentice's shirt, holding on for dear life.

After running like a track star for what felt like miles, The Apprentice came to a halt. Isis flew from her shoulder and slammed into the grass. She rolled until her fingers snatched handfuls of the grass, stopping her body's momentum. She gasped upon realizing she was inches from a cliff. How far down that drop went, Isis had no idea. Did The Apprentice? Did she even care?

Isis pulled herself to her knees and peeked over her shoulder. But her captor was gone. Unfortunately, the pain in her stomach was not. The only trace of The Apprentice was a slight rustling of the branches high above. Isis peeked up, but she couldn't see her anywhere. With The Apprentice's speed, she could have been anywhere. But whether she was still above the trees, or miles away exploring the Other World, it still left Isis by herself on a strange planet in another dimension. There was still one hope. Perhaps she didn't have to face this place all by herself.

"*Luther*!" Isis screamed. "*Luther, can you hear me? Where are you?*"

The sound of galloping turned Isis' head. It wasn't Luther or anyone else she would have recognized. Her eyes went wide. "Oh, crap," she mumbled.

Two four-legged animals approached. They were huge like horses, but unlike the animals Isis knew from Earth, these had black fur and plump bodies that resembled bulls. Their paws had long claws that were sharp like knives. The heavy breathing from both animals triggered danger warnings in Isis' brain. Her first thought was to teleport, but she couldn't sense Wiccan energy on this world. The animals stopped directly in front of her.

Isis slowly stood up and looked into their large grayish eyes. "Hi there," she said in as soft of a voice as her dry throat could muster. "I'm not here to hurt you. I'm not a threat. I promise."

One of the animals opened its long snout. The teeth it showed were many, and all of them looked like razor blades. A puff of smoke blew out of its brown nostrils. The animal made a loud noise that sounded like it came from a bad trumpet player. Isis wasn't sure if it was attempting communication or readying itself to attack. The second one made the same sound, flashed its teeth, and then stood on its hind legs. Isis jumped back. She considered running but it was doubtful her legs could outrace these huge animals.

With each step the two animals took, Isis backpedaled until she pressed against a tree. She eyed the cliff as a means to flee, but if it was a far drop, she could end up breaking every bone in her body. The last thing she expected when The Apprentice dragged her to the Other World was meeting her end by getting eaten by two alien creatures…although technically Isis was on their planet. She was the alien—

From out of nowhere, a tall woman appeared. She jumped in front of Isis, facing the two animals in a battle stance. Dark but dirty straight hair hung to her waist. Her black skirt and blouse were filthy and torn in several places. She let out a loud snake-like hiss. The animals backed away, then galloped in separate directions. The woman slowly turned around and faced Isis with her dark purple irises. Isis' back rubbed hard against the tree. Her shirt tore.

The woman's lips stretched open, showing off her corroded teeth.

"Valeria," Isis gasped. "Wh-where is Luther?"

Valeria leaned in with a scowl. If her intention was to frighten, it worked. Every memory that filled Isis' nightmares, memories both from her life and that of Isis from the previous timeline, ran through her brain. A shiver rolled down her spine like a dull knife. Her jaw trembled. If not for the tree, she may have toppled over.

"Luther is on the other side of this land hunting those creatures for blood." Valeria's teeth ground. Two long fangs protruded from her upper lip. "The real question, young witch, is what are *you* doing here?"

"I…I'm…" The words wouldn't come out of Isis' mouth. Their history of conflict was far longer and more horrifying than what this timeline's Valeria had known. Now the monster was staring her down again. At least here Valeria didn't have her Wiccan connection…but neither did Isis. Meanwhile, Valeria was still a dangerous centuries-old vampire.

"Well?" Valeria snapped. "I await an answer.

Wha—"

The Apprentice leapt from the branches above Isis' head. She swung her makeshift weapon in mid-air, slamming the thicker end against Valeria's ear. The elder vampire went down and rolled to the edge of the cliff, perhaps more out of sheer surprise than pain. The Apprentice swung the branch around so the pointy end faced forward. She bent her knees, ready to pounce.

Valeria stood up, holding the side of her head. Her gaze shifted from The Apprentice to Isis and then back. "What in damnation?"

The Apprentice flung the branch at Valeria like a dart. Valeria caught it in mid-air, but it was a distraction. The other Isis charged, ramming her shoulder into Valeria's midsection. The Apprentice thrust the elder Wiccan vampire backward. The momentum sent them both over the cliff. The sharpened branch flew from Valeria's hand, taking the plunge along with her.

At least now Isis' escape would be easy, so long as she wasn't mauled by one of those alien animals. Isis picked herself up and ran. But where would she run to? What if Zack never received the message, or her family couldn't open a hole between this location and theirs? Even if they did arrive, they could be anywhere.

Isis did have one option; she had to find Luther. According to Valeria, he was at the other end of this land. Unfortunately, she had no idea in which direction.

****

Valeria pushed away from her attacker while both fell through the air. She landed on her stomach and bounced. Instinct took over, forcing her to roll back to a standing position. The other Isis did the same, rising up with darkened eyes and protruding fangs. Valeria dodged a step back, realizing that her newfound enemy was already in attack mode. The hate and anger in her face were as baffling as her resemblance to the child their battle left behind. For the first time in perhaps her entire four-century existence, Valeria was at a loss.

It was as if she had picked up a book and started reading it from the middle instead of the beginning. Right now, she had to push past the confusion and focus on what she did know. This vampire—whoever she was—represented a threat to Valeria's continued existence. She had to be neutralized quickly. But first, Valeria needed to stall so she could get her bearings.

"You look and smell like Isis Rivera," Valeria said, keeping a healthy distance from her attacker. "Except you are far older. I know I did not turn you, yet I sense my essence within you. How can that be?"

The younger vampire looked back and forth at the hundreds of decaying animal carcasses around them. They were at the bottom of the cliff where the creatures dragged their dead, then pushed the bodies over. Valeria suspected it was out of some sort of instinctive ritual. In truth, their reason did not matter so long as they continued to repopulate and provide more blood for her vampiric needs.

It was time to alleviate the threat. Valeria charged. Her opponent did the same. At the last possible moment Valeria reached out to clutch her opponent's throat. The girl slapped Valeria's hand away and dodged to the left. Valeria's balance was thrown off, which left her vulnerable to a tackle from behind. It was as if this undead Isis lookalike knew exactly what to expect.

An arm from behind wrapped around Valeria's

throat. A back elbow did not budge the grip. A second one, however, felt nose cartilage. The impact broke the hold and moved her opponent back. Valeria clenched her fist, then spun, launching a roundhouse right. It contacted only air. The Isis vampire charged and grabbed Valeria's outstretched arm. She bit down on Valeria's forearm. The fangs dug through Valeria's muscle with a sting that rocketed straight up her arm and into her reanimated brain. For the first time in centuries, she screamed. Almost on instinct, Valeria jabbed her sharp fingernails into the smaller and skinnier vampire's eyes. She had never been bitten by another vampire before. With the grip broken, Valeria stumbled backward, giving herself some space.

"Who are you?" Valeria screamed. "What did I do to you? Why do you hate me so?"

The Isis vampire rubbed an arm across her eyes. When the arm came down, her pitch-black eyes were filled with determination. Dark red soot covered her mouth and fangs; it was Valeria's blood. Then, she spoke. "Your…" Her voice sounded more like a growl. "App-ren-tice."

Apprentice? The name rang a bell. It was what Valeria intended to rename Isis after turning and then training her. But Valeria had changed her mind. Instead, she decided to kill the wretched girl on a public street as an example to the world. It was a plan that failed miserably and began Valeria's second exile, thanks to that boy and Isis' wretched family.

Valeria had replayed the battle many times in her head. There was much she could have done differently, but she never once questioned her decision not to make Isis a member of the undead. Yet, here she was, a vampire turned by Valeria with a body that had to be hundreds of years old. What was going on here? No. Right now it was better to focus on what she could deduce from the situation.

This…Apprentice, she was here seeking revenge for acts Valeria had not yet committed, so survival was the priority. After that, she focused on the fact that her attacker had to have come from somewhere. Unless this monstrosity planned on staying, there must have been a door from somewhere in the Other World. Perhaps it led back to Mother Earth.

The Apprentice, as she called herself, peered at the roots of the nearest tree. Her weapon, the sharpened branch, lay in front. She dove for it. Valeria did as well, but realizing she was a step behind, pulled back. The Apprentice, meanwhile, rolled to her feet and held the branch with the sharp end facing Valeria. There was very little that could end a vampire's existence, but wood was one of those rare materials that required caution. Wood could cause an infection throughout a body's cells, even an undead one. It was a formidable weapon against a vampire.

Valeria jumped in the air and grabbed onto a high branch. She barely avoided the charging Apprentice, but at least she now had the high ground. Her opponent, meanwhile, had the weapon so it wasn't exactly a fair match. What mattered most, Valeria realized, was the futility of prolonging this confrontation.

The Apprentice was determined, but so was Valeria. That meant the battle could turn into a war that would last for all of eternity with neither succumbing to the other's attacks. It was time for Valeria to utilize her one distinct advantage. She had lived in the Other

World for three hundred years before finding a way to escape. She was sent back, along with Luther, for however long they had been here. About a year? Maybe more. The fact was, no one knew the land as well as she did. Time to utilize that knowledge.

"You wish to end me?" Valeria shouted from her branch. "Then come and try!"

She climbed the branches until she made it to the top of the tree. Her next move became obvious. A devious grin formed across her face. Valeria ran across the branch and jumped onto a nearby tree. From there she jumped to another. Rustling from behind meant The Apprentice took the bait. She must have believed Valeria was running from the fight, as intended.

After several more leaps, Valeria reached her destination. The forest of trees led to another cliff, one overlooking a rocky terrain. The area sitting dead center on this particular land was filled with huge crevices between the large rocks and covered with mostly gray moss.

Valeria stood at the edge of the thick branch overlooking the terrain. If her plan were to work, the timing would have to be perfect. The rustling coming her way grew with frequency and intensity. She waited until the last possible moment, then dropped from the tree, landing at the cliff's edge.

The Apprentice could not stop her momentum. Her body flew past the trees straight down into the terrain. She hit the rocks, bounced, and then rolled. Refusing to be denied, The Apprentice shot to her feet and gazed straight up at the cliff's edge and Valeria. Her focus shifted to one of the rocky caverns. Two of the native animals stepped out and snarled. Three more approached The Apprentice from the caverns behind her. Another one charged from the right.

This was an area Valeria and Luther avoided at all costs. It was where the native species gathered when they weren't roaming the land. It was an open space with enough enclosed areas for hiding and sleeping in packs. The one and only time Valeria tracked them into this terrain, she had been overwhelmed and barely escaped, but not before suffering brutal injuries. The area was a great defense against vampires seeking their blood. The animals' instinct to go there, especially at nighttime, had evolved over generations.

The Apprentice now realized she was caught in the trap. A dozen of the creatures surrounded her. One reared on its hind legs, which Valeria knew was a message for the others to attack. As much as Valeria would have loved to stay at the top of the cliff and watch The Apprentice have the boldness ripped from her body by these creatures, she had a far more important goal ahead of her.

A portal. There had to be one. It was the only explanation of how The Apprentice and Isis could be here. Wherever it was, Valeria was determined to find it so she could be whole once more.

Chapter Seventeen

Zack stood back with one eye on Selena and Sacha who were placing the stones in a pentagon-like shape. His other eye stayed on the village. There were a number of witches over there, and any of them could have sensed what they were doing. This was an act in direct violation of the task force and administration's expressed orders. If they were caught, they'd all get in huge trouble, whatever that meant in New Salem. Although they were past the cottages and in the cemetery, it was still technically within New Salem's borderlines.

With good reason, Zack was worried, but the wide-eyed face staring at the crystals showed even more stress and angst. He peeked toward the village. Zack tapped Harry's shoulder. It shook him out of his trance. His head spun to face Zack. It wasn't a good look on the guy from the future. "Hey, are you all right?"

The picture of worry gave way to a huge grin. "Nah, man, I'm great," Harry answered. "Let's just do this, okay?"

"Yeah, sure."

Harry trotted and stood by Sebastian. Zack wasn't buying the bravado; something was worrying him. Something he wasn't sharing with the rest of the group.

"We're ready," Selena said. Sacha nodded her agreement.

"Great." Sebastian folded his hands and gave the others a hard glance. "Let's do this fast."

A rough female voice shouted from behind, "None of this is a good idea!"

Carolyn marched past the tombstones, her hand resting against the pistol holstered on her belt clip. Zack jumped out of her way as if she were a freight train and he was standing on the tracks. The others gawked, frozen in place.

"Carolyn!" Sacha sprang in front blocking her path to the crystals. "Hey, Hon, what are you doing here?"

Zack felt a need to say something. He thought quickly. "You're just in time for a…umm…Wiccan ceremony, from Vegas—" Maybe speaking wasn't his best move.

"I know exactly what you're all here to do," Carolyn growled. The side-glance she gave Zack nearly knocked him off his feet. "It's a bad idea. This plan is doomed to fail."

"We have no choice," Selena pleaded. "Isis is trapped over there. You have to understand…"

"I do understand!" Carolyn snapped. "This isn't about defying Paul's orders. This is about you going over there unmanned and unprepared. That's why we are here."

"We?" Sebastian asked.

A distortion formed in front of Carolyn. It looked like a huge soap bubble, which couldn't have been her doing, not unless she was secretly a witch that none of the others could sense. The distortion faded. Standing in its place was the last person Zack, or the rest of the family, expected to see.

"Doctor Mac?" Sacha exclaimed. "I didn't think

catching offenders was part of your duties."

Without an answer, Doctor Mac stepped between Selena and Sacha. "I take it the two of you will be holding the wormhole open from this side?"

"That is the plan," Sacha replied.

The doctor swung around to the men. "And that leaves just the three of you to search an unknown alien land for Isis."

Harry raised a finger. "Actually, I'm on wormhole guard duty once we get to the other side."

"Oh, even better."

"Isis needs us to bring her home." Sebastian came nose to nose with the doctor. "You're not going to stop us."

"How successful will you be if it's just the two of you out there?"

"We're willing to take our chances."

"Damn right," Zack said, backing up Sebastian.

"You won't be enough." Doctor Mac looked to the clear sky. He took a deep breath and shook his head. "Selena, Sacha, create the portal to the Other World. Then give me control of it. My connection is strong enough to hold it open. You will need as many hands on the other side as possible."

"Really?" Zack gasped in disbelief.

"Yes, it's true!" Harry raised his hands in the air as if he had just won a race. "I remember, in the stories they're part of this, too."

"I knew I would have to intervene one way or another. That's why I researched Einstein-Rosen bridge theories." Doctor Mac walked to the pentagon with his eyes aimed at the crystals. "Most of it was speculative, of course, but I believe I can hold it in place for a total of ninety minutes before the strain on our planet causes the rotation to halt."

"Thank you, Doctor," Sebastian said. "We appreciate your assistance in bringing Isis home."

"I'm coming with you as well," Carolyn announced.

Selena spun to her. "Oh, Carolyn, thank you for the offer, but we can't ask that of you."

Carolyn scoffed. "You have no idea what you'll be facing there except for the two vampires." She smacked her holster. "I'm the only one here who is armed."

"You shouldn't come." Sacha faced Carolyn with a hand on Zack's shoulder. "Remember what they told us happened in the old timeline—"

"Yeah, Valeria killed me. But I'm ready. If it happens this time, I promise I'm taking her down, too."

Zack glanced at Harry who wore a huge grin across his face. He knew Doctor Mac and Carolyn would get involved in the rescue attempt, yet never said a word about it to any of them. A huge question filled Zack's mind...what else did Harry know that he wasn't telling them? More importantly, why?

Sebastian cleared his throat, grabbing everyone's attention. "Okay, if we're set on who is going, now is the time. Carolyn, we appreciate the assistance."

"You're going to need it," Carolyn muttered under her breath.

Selena eyed her sister, who walked to her side. "Let's hope we remember this spell as well as we think we do."

Without another word, she and Sacha stood in front of the crystals. They clutched hands as Doctor Mac positioned himself behind them. Zack's shoulders tensed. He never thought he'd end up in the Other World again. Somehow, he wasn't as anxious as he thought he'd be. But someone was.

Harry swung his arms in circles, his left hand almost hitting Zack. He kept taking deep breaths. "This is really happening," he mumbled. "Yup, I'm doing this, let's do this."

Harry flashed another grin before skipping toward the crystals on the ground. Zack had seen, and formed, enough fake smiles on the stage to be able to recognize one.

The sisters jumped into a fast-paced chant that was nearly impossible for Zack's ears to follow. To him, it sounded like gibberish, but it was an actual spell. Proof came in the form of sparks shooting within the perimeter of the crystals. A loud hum was soon joined by a static-filled circle. On the other side of this wormhole was the Other World. The ground around the circle vibrated.

"All righty, then," Harry said. "No stopping it now. It's time."

The tension of reluctance filled the air. Sebastian took a deep breath, then stepped through the static and disappeared. Zack followed him through into the unknown. They had no idea what they would face on the other side, but it didn't matter. They needed to find Isis and bring her home.

Chapter Eighteen

Zack twisted his head from far left to far right, taking in the Other World. It should have all been familiar since he had been here before. Well, technically that was the Zack Galloway from before Isis changed time and he literally became another version of himself. Okay, so he had never actually been here before. That's why nothing looked familiar. Not the weird gray grass or the tall cactus-like trees. Zack was sure he'd remember branches stretched out in all directions with two that arched back to the base like hands on hips. If not the trees, then certainly the dusty smell in the air that reminded him of hay in a barn.

"We're here!" Sacha's screech forced Zack to look behind him.

They were at the bottom of a hill, and it looked steep. Selena and Sacha were the last two to join them. They probably needed a few moments to give Doctor Mac control of the portal…a portal that suddenly shrank to the size of a grape. While Harry stayed near it, Zack walked ahead, making sure not to stray too far from the group. The others may have had their Wiccan control while they were near the portal, but once they ventured out, they'd all be on the same level: powerless in a strange world with supernatural beings as threats.

"We have ninety minutes to get back, or we will be left behind," Sebastian announced. "We need to keep track of our time."

"No problem." Zack pulled his phone from his back pocket and raised it for all to see. "I can set a timer for—"

"*ZACK, LOOK OUT!*"

Zack couldn't be sure which voice called his name. He turned around in time to see three massive beasts. One was in mid-charge, dashing down the hill like a speeding locomotive aimed directly at Zack. Sacha screamed to the others. Selena raised a hand, but she was panicking, an emotion that deterred a witch from controlling the energy. The animal's two front paws pounced, its claws aimed for Zack's chest. There was no time to dodge…

"Switch!" Harry screamed as his hands clapped.

Zack was suddenly staring at the portal hole. He reached for his chest, but there were no slashes or holes. Sacha cried out. Harry was on his back with the huge animal straddling him. The creature lifted its paw. The claws were covered in crimson red.

"No!" Sacha raised her hands. "Four-legged creature, fly away!"

The creature levitated high in the air. It let out a high-pitched honk, a noise so loud that Zack had to cover his ears. Then, like an airplane, the animal flew what had to be miles into the far distance. The creature's flight came to a halt when it hit the branches of the highest tree. The tree timbered over taking the animal with it. The crash could barely be heard from so far away.

The other two animals let out what sounded like horns honking. One charged while the other jumped onto its hind legs. Carolyn shot two bullets in the air.

The charging animal stopped short, then both galloped away. Whether it was to run from the loud noise or to gather reinforcements was anyone's guess.

Sebastian and Selena dropped to their knees on opposite sides of Harry. His ripped shirt was covered in the blood gushing from his midsection. Sebastian held his hands over Harry's stomach while Selena leaned in for a closer look. "Heal," Sebastian chanted. "Heal." Frustration filled his face as he looked across to his wife.

"It won't work," Selena answered Sebastian's unspoken question. "He's losing blood too fast. I believe that animal's claws punctured an artery."

Sebastian pulled back his hands. "We can't heal that, not fast enough..." His head popped up. "But Doctor Mac could. Selena, we can teleport him onto the other side of the portal—"

"Sebastian, if we move him, even teleport him..." Selena shook her head back. She didn't want to finish her thought, but it was clear enough.

"It's okay..." Harry mumbled. "It's all good."

Zack dropped to his knees next to Selena. The grass around Harry was stained red, as was the guilt Zack felt in his gut. He had such harsh feelings toward the kid...who had sacrificed his life to save Zack's.

"Harry, why did you do it? Why did you take my place?"

Harry reached out and clutched Zack's hand. "I had to. It was the only way..." His words slurred.

"Harry, try not to move," Selena said.

"Had to?" Zack asked. His hand was being squeezed by Harry's shaky hand. "Why?"

"You...you had to live...so I can...too."

"Selena, we have to try," Sebastian shouted. "We have to teleport him."

"Nah, it's fine, I know I...die now." Blood from Harry's mouth ran down his cheeks. He gave a yank to Zack's hand. Zack took the sign and leaned in. "It all happened so...so much sooner, a little...different this time, but the same series of events. They said it would...but I did it. I saved you." Harry's grip went weak. Despite the horrible pain he must have been in, he managed a slight grin. "Mom and Sis...they were right. You're kind of awesome."

"What are you saying—"

"I finally got to know you...Dad." Harry's hand slipped from Zack's grip. It fell to the grass, lifeless, much like the rest of Harry's body.

Zack fell back. His eyes were open as wide as he could make them. Selena checked Harry for a pulse, then looked to the others and shut her eyes. "He's gone," she said.

Carolyn removed her camouflage baseball cap and placed it against her chest. Sebastian took Selena's hand and slowly rose, bringing them both to their feet. He looked back at Zack seated on the ground. "He's...my son?" Zack asked, having no idea what else to say. "Mine and Isis', I guess? Is that what he meant?" Damn, he barely got to know him.

Zack stood and ran to Sebastian's side. The silence lasted for what felt like forever as they stared down at Harry's body. In truth, it was only several moments, interrupted by Sacha. "What's the matter with all of you? What are we doing?" Her tone was loud and scolding. "We can still save him, so let's do that!"

"Sis, we can't," Selena said with tears in her eyes.

"He's gone."

Carolyn placed her hand across Sacha's stomach. "Sach," she whispered. "We have to accept it. We lost him—"

"None of you are listening to me!" Sacha pushed away from Carolyn and pointed down at Harry with both hands as if she were presenting something no one had noticed. "He's from our future, remember? We rescue Isis, we get the hell out of here and make sure we leave those vampires behind without a way back. Then she and Zack will birth this kid some day in the future, and this never happens! Harry will live."

"You're absolutely right," Sebastian replied. "We lost him today, but we can keep him safe tomorrow. We're still on a time limit, so let's go."

Carolyn holstered her pistol, placed her cap on her head, then eyed the portal. "Let's keep in mind, there's probably a lot more of those things out there. And as soon as we move away from that hole, you won't be connected anymore. You'll be vulnerable."

"We understand the risk." Selena turned to Sebastian and touched his cheek. "Let's find our girl."

Sebastian's head spun side to side, eyeing the many trees around them. Each direction looked exactly the same. "Should we split up?" he asked.

"I don't recommend it." Carolyn rubbed a hand against her holster, another reminder that she had their only weapon. "We're better off staying together in a group."

Sacha's hands waved all around. "How about…" Her right hand suddenly stopped, aimed to the left. "That way?"

"Good direction as any." Sebastian marched to the

left. "Keep an eye out for any clues, like footprints. If we can't find Isis, perhaps we can locate Luther for help."

Zack couldn't look away from Harry's corpse. This was his son. His and Isis', or at least he assumed Isis was the mother. Now that he had a good look at the kid's face, he realized Harry had her cheekbones. Harry's last words stuck with him. "I finally got to know you." An implication that Zack wasn't there to raise him. Because he died early in Harry's life. A hand suddenly clutched his shoulder making him jump. It was Selena's.

"Will you be okay, Zack?" she asked.

"Yeah," Zack lied. "It's just…should we bury the body or something?"

"There's no time." Her hand on his shoulder tightened. "It's as Sacha said. We're going to stop this from ever happening. We save Isis, we save Harry."

"Right." Zack took a deep breath and straightened his back. "Let's go save them both."

The group started their journey. Zack took one last look behind him, both at the small circular hole in space, and at his future son. *May he rest in peace, for now*. He ran and joined the others.

Chapter Nineteen

Paul entered the medical center's recovery room to check on his daughter. He had full confidence in Doctor Mac's medical and Wiccan abilities, but he was compelled to stop what he was doing and check on her with his own eyes. He stepped through the door with a momentary hesitation. Something about his being here seemed off. It was unlike Paul to put anything ahead of his duties, even his family. Then again, there hadn't ever been such a dire situation in New Salem, or with a member of his own family, where he had to make that choice. At least not until today.

Natasha floated behind him an inch from the ground with the same concern across her face. Paul wasn't a witch, but his human instincts were strong. He sensed his task force's second in command's concern. It made sense. In her teen years, Natasha babysat Maya who was an infant at the time. The two grew up together in the village, as did everyone else in New Salem. It was a dynamic he appreciated about the community. It was also one of the selling points that Tia's grandfather—the president at the time—sold Paul and his wife on in relocating to New Salem.

Maya lay in one of two beds with her right hand and wrist wrapped up in a thick cast. What looked to Paul like a metal clamp with wires and tubes which ran to a computer behind the headboard pressed against two sides of her hand. The computer constantly beeped as numbers scrolled across the screen. Five crystals surrounded the bed. With each beep, the crystals sparked. Amazing, Doctor Mac had combined medical technology with witchcraft in his practice. The man was truly a genius, although Paul would never say that out loud. The guy was smug enough without having his ego stroked.

Jeb was seated on a chair to Maya's right. His eyes were glazed over. The tall and beautiful blonde lady on Maya's left hunched over the bed and held her good hand tightly. She was using the energy on their daughter, possibly keeping her asleep. Paul waved a hand, signaling Natasha to stay by the door as he walked up to the bed.

"Paul," the woman whispered, never looking up from Maya.

"Helen, my dear." Paul embraced his wife. "How is she?"

Helen let out a deep exhale. "Doctor Mac says it will take time, but there is a strong possibility she will regain movement in her hand."

"Man, I'm so sorry," Jeb muttered. "That vampire came out of nowhere, and she was so damn powerful. Facing her ourselves; it was stupid. We never had a chance."

"Yes, Jeb, it was stupid!" Paul responded. "You are very brave, but bravery needs to be tempered with clear planning."

"I know. I'm sorry." Jeb sniffled. "I should have said no, should have talked her out of it, should have talked everyone out of it—"

"Tell me the truth. Was going there Maya's idea?"

Paul let his tone soften. "I know she cannot be talked into doing anything she doesn't want to."

Unfortunately, Paul couldn't say the same for Jeb. As fond as he had grown of his daughter's choice of a mate, he felt the boy's inner strength did not match his outer frame. This was also the case for his parents who were both kind and passive people. They were farm hands in New Salem who may have moved up the ranks if they were a bit more forceful. It was part of why Paul wanted Jeb as a future member of the New Salem Task Force. Under his tutelage, Jeb could gain the fortitude to temper his kind heart.

When Jeb looked up, Paul offered him a rare smile. "Thank you for being here with her."

"I'm surprised to see you so soon, Paul," Helen said. "Especially with that monster still out there, and one of our own still in its clutches. I didn't think we'd see you until Isis was back and safe."

"Unfortunately, The Apprentice took Isis to the Other World. I decided that we cannot afford the risk of opening a portal to retrieve her. Her family agreed."

Helen's head spun from Maya to Paul. "They agreed to stand down? So easily? *That* family?"

"It was a difficult conversation. But Sebastian is their coven leader, and he understood." Paul reached down and rested a hand on Maya's shoulder. "I sympathize with how hard it is for them to abandon their child. It's probably why I was so compelled to come here and see Maya."

Helen eyed him with suspicion. "You put sentiment over your duties to New Salem, Paul? That doesn't sound like you at all."

Paul's head popped up. Helen was right. It didn't

sound like him any more than Sebastian taking sides against his family wasn't like him. Just like Sebastian, Paul loved his family with all his heart, but his responsibilities to this village always took priority, especially when he knew Helen and Maya were safe. Maya was in the best hands possible with Doctor Mac. But despite his trust, he needed to see her with his own eyes. That was despite knowing that Helen was by her side the entire time.

He thought back. When did this need to go to the medical center hit him? After Sebastian agreed to Paul's demands and promised to convince the rest of his coven to accept the decision. He never suspected Sebastian was being anything but genuine, a witch with a Wiccan knack for persuasion and hypnosis. Paul's judgment in that moment was clouded with emotion, which was something a lifetime as a soldier trained him to put aside.

Damn it. Paul had been around witches long enough to know when one was trying to put a spell on him. But the guilt he felt over the decision he had to make for that family caused him to let down his guard. They were powerful, so he should have been ready for the attempt. Wow, he just accused Jeb of being naïve and stupid. Apparently, there was a lot of that going around today.

Paul eyed the entire recovery room, then Maya. She was resting comfortably, but she certainly wasn't out of the woods. She still needed to be monitored by the one doctor who could help her should a problem arise.

Paul's shoulders tightened. He faced Natasha. "Where is Doctor Mac right now?"

Natasha shut her eyes. "He is not anywhere in medical center. For Doctor Mac, this is odd."

"Quite." Paul walked around the bed. He clutched Maya's ankle and squeezed. "You have this?" he asked Helen.

"I'm not going anywhere," she replied. "And neither is Jeb. Go do what you must do."

Paul about-faced and marched up to Natasha. "Let's find him, now," he commanded.

Suspicion took over. Something was amiss. He had a hunch his orders were in the process of being defied, and, somehow, Doctor Mac was involved, too.

****

Isis heard what sounded like a mini explosion, and then another, from a distance away. They had to be gunshots, and they were followed by a loud crash from much closer. Based on what she had seen, there was no industry or technology in the Other World, or even a native species other than those wolf creatures. This had to be her family here to rescue her, but who—or what— were they battling? As far as she knew, the two Wiccan vampires were fighting each other.

She needed to go to them…if she could figure out which direction the gunshots came from. Then she'd need to get there without attracting the attention of those wild animals. The problem was that Isis had next to no experience when it came to navigating a forest. That was especially the case without her Wiccan connection. She needed a plan, and she needed one fast.

Isis pressed her body against one of the many trees in the area. After looking back and forth, she ran in a straight line to another tree. Then she did it again. Maybe not the most brilliant of strategies, but it was all she could come up with in the moment. She also had no idea how far away the others were, but from the sound of those explosions, they had to be pretty far.

A loud honking grabbed Isis' attention. It was in her path, but it didn't sound vicious like the last time she heard it. This one sounded like a baby's scream. Isis couldn't help herself; she had to check it out. Isis detoured to the left while being careful to stay near the trees. "Oh my God," she gasped.

It was one of those animals on its back, trapped between the branches of a downed tree. Two others, both much larger, stood on opposite sides looking confused, or as confused as a four-legged animal could. Now Isis knew where the crash had come from. The tree must have just fallen based on how fast the animal trapped underneath was flailing its paws in the air.

One of the two much larger creatures, maybe the parents, backpedaled, then charged and rammed its head into the trunk of the tree. The second animal did the same. With each ram, the trapped creature screamed in pain. It also didn't come any closer to freedom. This was Isis' chance to run past them without being noticed. Then she'd be well on her way, unseen.

It was simple. She just had to walk away, take one step after another, and keep going. But her conscience wouldn't let her take that first step. Ugh, she had to help the poor creature and hope the other two didn't maul her.

Isis ran past one of the animals who blew a sound from its snout. The second animal jumped to its hind legs and copied the horn-like sound. Isis, ignoring what she perceived as threatening snarls, squatted like a catcher and placed her left shoulder underneath the thickest branch. She pressed her hands against the same branch and, with all her might, tried to muscle the tree up.

"Come on, come on!" She grunted. Of all the times not to have the Wiccan connection…

With a loud grunt, Isis shoved with as much strength as she could muster. The tree was far heavier than she imagined. Her skinny frame was no match. Still, she couldn't relent. With a loud scream, Isis dug her heels into the ground, focusing on straightening her legs. The tree moved. It was only slight, but just enough for the animal to roll out from underneath the branches and jump to its feet.

Once the animal escaped, Isis' legs gave out. She fell on her back, and the huge log slammed against the grass. Isis clasped her left shoulder with her right hand. She had no feeling in her left arm whatsoever. It was like a huge charley horse that ran down to her fingers. Isis rose to her knees and kept an eye on the three creatures. The two sniffed the one who was trapped, making loud sucking sounds. At least it seemed okay, no visible injuries except for red blood covering its paw. But it was able to stand on its own four feet. The three animals all suddenly focused Isis' way.

She slowly stood up. "Okay, I see you're good now," Isis said, even though they wouldn't understand. She stepped back, still clutching her left arm. "I'm going to look for my family now. Please don't kill me, okay?"

Two of the animals trotted around the tree, surrounding Isis on two sides. The one she saved suddenly jumped over the downed tree, its eyes never wavering from her. Isis slowly turned around and took two slow and careful steps away. The animals did the same. They were now on three sides of her, but they were all facing her.

"I'm not sure what's going on," Isis said to herself.

She tried to dash, but the exhaustion from lifting the tree stopped her after a few steps. To her surprise, the three creatures copied her dash and stop action. The one she saved crept closer, moving to her left side and looking straight into her face. Isis was sure if they wanted to attack her, they would have already.

"Okay, I think I get it." Isis placed her hand on the smallest animal's head. "Let's find my family together. And keep an eye out for vampires, okay?"

Chapter Twenty

With each step through what looked like the biggest and widest grassland in the universe, Zack focused his thoughts on Isis. She was his love, and right now she needed to be rescued. He wanted to keep her, and only her, on his mind. But someone else kept slipping into his thoughts, even though they only recently met. Harry.

At first, Zack didn't care for Harry. He found him obnoxious and annoying. That's why he didn't try to get to know him. If he did, maybe he would have found out sooner that Harry was his future son. Maybe he would have figured out the real reason he came all the way through time. To give up his life in exchange for Zack's. He made that sacrifice for a future father he barely knew. Man, Doctor Mac would have a field day with this if Zack ever took him up on his offer for therapy—

He lifted his head to the sound of Sebastian calling his name. So lost in thought, he didn't realize how far behind he had fallen from the group. "Coming!" Zack shouted, then hurried until he caught up.

The group kept walking straight gazing in every direction. It was clear they had just chosen a random way with no idea how to find Isis. The only one who had thought ahead was Carolyn who brought a pocket full of buttons she must have taken from the marketplace. Every few steps, she'd drop one on the grass so they could find their way back. Under all those muscles, Carolyn was a smart and resourceful lady, that was for sure. No wonder Sacha was so fond of her.

Zack was usually the one member of their coven who thought ahead. Unfortunately, this time they were in a rush with no time to grab anything. At the very least, Zack should have had flash paper and a lighter, or something in his pockets. But a year living in New Salem put him in the habit of keeping nothing magic-related on him since they weren't useful or entertaining in a village of witches. No one there was impressed by card or coin tricks, so he just stopped carrying them around. Right now, he wished he had something on him that would help, even if it were just a match or a plastic magic wand he could throw at one of the animals.

Of course, it may not have been coincidence that the one latecomer to their group, Carolyn, was the most prepared. While he had come to care for, and even love, his new unofficial guardians, they tended to rely too heavily on their witchcraft to solve every problem. That was more than enough on Earth, but here where there was no energy to manipulate, they were at a horrible disadvantage.

Sebastian and Selena, who were leading the way, stopped in place, which prompted the rest to do the same. One of the animals had jumped in their path. Its backside shot up as if it was ready to attack. "Any chance this is the one that killed Harry?" Sacha asked.

Carolyn jumped in front and reached for her sidearm, stopping only when Selena held a hand out in front of her. "Wait!" Selena peered down at the animal. "It's not focused on us."

"Selena's right," Zack said, noticing the same thing. "It's looking up at the trees."

"Carolyn, draw your weapon!" Sebastian grabbed Selena's hand and pulled her back. "We're being tracked!"

A tall woman jumped out from the trees and landed in front of the group. The animal ran off, letting out a loud squeal that sounded like it came from a vehicle. Everyone else froze, especially Zack who felt his throat go cold. His mouth moved, but he couldn't say the name.

Sacha did say it. "Valeria!"

Zack lost his balance and dropped to the ground. He was once again face-to-face with the Wiccan vampire who made his life a living hell, both here and in a reality she wouldn't even know existed. Valeria, the one who went back in time and erased him from history. Now she stood in their path, staring them all down with those wicked purple irises, as smug as ever.

"Well, well," she cackled. "It seems this is a day for unexpected guests." Valeria walked up to Carolyn oblivious to the pistol targeted for her chest. "You, I do not know, yet I see rage in your eyes as if we have met before. I am receiving much of that, today."

"Don't take another step!" Carolyn placed her left hand under the gun in her right hand. "I heard you killed me once, but it won't happen again."

Valeria's head tilted with confusion. "What are you prattling on about?"

"Valeria, we are not here for a fight." Selena approached Valeria despite Sebastian reaching for her arm. "We simply want to find Isis. She's somewhere in the Other World."

"I am sure there is a story here," Valeria replied, "but, right now, I am looking at opportunity. How did you come to arrive here—"

The severed head of another of the native animals dropped at Valeria's feet. It was followed by The Apprentice who landed between her and Selena with a sharpened wood stake the same hue as the trees around them.

"That's her!" Zack called out.

Before anyone could react, The Apprentice jabbed the stake into Valeria's midsection, ran her backward, and pinned her to the closest tree.

With a scream, The Apprentice slammed her fist into the end of the stake, pushing it through Valeria until only the heavy end protruded from her stomach. Valeria swung an open hand, but The Apprentice jumped back, avoiding what would have been a hard chop, which may have ripped off her head.

Valeria tried to push forward, but the sharpened end of the stake was drilled into the tree. The elder witch eyed her midsection and gasped. She was stuck, trapped like a rat, a situation that Zack was not unhappy to see. Without hesitation, The Apprentice ran her two-hundred-year-old fingernails down Valeria's arms and chest, ripping off both the fabric of her blouse and skin from her body. Dried blood showed but did not drip.

Valeria eyed her body, then let out a fierce cackle. "I get it! Instead of killing me yourself, you plan to leave me a victim to the creatures of this plane who will seek vengeance on an injured and helpless predator." Valeria shook her head. "Clever, I must say. You truly were raised by me."

"Is that true?" Zack gasped. "You're going to leave

her here to get eaten by those creatures?"

The Apprentice eyed Zack, but her angry brown eyes showed no signs of knowing him. To this version of Isis, Zack was no more than a stranger. Selena, who was anything but a stranger, grabbed The Apprentice's hand and wrapped her own around it.

"Isis, please look at me and your dad. Focus on us." Selena waved her free hand at Sebastian. "I know you remember us. I also know in your timeline we weren't there for you. I'm so sorry about that, but I'm sure we would have been there if we could."

"Selena, be careful," Zack said through grinded teeth. He had seen how vicious The Apprentice could be, unfortunately at Maya's expense.

"We can be here for you now." Selena looked directly into The Apprentice's eyes. "Help us save our Isis, then let's all go back. We can figure out what to do. Together."

The Apprentice looked back and forth from Selena to Sebastian and then to the grass. A grin formed across her lips. She suddenly yanked her hand from Selena's grip and grabbed onto a high branch. The Apprentice swung herself over, ran across the branch, and jumped to the next tree past the group. From there, she dropped to the ground and ran.

"I don't get it," Sacha said watching The Apprentice take off. "I thought you were getting through to her. Why did she run away like that?"

"You naïve fools," Valeria shouted, yanking at the stake in her stomach, but to no avail. "She is *not* running from you!"

Confusion filled the group. Zack as well, until he realized The Apprentice's gaze was aimed at the ground. That's when he understood Valeria's sarcastic scoff. "The buttons!" he shouted. "She noticed the buttons!"

Sebastian gasped. "She's going for the portal!"

He and the sisters took off in the same direction as The Apprentice. Carolyn threw one last glare at Valeria, then did the same. Zack followed. They had to get there before The Apprentice, or New Salem—and possibly all of Earth—was doomed.

Chapter Twenty-One

Valeria was trapped. Worse yet, her enhanced vampiric senses said her time was limited. Animals were congregating. None of them were meat eaters, but it didn't mean Valeria was safe. She had been their natural enemy for generations. With her skin cut thanks to The Apprentice's sharpened fingernails, the creatures must have smelled her blood and knew she was vulnerable. They wouldn't hesitate to take advantage of the situation and tear her limb from limb to end the threat once and for all.

This was no doubt The Apprentice's plan, to punish Valeria for abuses that had not yet occurred. This entire conflict was confusing, but Valeria surmised this Apprentice had come from a future that no longer existed. It was one where Valeria had achieved her goal of conquering the Earth. In doing so, she must have turned Isis Rivera and molded her with an iron fist. It was an idea she contemplated, but then thought better of it. But every choice is like a fork in the road, which splits into different directions in events yet to come. Was it possible had she chosen to turn Isis, she would have won the battle with Luther's witches?

A creature's high-pitched scream caught Valeria's attention. It had to be a rallying cry to the others of its species. Valeria needed to escape, and quickly. But how? Her options were limited. She could drop all pretenses of dignity and call out to Luther, but was he close enough to hear her? The Other World was a huge place, and he had purposely put some distance between them in order to cool off.

Their philosophical argument over the evolution of the Other World's inhabitants and what role they would play in it had become heated. Despite the trivialness of the subject, it sent them on separate journeys for blood. Luther purposely took a long route for the sake of being alone with his thoughts. Of course, this was not the first hypothetical discussion that led to this result. There were times Valeria had gone days without seeing him. This was perhaps the worst time for one of his long journeys through the Other World—not that he could have known.

No, Luther was not an option. Valeria needed to free herself, and quickly. Unfortunately, there was only one way, and she would suffer for it. Valeria tossed back her hands and pressed them against the tree. The tree wouldn't budge, but her body could. Valeria pushed her body, sliding it along the wooden stake. Her midsection screamed with each movement, reminding her that even the dead could experience agony.

Ignoring the pain, Valeria kept pushing. The thicker end of the stake disappeared into her stomach. Lucky she had the foresight many years ago to use the energy to remove her vampiric vulnerability to wood. But it still felt like a saw rubbing against the inside of her abdomen, digging and clawing at her insides. "Block out the pain," she told herself. "I am a vampire, and I will heal…"

The sound of galloping in the distance raised Valeria's ears. It had to come from at least four of those creatures. Valeria pushed with all her might. Her back spasmed. Her black syrup-like blood rolled down her legs. At least the plan was working. She was almost free.

The galloping came closer. With a loud scream, Valeria pulled away from the tree. Her body slid along the wooden stake until, finally, she fell straight down onto her face. Valeria clutched her stomach and back which both felt like they had been stung by a countless number of bees. As a vampire she would heal quickly. But would it be in time?

She had her answer when the galloping stopped. Valeria lifted her head to see she was surrounded on three sides by six of the native creatures, all snarling at her like a pack of wild dogs who had cornered their prey.

Valeria's vision went dark. The fangs dropped from her upper jaw. One of the animals charged. Valeria pushed herself to her knees. She swung a hand, swatting away the animal's incoming claw. She rose to her feet, raised her hands over her head, and snarled. It was a bluff to convince her attackers that she was fully healed and ready for battle. It worked. All the animals took off, collectively deciding this was not the time to engage. How fortunate. Valeria's midsection felt like it had been used for a punching bag. But the skin was healing. The bleeding had already stopped.

Valeria stared at the long stake jammed into the tree. She grabbed hold of the end, and with all her might, yanked it from the bark. The momentum nearly pulled Valeria off her feet. The sharpened end was stained with her own blood and guts.

Damn that alternate version of Isis. But she did

have the right idea. It was time Valeria made her way to whatever portal stood open in the Other World as well. This was her first opportunity to leave this wretched place since her return. She planned to make the most of it, and in doing so, perhaps she'd leave the others behind. Then the Other World could become their prison instead.

****

Zack and Carolyn caught up with Sebastian and the sisters despite their head start. Not that Zack was an athlete—although Carolyn certainly looked like she spent a lot of time in New Salem's gym—but the three witches weren't used to stressing their muscles too often. Wherever they needed to go, they were always a simple teleport away. Luckily, they all made it to the top of the hill where Carolyn's buttons had led them, but was it too late?

No, the portal at the bottom of the hill was still barely big enough to stick a finger through. The Apprentice stood in front of it, eyeing it from every angle. From her proximity, she must have felt the energy from the other end coursing through her body. If she had noticed the body of Harry several feet away, it either did not faze her or she chose to ignore it. Apparently, this version of Isis had lost all of her compassion a long time ago. Zack couldn't turn a blind eye even if he wanted to. The guy was his future son…and he died in front of his eyes.

The Apprentice held a hand in front of the portal. At the moment, her arm wouldn't fit through. Perhaps she was seeking a way to expand it so her entire body would fit. Unless Doctor Mac on the other side sensed her and could stop her, she'd be unleashed on an unsuspecting New Salem.

"We have to do something, like, right now!" Zack heard the desperation in his own voice.

"Okay, coven leader." Sacha nudged her elbow into Sebastian's ribcage. "What's the game plan?"

Sebastian looked up to the sky, then down to The Apprentice. Zack could practically see the wheels turning. "Let's get to the portal," he said. "Once we have use of the energy, I'll make us invisible. Selena, Sacha, the two of you can freeze her in place."

"Then what?" Selena asked. "I realize this isn't our Isis, but it's still Isis. I can't just kill her as if she was never under our care."

"I know exactly how you feel, Selena." Sebastian's eyes never wavered from The Apprentice, even as he spoke to Selena. "But we always understood Isis' potential. That's why we agreed when we first took her in that if she ever went dark, it would be up to us to stop her." Sebastian's gaze shifted to Selena. "This is as dark as Isis can ever get."

Selena nodded, although it was clear she still didn't like the idea even if she couldn't argue his logic.

"What about us?" Zack motioned back and forth from himself to Carolyn. "What do you want us to do?"

"Stay here, out of range from the Earth's energy," came their coven leader's response. "You're our backup. If you see an opportunity, take it."

Zack opened his mouth to protest, but before he could say anything, Carolyn responded, "Copy that."

The easy agreement took Zack by surprise. He hated the idea that Sebastian's plan involved leaving the two non-witches behind, as if they needed protecting. Hell, Zack had more dealings with witches than anyone else here could claim. Okay, that was in the other timeline, but he still had the memories in his head.

But Carolyn was a soldier, and a warrior. She certainly wasn't the type to shy away from a battle, even one she was ill-equipped to fight. If she was willing to stand back without an argument, then Zack had to accept that plan as well. Maybe there really was a good reason behind it.

The sisters crept down the hill at a brisk pace with Sebastian a step behind them. They stopped midway just a few feet from The Apprentice who had her attention on the portal. Their quick glance meant they felt the energy from Earth within their control. Selena and Sacha clenched hands to combine their sibling connection. Sebastian stretched out his arms. All three disappeared.

Zack could now only see The Apprentice in front of the portal. Behind her, three sets of footprints pushed down the grass as they approached her. One set stopped in place while the other two inched their way closer. The energy crackled in front of the two sets of footprints. Could it be this simple?

No! The Apprentice's body swung around, her eyes dark and fangs protruding from her mouth. She raised her hands, then spread her arms. Selena and Sacha both suddenly appeared in the air, reaching for each other. And then flying in opposite directions. Selena hit the ground hard and bounced. Sacha slammed into a nearby tree.

"Oh no!" Zack tried to run to help, but Carolyn snatched his arm, stopping him in place. Whatever their role, it wasn't the time to get involved yet.

Sebastian appeared; his invisibility spell was

broken. Seven identical versions of himself appeared, three on one side, four on the other. They stood in a semi-circle, each with a hand aimed at The Apprentice. An energy wave shot out distorting the space in front of Sebastian. In turn, The Apprentice thrust her arms ahead. The energy wave reversed. All eight Sebastians fell to the ground. Seven disappeared, leaving only one left, who was visibly shaken.

"We have to do something!" Zack screeched.

"We're waiting for the opportunity." Carolyn pulled out her pistol and aimed it with both hands wrapped around it.

It wasn't as if those bullets could kill a vampire, but if they'd stagger The Apprentice enough for Sebastian and the sisters to get their bearings, then maybe they'd have a shot at her. But to Zack's surprise, Carolyn didn't fire. "She's open. Do it!" Zack shouted.

Sebastian's body suddenly rose off the ground as if he was a puppet yanked by the strings. He now blocked any opening Carolyn had. "Crap," Carolyn muttered, lowering her arms and the pistol.

The Apprentice hovered in the air, going eye level with Sebastian. His shoulders shuddered, meaning he was struggling but unable to move. "Think back, Isis," Sebastian said to her. "To when you were nine and I found you. We bonded almost immediately." His words were rhythmic and hypnotic. "I brought you into our coven where you bonded with us all. We became a family. Do you remember?"

The Apprentice's eyes narrowed. Her jaw shook. She hovered a few inches over Sebastian. Her right hand suddenly shot out. "Not you," she growled.

The Apprentice's hand balled into a fist.

Sebastian's throat turned red. His head pulled back, and his eyes shut. Carolyn aimed the gun again. If she had a shot past Sebastian, she was still hesitating. Zack eyed Selena and Sacha. They were pulling themselves to their feet, but slowly.

"She's choking him to death!" Zack hollered. "Carolyn, take the shot!"

"I want to…" Carolyn's hands trembled ever so slightly. "I-I can't just shoot a kid…especially that one…"

"That's not our Isis, and she's not a kid!" Zack shouted. "She's two-hundred years old!"

Carolyn closed one eye. Her finger squeezed…

A heavy piece of tree bark slammed across the back of her head. Carolyn dropped. The gun flew out of her hands and rolled down the hill.

Just when things couldn't get worse, Zack spun around to realize they had just gotten a lot worse.

"Valeria!"

Chapter Twenty-Two

Valeria charged past Zack, dismissing him with a wave of her hand. She marched down the hill, the stake held firmly, and the sharp end leading the way. Zack kneeled to check on Carolyn. She was unconscious with a splatter of blood dripping from underneath her baseball cap. He placed a finger against her neck to see if she still had a pulse, but truth be told, he had no idea what he should be looking for.

At the bottom of the hill, Sebastian slammed into the ground like a dead weight being dropped from several stories up. The wind must have been knocked out of him because he didn't move. The Apprentice lowered herself to the ground in front of Sebastian, staring down at him and snarling. The resentment she had for her former family was made clear by the angry blackened eyes.

The Apprentice fired a blast of energy at Sebastian, one that was blocked by a clear dome that formed over his body. Nearby, Selena was back on her feet, her hands glowing. The gray grass suddenly grew, tying up The Apprentice's feet. Her head spun to Sacha charging her way. "Kiddo, you desperately need a time out," Sacha shouted. Had any of them noticed Valeria stalking their way?

Zack's eyes shifted to the pistol midway down the hill. He was tired of sitting on the sidelines and watching everyone try to stop these witches. Everyone except for him. The sisters were both up and facing The Apprentice. Valeria, meanwhile, inched her way closer, which certainly would not help the situation. It was time to take a stand, even if it killed him.

Zack ran past Valeria. He dropped to his knees in front of the gun and scooped it up. He aimed it directly at her chest. The gesture made the Wiccan vampire stop in place. At least he had her attention. "What do you expect to do with that?" she cackled.

"Drop the weapon and back away, Valeria," Zack answered. "I'm not afraid to empty this chamber all over your body! I know it won't kill you, but I'd bet it'll hurt really bad."

"So, the boyfriend has finally found his spine." Valeria held out her palm. "But, in this case, your bravery has come exactly two steps too late."

"Meaning what?"

"True fears always linger within our minds."

A blast of light shot from Valeria's palm and hit Zack in the face. Damn, he didn't realize they were within range of the portal. The ground opened underneath Zack's feet. He fell straight down through pure darkness for what felt like an eternity. He reached out, but there was nothing to grab onto, nothing to stop his fall—

He finally landed, dropping on all fours. Zack lifted his upper body to find himself in a long and dark hallway. He looked up at the ceiling. There was no hole that he could have fallen from. "What the hell?" This couldn't have been part of the Other World. So, where was he?

Zack's eyes shifted to the ugly green lockers across

the walls separated by thick wood doors. He now realized where he was: his old high school in Las Vegas. It had been over a year since he last attended, and it was never this dark and dreary, at least not as far as he remembered. "Hello?" Zack shouted, but his voice didn't echo. "Where did you send me, Valeria?" Somehow, it didn't feel real...

The classroom door to Zack's immediate left swung open. A massive figure stepped through the doorway gripping a metal baseball bat in his hand. Zack felt his blood go cold. The boy who walked out was a lot taller and wider than Zack recalled. His eyes never glowed red like they were doing right now. But, despite all the exaggerated features, Zack knew that face and build. It was him...Glen Dobbs, the bane of Zack's entire school experience.

"Glen...what are you doing here—"

Glen slammed the bat into the lockers. The clang echoed which made Zack's eardrums want to explode. He pressed his hands against the sides of his head.

"It's been a while, Nerdini." Glen's voice boomed throughout the dark and empty hallway. "Did you think you could hide from me forever?"

"This has to be in my head," Zack whispered. "There's just no way—"

"It's going to feel real when I pound your face in, you puny magic punk!" Glen smacked the end of the bat against his palm. "It's time we settled our beef once and for all!"

"There's nothing to settle." Zack's voice croaked. "We're out of each other's lives. I live halfway across the globe now. We can just move on—"

Glen cackled in much the way Valeria did. "I'm

going to give you to the count of three to run, then when I catch you, I'm going to do what I've always promised I'd do. I'm going to perform a magic trick by removing your head from your neck!"

Zack had heard that threat too often. He heard it almost every day since junior high school. Each time, he ran and hid. Once, he even stuffed himself in a locker. Glen never found him, if he was even looking for him in the first place. But it didn't save him from all the insults, shoving, and manhandling he endured for years. This was a chance to finally stand up to his bully, even if it wasn't real. He wanted to, but Zack's instincts took over. Those instincts told him to turn around and run as soon as Glen counted "one."

His feet moved fast, past every locker and door. Behind him, Glen's voice grew louder. "Two!" Footsteps charged at him from behind. "Three!"

Zack stopped and stood in place when the end of the hallway suddenly filled with a crowd of students looking on and laughing. There were even some cheers for Zack and Glen to fight. This was his worst childhood nightmare come true.

Except he wasn't that child anymore. Back then he was a loner who avoided people like the plague, mostly because of Glen. The stage served as a safe space for Zack since he knew even if the bullies were in the audience, they had to stay in their seats. The theater was his heaven, but the school hallway was his hell.

A locker behind the crowd creaked open. Zack felt the pull to climb in and shut the door just as he had done years ago. This time, he resisted the temptation.

"What am I doing?"

Zack stood in place, refusing to budge another step,

even as Glen's shadow covered him. So what if Glen hit him with a baseball bat? Zack had been shot with a witch's blast directly in the chest. And he survived.

The footsteps stopped, replaced by loud breathing. The metal bat hit the lockers again. "You're out of time and out of luck! Time to end you once and for all, Nerdini!"

"No need. It's already over." Zack kept his back to Glen. "I've spent a lot of my childhood being intimidated by you, Glen Dobbs. Yeah, you were the face in many of my nightmares. But that was before I faced real threats like Wiccan vampires and a nuclear war. That was before I was a two-hundred-year-old vampire. That was before I helped save the world."

"What the hell are you talking about?" Glenn asked. "Turn around and face me, Nerdini!"

The crowd noise died down. Zack peeked over his shoulder. "I've faced threats that make you pale in comparison. I don't scare so easily anymore."

Glen raised the bat high over his head. "I'm going to hammer you into the ground like a nail!"

Zack turned around and straightened his back with his arms at his sides. "Go ahead, do your worst. I'm no longer afraid of you. I take your power of fear and intimidation away, once and for all."

Glen swung his arms, bringing the bat to Zack's head. But it never connected. Both the bat and the bully disappeared into a puff of smoke. Zack looked behind him. The crowd of excited students was gone as well. The ceiling split open. A bright light fell over Zack. It was the way back to reality. It was time to go where he was needed...

Zack lifted his head from the grass and shook away

the grogginess. His eyes were heavy as if he had just awakened from a dream. He rolled to his feet. Valeria hadn't made it even halfway down the hill yet, meaning Zack was only out for a few moments, if that. There was still time to do something. But having the confidence to do something wasn't the same as knowing what to do. He checked on Carolyn who was still facedown and unconscious. At least the bleeding from the back of her head had stopped.

At the bottom of the hill, the grass under Sacha's control had grown and wrapped The Apprentice's arms along with her legs. Selena, meanwhile, kneeled at her coughing husband's side, checking his condition. The Apprentice suddenly faded away, causing the long strands of grass to fall to the ground.

Selena stood up, as did Sacha. Both sisters looked back and forth. Zack also looked from left to right, trying to figure out where The Apprentice had gone. He suddenly noticed that Valeria had stopped her descent down the hill. Her attention was aimed at the top of a tree near Sebastian and the sisters.

"Look out from above!" Zack shouted.

Before either Selena or Sacha could react, The Apprentice leaped from the tree, landing on her feet between the sisters. Lightning shot from her hands. One bolt hit Selena. The other caught Sacha in the chest. Their bodies convulsed as if they were strapped to electric chairs. Zack watched in horror as they collapsed to the ground, lifeless.

The Apprentice peered down at all three members of what was once her family, not with the love and admiration that Isis always had for them, but with clear disdain. Apparently, The Apprentice still blamed them for the torturous immortal life she had lived under Queen Valeria. Her head popped up toward her primary target who was several feet away.

Zack grabbed the gun from the ground and stood. Now what? The bullets in the chamber couldn't stop either of the Wiccan vampires. The Witches of Vegas, meanwhile, were down and out. Zack was the only one left standing. Their plans to find Isis and return safely to New Salem had failed miserably.

The Apprentice's eyes lit up and aimed at Valeria's. Zack knew that the worst of their problems had yet to come. The battle was about to resume, and directly in front of the portal. That meant whoever won could soon claim the Earth.

Chapter Twenty-Three

Isis had been walking for what felt like miles, at least that's what the throbbing in her ankles indicated. It wasn't so bad. At least she felt a little safer touring this strange terrain with her three new friends. But she still had no idea where to go. She did hear loud eruptions, like blasts in a battle, echoing in the distance. Isis tried moving toward them, but was she heading in a direct path? Was it farther east or west? There was no way to truly know how far to go.

One of the animals stopped and picked up something with its mouth. It was probably another strand of grass. Isis couldn't help but notice they stopped constantly, never gaining momentum in their strides. Waiting on at least one of them each time left Isis with her thoughts, most of which were filled with paranoia. If she was moving toward the sounds of battle—and it involved her family—were they dealing with The Apprentice, Valeria, or both? For all Isis knew, they couldn't find their way here, and she was heading into a fight between the two Wiccan vampires—

The animal spit up the tiny object it had nabbed. Its hack sounded like a human's throat gagging. Curiosity took over, and Isis approached the native creature to see what it had rejected. It was a small circular object with four holes in the center. Isis looked down at her shirt, realizing the identity of the plastic item in her hand.

"It's a button!" she screamed. It looked exactly like the ones on her shirt, on every shirt sewn together in the New Salem market. "They're here! My family is here!"

Ahead, the animal Isis had saved dropped its head toward the grass and blew its horn. Isis ran to it and reached down into the gray pasture. She picked up another button. After a couple more yards, she found yet another.

"It's a trail!" She frantically pointed. "This is the way."

A huge smile formed across her face; she finally got a break. The buttons had to lead her to the rescue party—her family—and home.

****

Zack tiptoed down the hill, staying a distance behind Valeria. In truth, he didn't exactly have a plan of attack. He just knew he had to do something. He couldn't stop one, much less two, all-powerful immortal witches. He needed to think outside the box and find another way. In other words, he needed to think like a magician.

Halting the Wiccan vampires' path to the portal was out. But if he could get to the portal, he could shout a warning to Doctor Mac. He must not know what was happening on this side, otherwise he would have acted already. Of course, the doctor's best plan of action would be to close the portal completely. Then they'd all be stuck there forever. Unfortunately, that was the only way to win. They'd have to sacrifice themselves. Hopefully, saving Earth would be enough consolation for everyone.

The Apprentice levitated a few inches off the

ground. Her face squeezed like a wild animal readying to pounce, until a rustling sound caused her back to straighten and her head to shift. The nearest tree tipped over and crashed on top of The Apprentice, sandwiching her between the heavy trunk and the ground. Valeria stopped in front and stared down, admiring her handiwork.

"I have to thank you," Valeria said to The Apprentice who pushed her hands and knees against the ground, lifting the tree with her back. "I had resigned myself to living eternity here in the Other World with my dreams to recreate our home planet a nearly forgotten memory."

Zack slowly closed in, his gun aimed at Valeria. He paused when he saw panic on The Apprentice's face. Her hands and legs had melted into the grassy ground.

"But your presence here," Valeria went on, "is evidence that my destiny is on Earth, and I shall win. The people will accept witches as the dominant species, and I am the instrument of that change."

The Apprentice's body sank as if she were in quicksand. She tried to lift her head but within seconds, it was gone, buried under the grass. The ground was once again solid. It was as if The Apprentice was never there.

"My God, she buried her." Zack gasped.

This was his opportunity. He had to fire the weapon and hope it did some sort of damage, or at least enough to give The Witches a chance to recover and take advantage. *Zack, hold on*! Sebastian's voice popped into his head. It sounded like an echo. *You'll only get one chance to catch her unaware. I'm going to give you the opening.*

Zack clutched the side of his head. He had no idea witches could project their thoughts into someone's brain. None of them had ever done that to him. Well, no one except for Isis, which he thought was because of their bond. *What are you going to do?* Zack asked in his head. *You know a bullet won't put her down for long, even close up.*

It doesn't have to. You're right in thinking it will give us the moment we need. When she focuses on me, move in as close as you can and aim for the neck.

Will that give Selena and Sacha the chance to get back into the fight?

Let's hope so. If not, I may have something else in mind.

Okay. Zack held his ground, waiting as much out of curiosity to see what Sebastian had planned.

Valeria turned to the portal...except it was gone. Seeing that hole missing took Zack by surprise as well. He expected Valeria to explode in a fiery rage. Instead, she looked down at her hands, then grinned. "An illusion," she scoffed, then about-faced to see Sebastian back on his feet. "The energy is still with me, meaning your ploy was fruitless from the start." Valeria waved a hand. The tiny portal reappeared.

"Then I guess my only option is to face you and stop you!" Sebastian's fists clenched. "It is time we finished this once and for all!"

Valeria scoffed and formed a fireball in her right palm. Sebastian's threat was false bravado equivalent to spitting in the wind. But to stand his ground in the face of death, even if it was just a distraction, was impressive. Once Zack received the signal, he was determined not to let down this brave man.

Selena and Sacha pulled themselves off the ground. It went unnoticed by Valeria, meaning Sebastian's plan was working. The sisters eyed one another and nodded; they had a plan of attack as well. Valeria flung the fireball at Sebastian. It went straight through him, which meant he wasn't really there. His presence was an illusion.

Valeria's eyebrows rose. She shot out her hand. Sebastian suddenly appeared; his invisibility spell cancelled out. Valeria growled at him and raised her hands over her head. Whatever she was planning, it wouldn't be good. Somehow, he didn't look worried at all. A slight grin formed.

Now, Zack! Sebastian's voice rang through his head. *Now*!

Zack charged and lined up the pistol with Valeria's neck. He was only a few feet away, which should have made this an easy shot even without much experience shooting a gun. He had only fired a gun at an actual person one time before, and it was also Valeria. At the time, she was ready for it, so it did little good. This time, her attention was on Sebastian. Zack pressed his finger against the trigger…

Before he could shoot, the ground shook like an earthquake. Zack went off balance and fell over. The widened eyes of both Valeria and Sebastian meant the shaking wasn't either of their doing. The ground between Valeria and the portal suddenly split open. The Apprentice flew out and landed in front of Valeria who backpedaled a few steps before regaining her balance. The Apprentice's blackened eyes narrowed. Her fists clenched. Zack had a hunch this was not the distraction Sebastian had planned.

Valeria looked directly into the dark eyes of hate, anger, and rage. They belonged to a two-hundred-year-old vampire with destructive Wiccan power who was set on destruction. To Zack's surprise and horror, she reacted with a sneer. "So, you wish to settle a score from a future that will never be, My Apprentice?" Her eyes darkened to match her opponent's. "Then let's find out if you have truly surpassed your master."

Both vampires flexed their fangs and circled one another. They looked like cowboys readying themselves for a showdown. Even Zack, who was not a witch and had no connection to the Wiccan power, felt the energy surging around them. Sebastian and Sacha backed up. An arm grabbed Zack's from behind. It was Selena, pulling them away from a fight that could very well destroy the Other World. Could they possibly gain enough distance before getting swallowed by what was about to be a war between two powerful beings?

Then, both Valeria and The Apprentice's attention were diverted to the portal, which hummed as it expanded. The blurred hole had now become wide enough for either, or both, Wiccan vampires to step through. "What…what is happening?" Zack asked Selena, but she looked as lost as he felt.

Natasha and Paul stepped out with Jasper and Jeb behind them. They hadn't come empty handed. Jasper wore a rifle draped across his back. A hollowed-out steel tube with what looked like a small missile protruding from the front rested on Paul's right shoulder. Zack was sure it was a bazooka although he had never seen one in person, at least not until today. Natasha raised her hands high in the air. After a Russian word was spoken, a light as bright as the sun shined over Valeria and The Apprentice, both of whom were forced to stop what they were doing and cover their eyes with their arms.

Paul pulled the trigger. The loud hissing sound detonated from both ends of the cannon. It was accompanied by opaque snow-white smoke. The missile launched at the two Wiccan vampires and exploded. Valeria and The Apprentice flew like rockets in separate directions. Smoke flooded from their bodies. It was the same white smoke that now surrounded everyone. Zack swatted the air in front of his face.

Jasper eased the bazooka from Paul's shoulder and dropped it by his feet. "Nice shot, Mister Vice President," he said, with what sounded like a hint of glee.

Without a response, Paul marched up to Selena and Zack, who were joined by Sebastian. He didn't look particularly happy to see them. His grimace was far more pronounced than usual. "Hey!" Sacha cried out to him from behind. Paul turned. Sacha motioned up the hill. "Carolyn is over there, hurt. Valeria knocked her out."

"Jeb, help her," New Salem's vice president commanded. He then resumed his trudge, finally stopping in front of Sebastian who met him halfway.

"Thank you for the assist—"

Paul cut him off. "We are closing this portal right now!" He spoke like a drill sergeant chastising a crew of trainees he'd caught fooling around. "If you are leaving with us, let's go!"

"Not yet!" Selena shot back, joining Sebastian at his side. "We still haven't found Isis!"

"Damn it, you're out of time!"

Zack's head lifted. A tall shadow grew through the smoke, and it was heading their way. "Um…guys?"

"Paul, please," Sebastian pleaded. "We didn't go through all of this just to leave our girl behind."

The shadow moved closer, revealing darkened eyes through the white smoke.

"This is not me being unreasonable! This is coming from Doctor Mac!" Paul's grimace turned into a look of concern. "We close this now or we risk our planet's stability—"

"Heads up!" Zack shouted at the top of his lungs. "She's back!"

Valeria stepped through the smoke, making a beeline for Paul. Her hand swung. In response, Selena and Sebastian were knocked over as if a huge tidal wave had engulfed and dragged them away.

From the front of the portal, Natasha cried out, "Paul!"

Valeria's body floated from the ground. She hovered closer. Paul whipped a pistol from his belt and fired a shot at Valeria's chest. The Wiccan vampire raised a hand. The bullet reversed course and hit Paul in the thigh. He let out a scream as his body dropped to the ground.

Instinct took over for Zack who backpedaled. There were enough witches with far better training in war to engage. Sure enough, Natasha hovered a few feet away from Valeria to face the ancient witch. At the same time, Jasper dropped the empty bazooka, grabbed the rifle from his back, and pointed it. Before either could attack, Paul lifted off the ground and hung in midair. Jasper lowered his weapon.

"Let him go," Natasha roared.

"Oh, I will," Valeria answered. "Once I find myself on the other side of your portal."

Valeria walked ahead with Paul floating in front of her. Natasha blocked her path, but her options were limited with Paul hovering like a human shield.

"Stand aside, young witch," Valeria said to her. "Or become the first casualty in my revolution against humanity."

Chapter Twenty-Four

Isis picked up another button, then eyed the top of the next hill. It looked just as high as the last dozen or so she had to walk up then down just to get where she was at now. This hill, however, was different. Dense smoke rose from the other side and filled the sky. Her three travel companions were all staring Isis' way, perhaps waiting for her to make the decision as to whether they should continue on toward the smoke. God, when did she become a leader? Now, she supposed.

Isis looked back and forth at the animals and nodded. "Let's check it out," she said with renewed determination.

Her calf muscles felt like they had gone through a meat grinder several times. She had to put that aside. That smoke couldn't be a natural occurrence here in the Other World, meaning they had to investigate. The best case scenario was that it was created by her rescue party. Worst-case: they were at least another long hill away from where they needed to be.

Isis walked up the hill, as did the animals. At the top, she could see everything on the other side. A loud gasp shot from her throat. The smoke was finally clearing up, but things were hardly calm. Valeria levitated in the air with Paul—who looked like he was trapped in an invisible coffin—in front of her. Blood dripped from his right leg. The Witches of Vegas faced her along with Natasha and Jasper. They were all in front of an oval-shaped blur, which Isis was sure led to home. The only one not in front of the portal was Jeb, who stood to the side cradling an unconscious Carolyn in his arms.

Isis heard Paul even from the top of the hill. "Forget about me!" he shouted. "You cannot allow her access to our home!"

The only one Isis didn't see was Zack, until she caught him sneaking up behind Valeria. He charged with a pistol in both of his unsteady hands. He aimed for the back of Valeria's head. Before he could get off a shot, his body lifted in the air and slammed against the ground. The pistol flew out of his hands, but stayed in the air, floating near Valeria and with the barrel directed at Natasha. The Russian witch froze in her tracks.

"We have to stop Valeria!" Isis yelled to her new allies. "This is our chance! Go! Attack!"

The animals let out horn-like squeals. The troops—all three of them—were rallied. As one, they charged. Isis managed to grab hold of the fur of the smallest one as it passed. She held on, running at its side until she was able to swing a leg to climb onto its back. Isis braced her thighs on either side and held on as it picked up speed.

While all eyes were on Valeria and her hostage, Zack lifted his head from the ground in time to see the animals stampeding down the hill. He quickly rolled out of the way.

The gun went off creating a small sonic boom. The bullet passed through Natasha—who managed to phase her body—and traveled through the portal. Natasha flew aside like a sheet of paper in the wind. The pistol slowly turned itself. It lined up with Sebastian and Selena.

"You will interfere with me never again!" Valeria's voice roared, making known her intention to leave them for dead.

The two animals in the lead jumped in the air and dug their teeth into Valeria's feet, pulling her to the ground. The pistol dropped to the ground, as did Paul. Valeria was taken by surprise, but being a witch who had lived for four centuries, she quickly regained her composure. The animals shrieked. Isis couldn't imagine what was done to them as they thundered off in opposite directions.

"I will not be denied my destiny, not by these pathetic creatures, or any of you!" Valeria held a glowing hand over Paul, who had rolled to his knees. "Away from the portal!" The ground around her shook, causing everyone to topple over.

Isis and her ride moved at an amazing speed. She sensed the energy. It was everywhere, including inside her. She eyed Valeria's back and focused on one thought. "Teleport!" she chanted.

Isis was suddenly exactly where she imagined herself, on Valeria's back with her left arm wrapped around the elder witch's neck. Paul slid out of their way as if a hook had wrapped around his waist and yanked him, the work of one of the others surrounding them. Isis, meanwhile, willed Valeria's right hand up and inches in front of the elder witch's face. The palm pointed her way.

"Look at the lines on your hand and feel your

eyelids sag," she chanted into Valeria's ear. "Feel yourself grow tired. Let the need for sleep take over."

"What…what do you think you're doing?" Valeria screeched.

The first time they met, Valeria put Isis to sleep. Now it was time to turn the tables. Hypnosis was one of Dad's strengths in manipulating the energy. He hadn't taught it to Isis, at least not yet. But in the original timeline, he did teach it to her a few years from now. That was one of many memories from the original Isis' life that circled around her brain. Like when that version of Isis used those lessons on Valeria to save every living being on Earth. Just as she was about to do right now.

Valeria lifted her left hand over her head. It ignited into flames. She was about to use fire as a weapon against Isis, just as she had done in their previous battles. But Isis wouldn't release her grip or lose concentration. She was determined to see her spell work.

"Fall asleep," she said rhythmically. "Fall asleep."

Isis braced herself for the heat of Valeria's blaze. But the Wiccan vampire's left arm suddenly stretched out. Selena and Sacha were nearby to their left, their hands locked. The energy crackled around them, and around Valeria's arm, meaning they had a tight grip. "No!" Valeria mumbled. "No…I will not…fall…"

"You need to sleep." Isis felt her presence in Valeria's brain. It was a strong brain resisting her entry, but Isis had the advantage. "Sleep…sleep…"

The flames around Valeria's left hand faded. Finally, her legs gave out. She tumbled, taking Isis to the ground with her. The Wiccan vampire lay face down on the grass. Isis rolled away, let out a deep exhale, then stood to face the many surprised stares that surrounded her.

Two arms suddenly wrapped around Isis and squeezed. They belonged to Mom. "You're okay," Selena sobbed. Her cheek pressed against Isis' head. "And you found us. We had no idea how to find you, but you came to us."

"I saw the buttons." Isis embraced her mother, returning her tight squeeze. "I followed them."

"Hey." Sacha motioned a thumb over her shoulder. "Kiddo looks okay to me, so I'm going to check on Carolyn. All right?"

Selena nodded to her sister, who ran off. She placed her hands on Isis' cheeks and looked down into her eyes. Zack and Sebastian approached from opposite sides.

"I'm okay," she insisted. "I really am." Sebastian's hand rubbed against the back of Isis' neck. He helped both her and Selena to their feet.

"We're really glad about that," Zack shouted. "Because we were worried about you." Isis turned from her parents to Zack and gave him a hug as passionate as she gave her mother.

"Heads up!"

Sebastian's sudden warning forced Isis to pull away from Zack. Her immediate thought was that Valeria had awakened from the sleep spell. But it wasn't a vampire threat that caused the warning.

Sebastian pointed at the animal Isis had saved. From just a few feet away, its head leaned toward Sebastian, then tilted. Zack took two steps back. His eyes dropped to the pistol on the ground. Isis sensed the energy building up in Sebastian. The creature flashed its sharp teeth.

"Wait!" She ran in front of Sebastian and stretched out her arms to block his way. "It's okay. That's my friend."

"Your friend?" Selena asked.

"Yes, my friend." Isis nodded at the confused looks her way. The animal ran up the hill. From the top it looked back, let out a loud horn-like howl, then resumed its path. Isis waved her hand to say goodbye.

"Witches of Vegas!" Paul's commanding voice turned the group's attention to the portal. His arms were draped across an invisible barrier created by Natasha who held a glowing hand his way. "If there are no other objections," he said with a hint of frustrated sarcasm, "we need to go!"

Sebastian wrapped his arms around Selena and Isis. "We have no objections—"

"Um, Mister Vice President, sir?" Zack stepped in front. He looked back and forth from Sebastian and Selena to Paul. He motioned to the corpse several feet away. "Can we take Harry's body back with us so we can give him a proper burial?"

"*Burial*?" Isis pulled away from Sebastian and gawked at the body. Harry lay on his back, unmoving with his eyes closed. She shrieked with a hand over her mouth. "Oh no."

Isis had no idea that Harry was a victim of her rescue. She tipped her head down and wiped an arm across her eyes. No one should have died trying to save her. But someone did.

"Grab him, quickly!" Paul ordered. "We need to close that portal now!"

"You don't have to tell me twice," Sacha replied while eyeing Valeria in her slumber.

She and Jeb entered the portal with Carolyn who had an arm draped over each of their shoulders. Her eyes were barely open, but she was conscious and speaking with Sacha as they entered the circular blur. Natasha sent Paul through next, then followed him in. That left Jasper. He stopped and stood to the side of the portal waiting for Isis and her family to step through.

Zack followed Sebastian to Harry's corpse. They squatted on opposite sides. Sebastian lifted Harry by his shoulders while Zack took the legs. Then they caught up to Isis and Selena by the portal. Before entering, Isis noticed Jasper's gaze at the sky and the hills.

"What is it?" she asked.

"I am just taken in by the idea that we are on an entirely different planet far away from our own."

"Technically," Zack replied, "we're actually on another plane of existence. This planet shares the same space as Earth."

"He's right. It does." Isis poked Jasper on the chest. That was a fact Isis remembered learning in the original timeline.

"Wherever we are," Sebastian said, struggling to keep his grip on Harry. "Let's leave it behind."

Isis and Selena stepped aside to let Sebastian and Zack take Harry through. Then, they, along with Jasper, exited the Other World. They were back on New Salem land. Jeb ran over and took Sebastian's place, wrapping his arms around Harry's chest. He and Zack took the body aside. Soon, it would be prepared for burial. Sebastian and Selena—Isis' folks who once again risked everything and everyone to save her—exchanged a relieved hug. They were all finally safe.

Natasha, wasting no time, dropped to her knees and held her hands over Paul's horizontal body. The bullet ripped from his leg and dropped onto the ground. Natasha focused her healing spell on stopping the bleeding and healing the wound.

Isis, meanwhile, ran as far ahead as her swollen ankles allowed. They were in the middle of the cemetery with the cottages on one side and the swamp forest surrounding them on the other. She took a deep inhale. The air had never tasted so sweet. Same with the relief that it was all over.

Jasper was the last one through. He nodded to Doctor Mac who stood at the edge of the portal with his arms stretched out and his hands glowing. "We are all here. Please close the portal immediately," Jasper said in case the doctor didn't understand his nonverbal cue.

"I can't!" The doctor's voice was filled with panic.

Isis spun around like a top. Natasha lifted her head from healing Paul's injury. Doctor Mac still had the portal open. "Doctor!" Natasha shouted. "What are you doing? Close the portal immediately." Paul pushed his elbows against the ground to lift his upper body. The same disbelief was written across his face.

"It…it's not me." Doctor Mac's jaw shook. "I am no longer in control of the energy holding it open."

A foot shot out of the blurred oval circle leading to the Other World. It was joined by an arm, and then the rest of a body.

Isis gasped. It was her foot, her arm, her body. The Apprentice stepped out of the portal.

"I can't take control, can't send her back!" Doctor Mac exclaimed. "Someone do something, quickly!"

Sebastian and Selena ran toward the portal, as did Sacha who had rested Carolyn on a nearby bench bordering the circular cemetery. "We have to push her through!" Sebastian called out to everyone. "Together, we can do it! With a force blast spell from all of us, we can overwhelm her—"

The Apprentice whipped her arms from far left to far right. A burst of clear energy shot out from her body, engulfing the area in front of the portal.

"Shield!" Isis shouted, thrusting her palms in front of her. The energy burst on impact in front of her like water smacking a shower door. Following her dad's command, Isis focused on The Apprentice.

"Force blast!" she chanted. A wave of energy shot from her outstretched hands and traveled to its target. The Apprentice held out one hand. It blocked Isis' blast, crackling as their witchcraft connected.

Isis focused on the energy, pushing with all her might. She had no idea how many witches were working with her to force The Apprentice just two steps back. But, however many, it was to no avail. The Apprentice was too strong, too powerful. Instead of falling back into the portal, she took a step forward. Isis' shirtsleeves tore from the energy's strain around her body. They needed a distraction to break The Apprentice's concentration, something to throw her off so she'd lose her grip of her powerful connection.

Isis' mind raced, trying to come up with a solution. She could only think of one possibility, one deadly possibility. She hated the idea, but there was no other choice. Keeping her focus on her energy blast, Isis pulled back her right hand and brought it up in front of her face. Crazy, maybe even stupid, but it was the only way to stop her other self. "Fire!" she chanted.

In response, the energy formed a circular flame that hovered in Isis' palm. The Apprentice eyed the fire and smirked. It was as if she was daring her less powerful self to try and use it on her.

The Apprentice took another step, putting a bit more distance from the portal. Her head turned to Doctor Mac who, now in control of his own connection, kept the entryway back to the Other World open. He had no choice.

The idea of what she was about to do made Isis' stomach muscles cringe, but she was committed. The flame grew in size until it became as big as a soccer ball. Isis hesitated, but as she stared into the confident but enraged mirror image of her own face, daring her to throw the fireball, she knew there was no other choice. No other way. At least even The Apprentice wouldn't see this coming…

Isis turned her palm until it faced herself…the flame jumped from her grip and ignited her left arm. The fire overtook Isis' arm from the shoulder to the wrist. She screamed, as did every pore in her arm. The fire sparked, catching the left side of her pants over her waist and thigh with tiny flames. Isis fell to her knees, shrieking like a coyote singing soprano. She had never felt such pain or agony before in her entire life. It was as if a dozen leather belts smacked her arm, shoulder, and waist a hundred times each. Quickly, the energy swirled around her like a swarm of insects. Static snapped in every direction. She sensed the tingling in the air, but she could no longer feel it in her brain.

Isis' eyes watered. Through the haze, she saw The Apprentice reach out. Which meant she was taking the bait. The energy around Isis turned into an invisible wind and traveled toward her doppelganger. The Apprentice looked to the sky with her eyes closed.

"Isis!" a voice called. It was Jeb's. "I'm here! Zack sent me to you! My God, what did you just do?"

Isis had no idea where Zack was, or if he was all right. Jeb held his hands over Isis' shoulder. A cold breeze blew over her making the flame slow then abate. It didn't ease the pain, but Isis didn't care about herself, not in this moment. She needed all the other witches around her to take advantage of the distraction.

"N-now!" It hurt to shout, but she needed everyone in earshot to hear her. "Send her back!"

Isis' right hand rubbed across her eyes, wiping away the heavy tears. That's when she saw it. The Apprentice's energy blast rendered everyone who could help unconscious. Mom, Dad, and Sacha were down on the ground, perhaps hurt, or just knocked cold. It was the case with Natasha as well. She was laid out next to Paul who, although conscious, was still off his feet. Even Jasper was down. Within her scope of vision, the only one on his feet was Doctor Mac, but he was too focused on keeping the portal open to intervene. He certainly couldn't close it with The Apprentice on this side.

This was the moment Isis' plan relied on, but there was no one left to follow through. The Apprentice was distracted, but that would only be momentary. Everything was now up to Isis. She focused on the energy to push The Apprentice the few steps necessary to send her back through the portal...but nothing happened. As expected, she no longer had her connection.

Isis had one option left, and it was drastic, even more so than setting herself on fire.

She thought back to what Zack had said the first Isis told him. "In order to defeat the threat to Earth, it would require a great sacrifice." This was that sacrifice. Isis had to physically run her other self through that portal and back into the Other World, even if it meant going in with her. It was a ransom she was willing to pay if it meant keeping her loved ones and their futures safe.

Isis blocked the pain in her mind and stood up. She looked over at Zack, who surveyed her from a distance through widened eyes, stunned at what he had just witnessed his girlfriend do to herself. When his gaze shifted to The Apprentice, she knew Zack understood why, and what had to happen next. Isis gave him a silent goodbye, and then one to the family that took her in and gave her the great life she enjoyed. She hoped they would understand that this was the only way.

"Isis, what are you doing?" Jeb screamed. But there was no time to explain, not to him or anyone else.

Isis put one foot in front of the other, picking up speed as she approached the target. The Apprentice, slowly regaining her senses, snarled at Isis, displaying her fangs.

She couldn't feel or move her left arm, but she was able to stretch out her right. She needed to ram her shoulder into The Apprentice's gut and run her back before she could adjust to the increase in her connection to the energy. Isis ducked her head, charging as fast as she could toward the target…this was her only chance, the entire planet's only chance…

A hand pushed against Isis' scorched shoulder. The

striking pain knocked her off balance. Isis fell to the ground and rolled across the grass. She looked up to see Zack, hunched down and charging. His arms wrapped around The Apprentice's waist.

"*No!*" Isis cried.

Zack lifted The Apprentice off her feet and barreled forward, taking the vampire with him. They passed by Doctor Mac and plunged through the blurred oval-shaped portal.

And disappeared.

"*Zack, No!*" Isis' eyes watered again, but not from the blistering that engulfed her left side. "*Not like this! Get out, come back to me! Please!*"

Doctor Mac looked her way. His face was covered with sweat and guilt. "I'm sorry," he shouted. "I have to. There's no choice."

"Doctor Mac, please, just wait—"

The doctor lowered his hands. The portal faded away. The trees from the swamp forest were now in perfect focus behind Doctor Mac. Isis moaned as the fog in her brain took over. Her eyes shut. The last thing she remembered was the ground slamming against the side of her face.

Chapter Twenty-Five

Zack landed on top of The Apprentice and was quickly shoved off. He picked himself up, ready to either defend himself or run until he realized he was no longer the vampire's focus. She was fixated on the energy sparks in the air where the portal once stood. The Apprentice reached out, but the electric flickers diminished until they were gone.

Once again, Zack was surrounded by a planet that was not his own. For as far as he could see, he was surrounded by the gray grass and hills of the Other World along with trees sporting that cactus-like bark, and Valeria in a deep slumber by his feet. That was it, nothing else. And now he was stuck here with no way home.

After witnessing Isis burn herself, he realized what she was up to. It was the right move, and it was necessary, but she wasn't the one to make that sacrifice. Had Isis gone through the portal, no one in that family would have recovered. No one would have been able to move on, and that included Zack. In the moment, instincts took over. He charged and took her place, damn the consequences to himself.

Zack grabbed his right shoulder, which stung like a cramped muscle. The Apprentice, despite her skinny frame, was like slamming into a flagpole. After what Isis had done to the left side of her body, it was doubtful she would have had the strength to budge The Apprentice, let alone lift her up then run her through the portal back to the Other World—

The Apprentice spun around and faced Zack. Her eyes were pitch black. A scowl like that of a wild animal backed into a corner crossed her lips. The Apprentice didn't have her Wiccan connection here, but she was still a vampire, which made her dangerous. She eyed Zack with a body shaking from rage.

"Um, I know you don't really know me." Zack held his hands out while taking a step back. "In your timeline, we never met. But in this one, we grew close. We fell in love. We have a bond, a connection, one I'm hoping that deep down you can feel as well—"

The Apprentice pounced. Zack barely saw her coming. A hand wrapped around his throat and slammed him onto his back. Isis' face stared down at Zack while the fingers around his throat tightened like a noose. He felt the palm press against his windpipe. This was the closest he had been to The Apprentice. Her skin looked washed out and nearly pale. Her face was also covered in burn scars. But the dimples, the cheekbones, the smooth forehead up to the hairline, it was Isis, but nothing like the one Zack knew better than anyone else on Earth. This Isis was an angry and broken version who never experienced their love for one another.

Zack needed air. He tried to suck it in, but his trachea was blocked off and the grip was getting tighter. His eyes felt like they were about to explode inside of his skull. At first, he thought The Apprentice was looking to suffocate him until his death, then bring him back as the reanimated undead. But then he saw her lean down with her fangs exposed. This wasn't about creating a new vampire. She was looking to drink blood. His final contribution was to become The Apprentice's next meal.

One thought had run through Zack's mind…how would he survive in the Other World without a way home? He was glad Isis wouldn't have to figure it out, especially with what looked like third degree burns across half of her body. As it turned out, he wouldn't need to figure it out either. He was about to die…

The Apprentice was suddenly pulled into the air as if a crane snatched her by the pants. Her hand ripped from Zack's throat. Clutching his throat, he rolled over and hacked. A mouthful of air finally reached his lungs. It tasted like a bowl of boiling soup after not eating for days. He was appreciative, but who pulled The Apprentice from him? He opened his eyes to see Valeria was still face down on the ground. Whoever he had to thank for saving his life, it sure wasn't her.

Zack pushed to his knees and looked over his shoulder. His savior stood behind him and studied The Apprentice. He was tall, bald, and wearing the remains of a black button-down shirt and black dress pants that had seen better days. The same could be said for the black cape, which hung to his ankles with the bottom shredded. But his arrival couldn't have been any timelier.

It was The Witches of Vegas' mentor, Luther. The Apprentice eyed him with her head tilted in confusion as to how she should react. She let out a snarl. Both vampires stood in place, carefully examining one another, waiting for the other to pounce. Zack jumped to his feet and dashed out from between them. He needed some distance from what could turn into yet another lethal showdown between two relentless vampires.

A loud groan caused Luther's head to turn. It came from Valeria who hadn't moved a muscle. The Apprentice took advantage of the distraction and ran off, perhaps to regain her bearings. After several steps, she made a high jump, catching a tree's nearby branch. The Apprentice swung herself up and then leapt from one tree to the next. The ruffling of the branches moved farther away until Zack couldn't hear them at all.

Luther dropped to one knee by Valeria's side. The Wiccan vampire lifted her head. She tried to push her body up, but her arms gave out and fell back to her side. "Valeria," Luther said. "Are you all right?"

"Wh-where are they?" Valeria mumbled. "The portal…is it still… I-I think I need a moment."

"Rest, Valeria. You are groggy from a slumber, one I believe to be caused by a witch's spell."

Valeria's eyes closed. Luther stood and faced Zack. "It seems I have missed a lot during my excursion to the other side of this plane."

"Luther," Zack said. "I'm not sure if you remember me, but I'm—"

"I do remember you. You're Zack Galloway, Isis' friend." Luther marched up to Zack while eyeing the direction The Apprentice had gone. "At first, I presumed that was Isis and she had been turned. She certainly looked and smelled like Isis. Except she is hundreds of years old."

"Two hundred years old, to be precise—"

Luther charged and grabbed two handfuls of Zack's shirt. His body froze as Luther lifted him inches off the ground and pulled him close. Zack could taste the dead vampire's breath as it hit his face. It was similar to rotten onions.

"I need to know what is happening here," Luther demanded. "Tell me everything, and tell me quickly!"

Fine. Zack was looking to do exactly that, anyway.

Chapter Twenty-Six

Isis sat up from one of the two beds in the medical center's recovery room. Her left arm was wrapped tight in white gauze from her wrist to her elbow. It rested against her chest in a sling. The arm no longer stung, or even hurt. In fact, she couldn't feel it at all. It wasn't a "so painful it stopped hurting" feeling like she had when she set her arm and left side of her body on fire. It was more of a medicated numbness. An attempt to wiggle her fingers proved unsuccessful. Only her pinky finger moved ever so slightly.

Isis used her right hand to push herself off the bed. At first, she wobbled until she was able to hold her balance and plant two feet on the floor. Isis walked up to the other bed which had its own occupant reclined in an upright position with her face drooped from boredom. "Can't feel your arm, can you?" Maya asked.

"Not at all," Isis answered.

"Me neither." Maya raised her hand. It was wrapped in a cast that covered her fingers and wrist. "I think Doctor Mac purposely puts a spell on healing body parts. It keeps us from whining about the pain."

"How do I look?" Isis asked, noticing Maya's squinted eyes.

"From what I can see of your arm, it's a whole bunch of different colors. I don't know about the rest of your body underneath that ugly hospital gown." She gave off a cheese-faced grin. "But as far as your face goes, it still looks like you. Well, except for all those bruises around your eyes."

Isis placed a finger from her right hand against her left temple. The skin felt lumpy and sensitive to the touch.

"Hey, I heard you saved my dad's life over there. Thanks." Maya flashed Isis a devious grin. "Maybe I can use that as leverage in case he tries to ground me for my part in all of this. You think?"

Isis appreciated Maya's sense of humor, especially at this moment. But it didn't change the fact that she felt responsible for her best friend's injury. It was her other self that severed Maya's hand. Hell, she was the reason The Apprentice even existed in the first place. Everything was her fault. "Maya, I'm so sorry—"

"Hey! Stop with that right now." Maya waved her good hand at Isis. "Yes, going after The Apprentice was a dumb idea, but if you remember, it was *my* dumb idea."

"I could have said no. If I didn't agree, we wouldn't have gone—"

"You weren't going to say no. But if you had, I'd probably have talked you into it." Maya clutched her forehead. "I need to start thinking things through a bit more from now on. If I'm ever going to be president, I have to stop being such a rebel, you know?"

Isis stared at the cast around Maya's hand, and then through it. She didn't respond because her mind had drifted somewhere else. She pressed her right hand against the top of her head, but it did little to comfort the striking ache inside her skull. Maya reached out and gave Isis a shake to snap her back to reality.

"You'll bring him home," Maya whispered. "Your family will make sure of it. They have the power to make that happen even without you."

"I really hope you're right," Isis replied with a sniffle.

Her family. Mom, Dad, and Sacha. Isis hadn't spoken to any of them since before the battle ended and she passed out. Then she woke up in the medical center, presumably thanks to a teleportation spell by Doctor Mac. Before that moment, Isis was one of the most powerful witches on Earth. Now she couldn't even move a pencil. Could she ever again reconnect with the energy? Even more concerning, would Mom and Dad look at her any different now that she was no longer like them, no longer a witch? Her connection was the sole reason they brought her into the family in the first place. The pain around her brain tightened. It was interrupted by Maya's voice.

"Hey, Isis, can I ask a favor?"

Isis lifted her head. "Sure. What's up?"

"I heard you gave up your connection to save us. That's really cool and all. But you still know how a witch can use the energy to block pain, right?"

"I remember the spells I used to manipulate the energy like that, yeah." Even though she couldn't do it anymore. Maybe never again.

Maya held up her bandaged hand. "Connected or not, you're still like an expert with all the witchcraft stuff. When Doctor Mac's spell starts wearing off, can you teach me how to do that? Although, to be honest, I don't know if my connection is strong enough."

"It is." Somehow, Isis still sensed that about her even now. "Your connection is strong enough."

"You know what? I believe you." Maya let her hand drop. "So, what do you say? Can I be your student?"

Now that was something within Isis' abilities, and a fair request from Maya. Isis knew more about controlling and manipulating the energy than anyone else alive. There were two centuries of memories in her head; much of it was on witchcraft and how to control the energy. "Yeah, I can walk you through it—"

A blur formed next to Isis, which forced her to step back. Once it cleared, Doctor Mac stood in front of Maya's bed. He looked from her to Isis. "I see both of my patients are feeling better. Excellent."

Isis walked up to him. "Doctor Mac, I-I can't feel my left arm."

"Your burns are severe, Isis, particularly from your elbow to your wrist." The doctor held a hand over Isis' forearm, which was pressed against her stomach in the sling. A light formed around his fingers. "I healed it as best I could, both through medical and Wiccan means. You're going to need around six to nine months of physical therapy. However, I do believe in that time I can get you to at least ninety-percent mobility." The light around Doctor Mac's hand disappeared. His quick examination was apparently finished.

"Thank you, Doctor Mac." Ninety percent was better than less, so she'd take it.

"He promised me the same thing," Maya said. "Hey, maybe we can race to see who can move her fingers first. Sound like a bet?"

"Your healing process is not a race, ladies," Doctor Mac interrupted. "Nor should it be treated as such. Isis, how about I teleport you back to your cottage? I know your family is anxious to see you."

Isis nodded, then prepared herself for teleportation. It was a use of the Wiccan energy she was great at, or at least she used to be. But that was the least of her worries. Zack. They had to get him back before it was too late. What if it already was too late? The Apprentice could have killed him. Or Valeria. What if he wasn't killed but injured really badly while stuck in the Other World? The thought made Isis shiver.

"Hey, it's going to be okay, Hon," Maya shouted from the bed. "I'll see you in physical therapy. That's where we're both going to beat Doctor Mac's projection and come out one hundred percent. Sound good?"

Isis smiled in response. It was forced, but that wasn't Maya's fault. There was just too much to worry about.

Doctor Mac took Isis by the shoulders. The medical room disappeared into a haze. Once Isis' vision cleared, she was in her cottage's living room. Sebastian and Selena jumped from their seated positions on the couch. Sacha, who was standing by the open kitchen's table, dropped her sandwich and ran over. Doctor Mac stepped back as the family approached.

Sebastian wrapped his arms around Isis and squeezed her as tight as he ever had before. Once he let go, Selena grabbed Isis from the side, pulled her in close, and kissed the top of her head. She then gently clutched Isis' wrapped hand and wrist to check on them with her own eyes. Both embraces meant the world to Isis. It meant she could put at least one major concern aside. Her family still loved her whether she was a witch or not.

"Tell us your prognosis, Doctor Mac," Selena said. "How is she?"

"The worst is over," the doctor replied. "Now, we are looking at the healing stage."

"How are you feeling, Kiddo?" Sacha asked Isis with a hand against her back.

"Worried." Isis looked up into Selena's eyes. "Are we are going to—"

"Stop!" Sebastian's shout made Isis nearly jump out of her skin. Sebastian faced Doctor Mac, who stood across the room. "Doctor, it is unusual for you to bring a patient home, isn't it?" The suspicion across his face matched his tone.

"It is, and I'm sorry." Doctor Mac raised his arms. "But now that Isis has been released from my care, you are all expected for an important meeting."

Before anyone could react, the living room faded around them. The teleportation was quick and smooth; it took maybe seconds. They were suddenly in the president's office in front of her desk. Tia stood from her cushioned chair with Paul on her left and Jasper on her right. At least everyone was healed. Even Paul was back on his feet.

Isis peeked behind them where Natasha and Carolyn were positioned by the door. Jeb was there as well, a few feet away. His head dropped toward his boots, as did the pistol in his hand. When his hand finally picked up, he avoided eye contact with Isis.

Natasha's eyes sported a yellowish glow to them, which meant she was manipulating the energy in the room. With Doctor Mac to their right, the family was clearly outnumbered, and maybe outgunned. They were also in the middle of a pentagon formed by five sparking enchanted crystals. Sacha eyed her hand with a look that said she was cut off from the energy.

Selena's shoulders flexed back. "What is this about?"

Tia folded her hands together against her chest and let out a deep exhale. "We have come to a decision, and I wanted you to hear it from me directly."

Sebastian's fists clutched. "You don't expect us to leave Zack over there all alone, do you?"

"This is a difficult decision to make. Zack is one of us," Tia explained. "He is a member of this community. However, there are two serious threats to every single life on the entire planet in the Other World. Weighed against one life, we have no choice but to take precautions which will assure a portal between our lands is never opened again."

"Are you joking?" Sacha screamed. She rushed forward until Selena clutched her arm. She spun to her sister, stunned. "Selena, Sebastian, we can't just abandon him!"

"We're not going to," Selena answered.

"You don't have a choice!" Paul shouted. "Believe me when I say we don't like this any more than you do."

"What about you, Jeb?" Isis snarled his way. "You're okay being part of this? Zack is your best friend!" She received no answer, not even a glance.

Isis walked as far as she could to Doctor Mac. The sparks coming from the invisible pyramid around them stopped her in place. She looked up at the doctor with wide eyes. "Doctor Mac, I don't get it," she sobbed. "You helped save me. Why not Zack? Is it because he's not a witch?"

Isis braced herself for his answer. She always believed Doctor Mac viewed everyone in New Salem, witch or not, as equals. At least that was how he portrayed himself and why he was so well liked in New Salem. But what if, deep down, that was not the case? Then her new status meant their relationship was about to change.

Doctor Mac raised a hand and held out his palm. "It's not like that at all, Isis. I want to help Zack come home, and I would if I could."

"Then why not?" Her voice cracked. "What changed?"

"I've had the chance to see one of these Wiccan vampires up close, and it wasn't even the more powerful of the two!" The doctor shook his head. "We can't ever again give them the opportunity to come here. If it should happen, it's almost assured that we would go extinct."

"And Zack understands that," Tia added. "It was why he made the sacrifice he did in the first place. He would not want us to reopen a portal and take that chance."

"You don't know that," Sacha mumbled.

"You said you were taking precautions," Sebastian said. "What does that mean, exactly?"

Tia and Paul exchanged a glance. The president nodded, then waved a hand. Jeb shook his head. His face pinched which made him look like an adolescent who just soiled his pants. That couldn't have been a good sign.

"Selena and Sacha," Paul announced. "You are the only ones who are powerful enough and have the knowledge to open a portal to the Other World. Even then, it takes your sibling connection to do so. That is why we need to separate the two of you."

"Say what, now?" Sacha gasped.

Tia offered her presidential grin. "Selena and Sebastian, we ask that you remain in New Salem to raise Isis. I can promise the three of you will have a good life here. Sacha, however, will need to be relocated."

"Relocated?" Sacha's eyes went wide. "You can't be serious."

"We are," Paul replied. "We are setting you up in a location far from New Salem. You will be provided for until you have established a new life and no longer need us."

"After everything we've been through," Selena roared, "you want to break up our family? You can't possibly think we're going to be okay with this!"

Jasper slammed a boot against the tiled floor. "Please watch your temper. I understand this is distressing for you, but you are still addressing our president."

"That is not happening!" Sacha turned her attention to Carolyn. "Don't tell me *you're* in agreement with my relocation plan?"

"I don't like it either, but I understand why." Carolyn leaned in close to the crystals' barrier and whispered to Sacha, "I could come with you."

"Is that all you got?" Sacha growled.

"What if we refuse this plan?" Sebastian thrust his hands on his hips. "Is there no room for compromise? Perhaps we could agree never to open the portal."

"Then what about Zack?" Isis screamed.

"We've had that agreement from you before,

Sebastian," Paul snarled. "That was when you used the energy to hypnotize me. Be glad I am not holding that against you."

Tia stretched out her arm in front of Paul, a message for him to back down. "I accept that the offer you just made is genuine. However, the temptation and your need to rescue one of your own would still exist, which is understandable. Unfortunately, the danger outweighs the reward. This is the only way to assure those immortal vampire-witches never set foot in our reality. Reentry into the Other World can never happen, and this is the only way to assure it."

Sacha slammed a fist against the energy barrier, which sparked. "This is crap, and you know it!"

"You've been told to watch your tone," Paul growled.

Arguing erupted. Isis backpedaled as far away as she could within the crystals. She wanted to call out to Zack, make sure he was still alive and okay. But even if she still could control the energy, he wouldn't be able to hear her. Zack was lost to her, to all of them, forever. That was a fact she may never be able to accept.

Chapter Twenty-Seven

According to Luther, he and Valeria lived in a cabin she had built during her three-hundred-year isolation. It stood several miles away. Luther carried Valeria back to what was their home so she could recuperate from Isis' sleep spell. Zack followed until he tired out. They had passed a huge lone boulder in the middle of all the emptiness and a cliff out in the distance. He decided to use the huge rock as a place to sit, catch his breath, and ponder his new environment.

There were no streets here, no buildings, nothing. Just wilderness. There were no people except himself, at least none that were still alive. He pulled his phone from his back pocket and stared at the latest picture on the screen of Isis. It was the one he took in The Sapphire hallway on the morning they arrived in Vegas. The screen showed zero bars at the top, just a notification that read, "no signal."

Zack placed the phone back in his pocket. May as well save the battery life, although he wasn't sure for what. He hoped not to be here for too long, but if Isis and her family could rescue him, wouldn't they have tried already? He'd understand if they didn't want to chance accidentally freeing one, or both, of those Wiccan vampires trapped over here. Was that the decision they made? Were they still discussing it? Did they try and weren't able to cross over again? It was not knowing which made every second tough to get through.

Man, Zack always hated the forest, even when he was ten years old and Uncle Herb took him camping. His uncle loved it. He called it "getting in touch with nature." All Zack remembered was every part of his body getting in touch with bug bites. At least he wouldn't have to worry about that here. Zack hadn't seen a single insect anywhere, at least not so far. Maybe insects did live here and he had just been lucky so far. He'd certainly have plenty of time to find out.

A deep inhale told him that the air was different. It was like trying to fill his lungs in a rainforest. Guess that was something he'd have to get used to. That, and the company. A rustling broke him of his thoughts. Luckily, it was just Luther. Without a word, the vampire strolled Zack's way, then took a seat next to him on the boulder.

"Where are they?" Zack asked, still staring straight ahead at the woods.

"Valeria is recovering from the sleep spell, swearing revenge. The other Isis, I sensed a few miles to the east. She seems content exploring her new home. They are separated, at least for the time being."

"That's a good thing."

"Yes, now let's talk about you." Luther's eyes nearly burned a hole through Zack. He really was the type who went straight to the point. It was just how Isis described him.

"Okay, let's talk about me," Zack replied. "I don't suppose you have a way to send me home, do you?"

"I do not." Luther's answer came without hesitation.

"What about them?" Zack waved a hand toward the forest. "We are here with two powerful witches, maybe the most powerful of all time."

Luther rolled his eyes at what he clearly took as an ignorant comment. "Without the energy of Earth to tap into, they are simply vampires. Like me."

Zack knew this already. Hearing it didn't make him feel any better about the situation. It was only out of desperation that he brought up the idea in the first place. "What can we do?"

"Listen to me carefully." Luther yanked Zack's arm forcing eye contact. "There is no edible food for you here." He looked to the distance far beyond the cliff. "There are rivers down yonder, but I highly doubt you would find the water drinkable. It is mostly sludge which satisfies the animals."

Zack nodded his understanding. "Then my only option here is to die." It was exactly what he suspected.

"Yes, it is. However, you could continue to exist."

Zack opened his mouth wide. He jumped off the boulder and faced Luther. "You want to turn me into a vampire?"

"I can see no other way you can continue on. Even if you could survive here, I am sure the other two do not share my reluctance toward drinking human blood. Your only hope is to be killed, then resurrected."

"I've been a vampire before. I don't think I liked it."

Luther's did a doubletake. "I do not know what that means. However, as a mere human, you will not last for long. As a vampire, I can teach you to hunt the animals for their blood. That is all you would need every twenty-four hours to exist."

Zack took another long look around him. If he agreed to be turned, it meant accepting that he would never go home again. He'd never see Isis, or her family who accepted him as one of their own. That was most likely the case, so maybe he needed to realize that eventuality. This was his new home. It was now a decision of whether he wanted to live here for all of eternity or just a few days. And what if they did come after Luther turned him? After that, could he even go back? His relationship with Isis would be over.

"Can I...can I have time to think about it?"

Luther nodded. "Do not take too much time." His voice offered no sympathy. "Before long, your body will be dehydrated. You would not want to live in that state for all eternity."

"I guess not, but I don't know what I should do. It's a tough decision— Whoa!"

An oval-shaped light formed behind Luther. To Zack it looked like a bright flashlight flipping on and off. It had to be a portal. They were coming to rescue him after all. But every type of portal Zack had seen looked like either static or an aura of a distortion. There was never pure light, not like this.

Luther, catching Zack's eyes, peeked over his shoulder. The heat was already getting to Zack. His brain felt like it wanted to explode inside his skull. It was possible this distorted circle of light, which suddenly brightened, was a hallucination. "Luther, do you see that?" Zack asked.

"I do." The vampire leaped off the boulder and faced the light. Zack wasn't imagining it.

A dainty body stepped out from the light. It looked like Isis except for the pale skin and centuries of experience across her face. This was the first Isis, now a manifestation of the energy.

"You're here!" Zack exclaimed.

"I am." The Isis manifestation hovered inches over the boulder. Her body moved past Luther, then lowered until she was eye-to-eye with Zack. "I'm here to bring you home."

Luther circled Isis with an uncharacteristic look of surprise. "Another one?" he mumbled.

"I don't understand." Zack walked up to Isis blocking Luther's path around her. "I-I thought, as part of the energy, you can't interfere."

"Part of the *energy*?" Luther reached out to touch this version of Isis. His hand passed straight through her. "What in damnation?"

"You're right. We can't interfere under normal circumstances. But we have decided to make an exception."

"Sentiment?" Zack asked.

"No." She flashed a grin Zack was well familiar with from his Isis. "Necessity."

Zack's eyebrows rose. "What do you mean?"

"There's no time to have this conversation. We can only keep this rift open for so long." She turned to the light and waved for Zack to come along.

He glanced at Luther who stepped out of their way. The first Isis rose from the ground and faced the hole. It was a path back home. He wouldn't have to stay in the Other World after all—

Hope gave way to dread over a gray tree that suddenly fell from the sky, landing in front of the boulder. The branches shot out like bars to a cell. All heads turned to see Valeria. She was just a few feet away. Her right hand glowed.

"Valeria!" Luther shouted. "What are you doing?"

"I know not what transpires here." Valeria's body hovered inches from the ground. "But I sense the energy through this hole in space. It is strong, indeed. I can feel my connection to Mother Earth even from here." Valeria marched their way. "My apologies, Luther, but while I was content spending forever with you on this world, this is opportunity I cannot let pass—"

Another tree slammed into Valeria from behind, knocking her off her feet. The tree in front of the hole crumbled and scattered in all directions. A wind passed by Zack. It dragged Valeria, and the tree on top of her, through the forest with her fingernails scraping across the grass. The hysterical screams disappeared into the distance.

"Isis, did you?"

"No, Zack, I did not."

She gazed ahead, forcing both Zack and Luther to turn around. The Apprentice stood between the trees with a devious smile across her face. Both clenched fists glowed with a hue of energy. Zack's body tensed up, waiting to see what she was about to do. To his surprise, The Apprentice slowly turned around and walked through the forest. The energy glow around her hands faded. Apparently, she had made her choice. She decided it best to stay. It was the sort of self-sacrifice Zack expected Isis would make. Any Isis.

"You should go now," Luther commanded. "Do not wait any longer."

Not wasting a moment, Zack heeded Luther's warning and ran for the boulder. Isis hovered by his side and stretched her arm out in front of him. It stopped him in his tracks. She turned back to Luther who gazed at the white light, then to the forest behind him.

"You can come with us, Luther," she said. "Return to your world, and to your coven."

"As tempted as I may be"—Luther stared into the distance—"someone must keep those two from killing one another. Perhaps I can even cease their hostilities and bring them together. That may take hundreds of years to accomplish, but we do have the time."

"Once we step through," Isis said, "there will never be another opportunity for you to return to Earth. You will remain here forever."

"I understand." Luther waved for them to go.

Zack climbed up the boulder. He stopped when Luther shouted his name. "Make sure to tell the coven...my family...I wish them all the best. Tell them I have full confidence in them, to take care of each other, and the planet. Let them know that I truly do care for them. I always have."

"I will, Luther," Zack said, looking back at the vampire. "I hope you'll be okay—"

"Do not fret over me, boy," Luther barked. "There are far worse places for a vampire to spend his eternal retirement. Besides—" Luther flashed a slight grin. "—I have a hunch things will become far more interesting around here."

"Good luck, Luther," the original Isis replied.

Zack returned his attention to the light. He and Isis walked through. The brightness overtook his vision of the forest. It quickly became so bright that he couldn't even see his own hand in front of his face. A wave of euphoria traveled through his body.

Chapter Twenty-Eight

In her short tenure as president, Tia had good days and bad ones. But never before had the pressure of the job caused her to hate it as much as today. For the sake of the entire population of the world, she had to take steps to break up this close and loving family who had fit in New Salem so well in such a short time. Today, she had to inform them that they must strand one of their members on an alien world without a way home. The decision was too much to ask of Tia, but that is what was required today. Necessary as it may have been, she still felt like the bad guy in the room.

"Let me see if I understand this." Sebastian, their mutually appointed coven leader, made eye contact with everyone behind the desk, stopping on Tia. "You're leaving Zack to fend for himself in the Other World, and Sacha is being exiled. What about the rest of us? Are we now prisoners here?"

"No, of course you're not prisoners," Tia said through her presidential smile. "However—"

"However!" Sebastian snapped. "That's the operative word, isn't it?"

"Sebastian, please," Paul demanded. "Under the circumstances, I think we are trying very hard to be understanding, and reasonable."

"You are not being reasonable!" Selena stepped in front of her husband with clenched fists. Her face had turned as red as her hair. "Tell me, Paul. What would you do if Maya was the one trapped over there?"

"I would do everything in my power to get her back," he immediately answered. "And it would be the wrong move. Believe me, I do understand. This decision was not made easily. We do sympathize with your situation. But this is about a lot more than just you and your family. You must realize that."

"Yes, *however*," Sebastian said, mocking Tia.

Maybe she deserved it. She certainly deserved the guilt that ripped at her chest. She didn't suspect it would go away anytime soon. The thought of that poor boy trapped on an alien plane with monsters, she suspected, would haunt her dreams and keep her from restful slumbers for the rest of her life.

It didn't help seeing Natasha and Carolyn on the other side of the room wearing disapproving expressions on their faces. Natasha's head was down, focused on the crystals while Carolyn's eyes were on Sacha and filled with sympathy. Tia had become close with both ladies, especially Natasha who grew up with her. Neither of them fully agreed with this decision. But it wasn't their decision to make; neither of them held the burden of president.

Tia chose not to ask Jasper for his thoughts. Had they not coincided with hers, it may have damaged their relationship in ways they'd never recover from. Paul and Doctor Mac, however, were in full agreement, and neither backed away from that view during their earlier meeting. Having their support made this moment easier, but not by much.

"I realize this is a lot to take in." Tia leaned forward and tapped her manicured fingernails against the desk. "I wish there was another way, but there is not. Please try to accept this decision and the reasons we must implement it. All of humanity is at stake."

Isis raised her hand like a student in school. "Can I please say something?"

"Yes, of course you can, Isis."

Tia waved her to come closer, or at least as close as she could. The poor girl's face was filled with the stress of everything she had gone through, yet her eyes were narrow and certain. She was ready to make an impassioned argument. There was no changing their minds now; the decision was made. But, in the interest of fairness, Tia could at least give Isis the opportunity to state her case. She deserved at least that much.

Before Isis could get the first word out of her mouth, a bright light formed within the pentagon. The others trapped by the five crystals' force field backed away from it. The fear and surprise in their faces meant this wasn't their doing. Natasha had full control of the crystals, and she was blocking all use of the Wiccan energy within. Yet, as impossible as it should have been, a teleport was taking place.

"Paul!" Natasha's mouth dropped. "I am no longer connected to the crystals."

"What are you doing?" Paul yelled to their captives.

"This isn't us," Sacha shot back, a statement Tia had already concluded. The forcefield stopped sparking, meaning it had evaporated.

"Task force!" Paul ordered.

In response, Carolyn removed her pistol while Jasper ran around to the front of the desk. Jeb, with eyes wide, stayed in place by the office door, bringing his gun down to his side. Whoever was about to join them couldn't be stopped.

The light faded, and two teens were in its place. One was Zack. The other had pale skin and an uncanny resemblance to Isis, which was exactly how The Apprentice was described to her. Except her posture was straight and she wasn't filled with rage. There were no burn marks on her body. She clearly wasn't The Apprentice. Her head spun to every corner of the office as if it were a familiar friend.

"Damn, Isis," Jeb screeched. "How many of you are there?"

"*Zack*!" Isis' high-pitched screech nearly shook the room. She ran to him and wrapped her right arm around his neck. Her lips pressed against Zack's perhaps harder than Tia had ever noticed the two teens kiss before, at least in public. There was little reaction to the embrace from Zack. Apparently, Tia wasn't the only one to notice. Selena clutched Isis' shoulder and gave her a slight tug.

"Isis, give him some space," she said. "He looks to be in shock."

"Overwhelmed by trauma," Doctor Mac added. "He needs air, and to acclimate to where he is."

Isis stepped back, eyeing her boyfriend with concern. Sebastian approached Zack from the side and gripped his shoulder. "Zack, listen to me," he said in a rhythmic tone. "It's all over. Know that you are here. You are home. You are safe."

Tia had been around witches enough to realize that Sebastian was using a calming spell to alleviate the boy's shock. But would it work? They had no idea what he had gone through in the time he was in the Other

World.

"Say something, please." Isis clutched Zack's hand. "Let us know you're okay."

Zack's eyes suddenly opened wide. His head rotated to Isis who had Selena's arm draped across her shoulders, and then to Sebastian. He took a deep breath, then exhaled a sigh of relief. "Um, I saw Luther. He says hi."

"Whew." Sacha grabbed Zack from behind, wrapped her arms around his chest, and squeezed him tight. "Good to have you back, Kiddo." Sacha gave him a relieved peck on the top of his head. "So, you actually bumped into Luther?"

Selena threw her sister a glance. "Time for that later," she insisted.

Tia sauntered around the desk. Now that their biggest concern was removed, she felt a need to make amends with this family. But first, they had a unique guest. Tia walked up to the other Isis who appeared to be waiting on her.

"Are you…" Tia gestured to Isis who leaned her head against Zack's shoulder. The distraction and relief of having her love back safe and sound seemed to take Isis away from the fact that there was a whole other version of her just a few feet away.

"I am," the former two-hundred-year-old Wiccan vampire answered. The voice was definitely Isis' but without the usual anxiousness. Despite appearances, this was not a sixteen-year-old girl. She was, in fact, the eldest New Salem resident in the room. It showed in her tone and stance. "I am here to assure you that this plane of existence will never connect to the Other World again."

"Never?" Paul asked.

"Never," she replied. "We are separating the two dimensions right now as we speak, our final act before our individualities are reabsorbed."

Tia scrunched her face. She tried hard to understand what this entity was explaining, but it was well over her head. The older Isis turned to The Witches of Vegas. All but Isis shifted their focus away from Zack and gave her their attention.

"And you should know that their worries of your future actions were justified." Her tone remained calm and with barely a hint of emotion. "We looked ahead. In every scenario, you would find one another and attempt to rescue Zack." She looked toward Tia and Paul. "I'm sure you can understand why they would do this."

She turned her attention back to Sebastian and Selena. "Know that your actions would have unleashed one or both Wiccan vampires on Earth, and they'd have caused your portal to remain open, just as the original portal would have done. The results were the same as what we all worked together to prevent."

"Is that why you brought Zack back yourself?" Sebastian asked. "To prevent us from destroying the world?"

She flung a finger at Sebastian. It was a gesture Tia had noticed Isis make numerous times to tell someone they were correct.

"Okay, I have to ask." Sacha swung her head from one Isis to the other. "Is anyone else weirded out by this?"

If Tia weren't required to keep her composure, she would have jumped up and shouted a resounding *yes*.

247

Selena walked up to the familiar stranger. A motherly concern was all over her face. "Isis, are you…okay?"

The glance at the ceiling meant perhaps the question confused her. After a moment, she looked back at Selena with a smile. "I am. I know you wish to speak further, but I must go—"

"Wait!" Doctor Mac jumped in front of her, nearly knocking Selena over. His eyes were wide with excitement, as he looked deep into their guest's pupils. "According to Isis' accounts, you no longer exist. That would make you some sort of apparition from your existence before the change to the timeline. Am I correct?"

"My existence is right over there." She waved a hand toward Isis. "Before that, the energy absorbed my being before I was erased. It made me a part of it, as it had done with a select few upon their deaths. We were manifested as a precaution."

"A manifested precaution? Wait. Are you saying…" Doctor Mac reached out. His hand glowed inches from the girl in front of him. His head shot back. "Am I speaking directly to the energy right now?"

"It's a bit more complex than that, Doctor Mac," she answered. "I guess you can say sort of, kind of, but not really?"

"My God, I sense the energy around you. It's more than any witch I've ever encountered. I have so many questions." His head darted back and forth at everyone else in the room. "There is so much we don't know about how it all works and how it chooses who to connect with. Everything we think we know could change—"

"Doctor!" Jasper called out to get his attention. He nudged his head so Doctor Mac could realize what everyone else in the room already knew.

The energy's manifestation—or apparition, or whatever she was—of Isis was gone. There was no teleportation, no portal, no lingering sign of the energy. It was as if she was never there.

"Well—" Doctor Mac let out a deep sigh. "That was abruptly disappointing…yet so enlightening. We've learned quite a bit, but it also leaves more questions than answers. I need to document, hypothesize…" A huge smile formed across his face. "We just spoke with an actual expression of the energy…"

Doctor Mac faded away, most likely back to his medical office where he would fill a notebook with his thoughts. The five enchanted crystals suddenly levitated in the air. They shot across the room and into Natasha's open palms. The threat was over. Tia's presidential duties, however, were not yet finished. She walked up to The Witches of Vegas with both Jasper and Paul in tow. She folded her hands against her chest and approached the family she had, moments ago, looked to tear apart.

"It would seem our circumstances, fortunately, have changed," Tia said behind her presidential grin. "With Zack safe and the Other World now inaccessible, there is no longer a need to separate, or detain, you. You are free to go, if that is what you choose. Although, I think I speak for all of New Salem that we hope you'd rather stay."

Tia awaited a response. She truly wished that hard feelings would not linger. Their contributions to the village since their arrival were helpful, and they certainly seemed genuinely happy here. At least until today.

Selena and Sebastian exchanged a long glance. Isis eyed them, apparently also awaiting their feelings on the situation. Sacha and Zack did the same from behind. After several long moments, Selena nodded her agreement to their silent conversation.

"It's been a rather long day, Madam President." Sebastian wrapped an arm around his wife's waist. "With your permission, we would like to now go home and get some much-needed rest."

"Home?" Tia asked.

"Yes, home." Sebastian smirked. "To our cottages here in New Salem. We'll see you all in the morning."

The five about-faced and walked past Jeb who held the office door open. Sacha, the last one to leave, threw a flirtatious wink and a smile at Carolyn before jogging out the door to catch up with her coven and family. Jeb pushed the door shut behind them. Tia and Paul faced one another and let out deep exhales of relief.

"Well, damn!" Jeb's shout caused everyone in the room to nearly jump out of their socks. "That was a lot!"

"Yes, it was," Paul replied. "You handled yourself well, Jeb, and under the most extreme conditions. Good job today."

Jeb approached Paul, turning his pistol around in his hand. He held it up for Paul to take from him. "Mr. Vice President, Sir, I appreciate everything you've done to bring me into the New Salem Task Force. But I really don't think this is my path. I'm sorry."

"I agree with you." Paul removed the pistol from

Jeb's hand. To Tia's surprise, there was no displeasure on the vice president's face.

"I have seen your path in a dream," Jasper said from Tia's side. "You are correct. It is not with the task force."

"I don't suppose you're going to tell me what it is?" Jeb asked.

Jasper shook his head. There were rules and protocols the village's soothsayer had to follow when it came to sharing his visions. Jeb knew that as well, but Tia couldn't blame him for asking.

Paul placed a hand on Jeb's massive shoulder. "I am sure you will find your way soon."

Jeb nodded his head. "If you don't mind, I'm going to head to the medical center and check on Maya."

"I'm sure she'd appreciate your company," Paul replied.

Jeb about-faced and strolled out of the office. He slowly closed the door behind him so it wouldn't slam.

"I do agree with him, Madam President," Paul said with raised eyebrows. "This was one for the record books."

Tia clapped her hands, then strolled back to her desk. "Okay, I think we've had enough for today. Let's see what's on the agenda for tomorrow, then close up shop."

The president wiped the sweat from her forehead. It had, indeed, been a long and eventful day, as was the case a number of times with The Witches of Vegas. She hoped that was a habit they'd soon break.

Chapter Twenty-Nine

The Next Morning...

Isis was supposed to meet the family for breakfast once she finished her early morning appointment with Doctor Mac. She never made it back. Sebastian and Selena wanted to use their Wiccan connections to locate her, but Zack convinced them it wasn't necessary. He had a hunch where to find her. Zack entered the school and walked up all five flights of stairs with the last one taking him to the rooftop. Their previous selves spent a lot of time up here. They did now as well. According to Isis, seeing New Salem from its highest point gave her perspective.

Zack pushed open the door. Sure enough, Isis stood at the ledge looking down at the Quad. She always sensed his presence when he walked through that door, but that was no longer the case. Now he would have to use a more traditional technique of getting her attention.

"Isis."

Her head popped up. "Hey, Zack," she responded, never turning around. "It's going to rain tonight. Probably in the next hour."

Zack walked to Isis and stood at the edge on her right. "Is that your Wiccan connection returning?"

"No." Isis pointed to the clouds, many of which were dark.

Zack rubbed a hand along the sling, which kept Isis' arm secure. The bandages underneath were thick and covered her flesh. "How is it?"

"Medium well," she answered. "Like much of my left side from the neck down."

Zack wanted to find the right words to say. Nothing came to mind. He couldn't stop staring at the left side of her forehead. It looked like it had been through a twelve-round boxing match. After several awkward moments looking out at the Quad, Isis turned to Zack and spoke. "I was thinking about how we've been living here for a year, and before that, two centuries as vampires."

"Yeah, we have."

"We spent a lot of time on this rooftop." Isis used her good hand to motion behind them. "Yet today might be the first time I ever walked up the stairs. First, on instinct, I tried to teleport. I had to remind myself I can't do that anymore."

Zack stared at Isis' dimpled cheeks. Her eyes were wide, and her mouth was slightly hung open. This was an expression she always had after long periods of deep thought. "Level with me, Isis, how are you handling everything?"

She laughed. "I was about to ask you the same question. You've been through a lot, too."

"I asked first."

"Yeah, you did." Isis nodded, then shrugged. She turned back to the rooftop's edge. "Last night was hard. I actually crawled into Mom and Dad's bed and slept between them. I haven't done that since I was a kid. But I just didn't want to be alone all night. How about you? How did you sleep?"

"I guess about as well as could be expected."

"So, not much, huh?"

It was hard for Zack to get any sleep last night. Each time he opened his eyes, he caught Sacha by his bedroom doorway, checking on him. He assured her that he was okay, but he was lying, and she knew it. The truth was, no matter how hard he tried, he couldn't get his brain to shut off. When his thoughts weren't focused on almost being stuck in the Other World, or nearly getting killed by The Apprentice, or almost having to get turned into a vampire again, he was worrying about Isis. The girl set her body on fire, and Zack watched her do it from afar. Then, he was a world away, unable to comfort her when she probably needed him most.

By four a.m., Sacha, realizing Zack wasn't asleep, came into his room and sat at the end of his bed. The two of them talked about everything, including his interaction with Luther. With permission, Sacha cast a spell that allowed them to relive Zack's last memory on the Other World so she could see for herself that Luther was well.

Sacha, despite her nonchalant attitude, was a really good listener, and talking to her helped Zack get through the night. He didn't know if Sacha used the Wiccan energy to make him feel better, but he was pretty sure it was her natural conversational skills.

"Not really," he summed up his answer. "But I was okay. I wasn't left alone either."

Isis looked at Zack with confusion written all over her face. "I still sense the energy. I sense it around us. I can sense witches controlling it nearby. I just can't manipulate it at all. It's like a body part that I know is still there, but I can't use anymore. I wonder, does that still make me a witch? It might, but I don't think it does."

"What if you're not a witch anymore?" Zack asked. "How would you feel about that?"

"Honestly?"

"Yeah."

"I thought I'd be lost without it, but maybe I won't be." Isis took Zack's hand and squeezed it tight. "I still have my family. I still have you and our friends. I don't think I'm going to…miss being a witch."

Zack caught the hesitancy in Isis' voice. "But?"

"I've been practicing witchcraft since I was nine years old. Most of my free time—long hours every single day—went into learning how to control the energy. Now what am I going to do with myself?"

"There's lots you can do." Zack let go of Isis' hand and put his arm around her shoulders. "Our future is open. No impending crisis to worry about. No vampires out there…"

"Except for Simon."

"Well, yeah, but he's harmless, and seemingly happy on the stage." Zack grinned. Isis offered one as well. "What I'm saying is we can do anything we want, and we'll figure out what. We always have."

"I hope so." Isis rested her head on Zack's shoulder. "My appointment with Doctor Mac this morning went really well."

"Was it rehab or therapy?"

"I guess it was both at the same time. He had a really good idea for me, something to try, and I said I would. He wants to ask you to do it as well."

"What's the idea?" Zack rolled his eyes. Great,

another Doctor Mac idea.

"He thinks we should write our stories, the life we've lived and everything in our heads about the previous timeline. This way all the details won't get lost, and then new generations could learn from it."

"That's—" Zack raised his eyebrows. "—actually a really good idea."

"I know you don't like to talk to him about your feelings, but for me, it helps." Isis gave him that wide-eyed gaze. "I think it would help you, too. We could see him together. I have another session scheduled for later this week."

Zack had been avoiding those appointments with Doctor Mac. He disliked having his innermost thoughts thrown on display, especially to a professional doctor. But after everything they'd been through—everything he had just gone through—maybe he needed to be open to the idea. There was a lot to get off his chest. Why not to Isis and Doctor Mac?

"Okay. I'll come with you to the next session."

Isis' head shot up from his shoulder. "Really?"

"Yeah, I will." Zack flashed Isis a smile matching the one that had formed across her face. "The writing it all out idea—I like it a lot. Hell, with all we remember, we could fill at least five books. Although, that will take up a lot of our free time."

"Yeah, it will for a while." The smile faded from Isis' face. "But then what?"

"Then anything we want." Zack rubbed the back of Isis' neck. "Except be a witch. Well, unless your connection eventually returns. That could still happen."

"Maybe. But if it doesn't…" Isis sighed. "What am I going to do with myself?"

Man, just when it seemed the conversation was going well…the two refocused their view on the Quad. It was early enough that the farmers were still running their plows and planting seeds. They were hard at work as if it was just another day and not less than twenty-four hours removed from an attack by a Wiccan vampire fighting her way out of a portal from a land in another dimension. It seemed nothing could stop that group from doing their jobs every single day. Zack had to admit he admired the work ethic. Their dedication was unlike any he had seen anywhere else. Except from his uncle on the stage. The Witches of Vegas were a close second when it came to practicing their witchcraft and taking care of one another.

A peek over at Isis saw her eyes getting watery, although she was trying hard to keep it to herself. Zack understood the emotions well. He had similar feelings when he realized all of his training and practice in magic was useless in New Salem, his new permanent residence. He didn't know how to redefine himself in a place where card and coin tricks were irrelevant. He kept practicing his skills because there was always the likelihood of ending up back on a stage, which did happen. In fact, it happened more than once.

But what if there was no hope that he could ever again double-lift two playing cards, or make one disappear? Zack did leave magic behind in the other timeline, but that was after a few lifetimes. In that history, his focus had changed from card tricks to being a vampire, right up until the moment Valeria erased their entire reality. But in that history, just like this one, Isis always had her witchcraft. Until now. It must have felt like a hole in her heart that was begging to be refilled.

An idea suddenly hit. He flashed a cheese-faced grin at Isis. "What is it?" she asked with squinted eyes.

Zack reached into his back pocket where he had his old deck of cards; this morning, he just felt like having them on him. He popped open the box and slid one card from the stack. It was the queen of hearts. He waved it in his right hand for Isis to see, then held it against his palm facing her.

"Check this out." Zack closed his fingers then reopened them. The card had disappeared. He closed and reopened his fist again. The queen of diamonds reappeared in his hand.

"Cute," Isis said, "but I don't know if showing me a card trick is going to help. At least not right now."

"I'm not just showing it to you." Zack took Isis' right hand and placed the card against her palm and fingers. "Press your forefinger and pinky against the edges."

Zack positioned Isis' two fingers against the card's edges. "Now, fold your other two middle fingers underneath and put your knuckles against the back of the card."

Isis did as Zack instructed, rolling her fingers so her knuckles pushed against the back of the card. She wiggled her left hand in the sling which still had the brace wrapped around her wrist. "You know I can barely move my hand or my wrist on this side."

"You only need one hand for this particular trick." Zack gave the queen a slight tug to make sure it was secure within Isis' fingers. "Okay, now, I want you to lift your middle fingers up so the card rolls to the back of your hand. Make sure your end fingers keep a tight grip on those edges."

"Okay." Isis rolled the queen just as Zack described. The card popped out from her grip and fell like a tiny weight onto her left foot. "Hmm, that didn't go so well."

"It takes lots of practice," Zack replied. "It's not exactly witchcraft, but once you get it down pat, it'll look almost supernatural. We can spend a lot of time working on this trick and so many more, at least until you figure out something else. When we're not writing about our memories or talking about them with Doctor Mac. Sound good?"

Zack was sure he covered everything, and the bright face looking his way told him that at the very least, his effort was appreciated.

Isis leaned in and kissed his cheek. She whispered in his ear, "I love you so much."

"That's good," Zack replied. "Because I'm going to marry you someday. I promise."

Isis' stare moved to the top of Zack's head. "And on that day, your hair will probably still be a bit messy, won't it?"

"Probably, yeah." Zack ran a hand across the top of his head. "I blame it on the humidity here."

Isis let out a chuckle. "Says the boy who lived in the Vegas desert most of his life." Isis' smile faded. She gazed at Zack with flirtatious eyes that made his heart flutter. "I'm really looking forward to that day," she said in a whisper.

Zack's arms wrapped around Isis and held her tight. He really loved this girl. The two of them could stare into each other's eyes all day without saying a word. But one lingering thought ran through Zack's head. It was something Isis needed to know, if she didn't already.

"Isis, how much of everything that happened did you and your folks talk about last night?"

She pulled away and tilted her head. "Not too much. Just a bit. We were exhausted and kept saying we'd talk more in the morning, but I was running late and had to get to my appointment with Doctor Mac. Why are you asking?"

"There is something I need to tell you." Was she ready to hear it? After everything they had gone through, could she handle another huge revelation? Her folks must have thought otherwise since they didn't bring it up, or maybe they just didn't have the chance. Right now, Isis was already dealing with charred skin and losing her connection. "Maybe we should talk about it another time. Okay?"

Isis eyed Zack. Her right hand wrapped around his. "You know you can tell me anything. Whatever it is."

Damn. Zack wanted to bite off his own tongue. Why in the world did he bring it up? But now that he sparked her curiosity, it was too late to back off. Isis did have every right to know. Hopefully she was braced.

"It's about Harry, and who he really was…or will be…"

Chapter Thirty

One Week Later...

The last thing Isis remembered was lying in her bed and her eyelids feeling heavy. She couldn't keep them open even if she wanted to. But somehow, she was now awake, aware, and no longer in her bed. Isis was surrounded by a fog that was so thick she could reach out and hold some of it in her hands. It reminded her of the foam that formed when she used too much soap in the bathtub.

Isis held her left hand in front of her face. Her arm no longer had Doctor Mac's wrapping around it. Her fingers moved freely and without pain. Suddenly, the thickness of the fog thinned, and she could somewhat make out the land, or lack of it, around her. There were no buildings, and no landmarks; it was as if she was literally nowhere. There wasn't even ground beneath her feet, just more thick fog.

A shadow of a person suddenly appeared in the distance. Isis ran forward. As she moved closer, she made out that it was another girl, one of her height, frame, and the exact same face. It was like a mirror image, except the other's skin was faded out, like a two-hundred-year-old vampire.

"Oh no!" Isis froze in place.

She jumped into a defensive stance, forced to once

261

again come face-to-face with The Apprentice. But the other one walked her way with a posture and demeanor that radiated confidence. There were no burn marks on her pale skin. The eyes weren't filled with rage, but with compassion. "It's you," Isis said with relief. "The other me. The first me…or the first you, and I'm the second one?" Wow, this still confused the hell out of her.

"You're the only us," the other Isis answered. "We were the same girl living the same life for the first fourteen years and seven months. Now, you exist, and I no longer do."

"But you're still here."

"Just a bit longer. I'm not needed anymore. Neither are the others. We've served our purpose. The world is safe, thanks to you."

"The others?" Isis peeked over the apparition's—as Doctor Mac called her—shoulder. Through the fog she made out three ghostly figures standing several feet back. One of the two men had shoulder length brown hair. He was dressed in a brown vest with a green cape. The other man looked middle-aged. He had on a top hat and a black three-piece suit. The girl who stood in front of them Isis recognized from memories of the previous timeline.

"Domina," she whispered.

"I chose Domina right before her death," the other Isis explained. "Then, together, we chose the two men. We wanted male perspectives to balance ours."

"Who chose you?" Isis asked.

"They did."

Isis' face scrunched. "What?"

"Time works differently outside of reality. It's

more circular than linear. No big deal if you're not grasping it. I probably shouldn't be telling you all that, anyway. It's also not why you're here."

Isis clearly wasn't grasping it, but at least she knew what tomorrow morning's journal entry would be about. She waved to the three figures in the fog. Domina waved back.

"Why *am* I here?" Isis finally asked. "Last week, you said you were being reabsorbed into the energy and we'd never see you again. You said the world is safe—" Her jaw dropped. She opened her eyes wide. "Is this another warning like you gave Zack?"

"No, not that at all. You sacrificed a lot to save our world." The apparition looked back to the others and nodded. "We felt before we become one with the energy, we have one final loose end to tie. To make up for all you've suffered, you deserve something in return. We're here to gift it to you."

"You're giving me my connection back?"

She made a slant-eyed glance that Isis had seen in the mirror too many times. "We both know that's not what you want."

Isis nodded. She had gone a week so far without being able to manipulate the energy. Objects no longer floated or obeyed her telepathic commands. She couldn't teleport or do anything of the sort. In all honesty, she didn't miss it. She was even becoming more intimate with some of her natural abilities, like powerwalking through the Quad once Doctor Mac removed her sling. She couldn't wait to fully heal and turn it into a jog. Zack's card trick lessons helped her memorization skills and coordination in her right hand. She enjoyed the movement and the venture it took to accomplish these tasks. It was also nice to converse with her folks about something other than Wiccan training.

"So, if not that, what do I want?" After two hundred years being them, Isis figured this version of her was probably more of an expert on the subject.

The other Isis grinned. Of course, she had an answer ready. "A glimpse," she said.

"A glimpse? I don't understand. A glimpse of what?"

The former Wiccan vampire pressed her palm against Isis' forehead. Everything went dark. Then her vision cleared. The fog was gone, as were the other Isis, Domina, and the two men. She looked down to find herself seated at the end of a rectangular oak table meant for family meals. She liked the look and feel of the hard wood. Four matching chairs were placed at each side.

From the structure of the doors and walls surrounding this large room, Isis was in a New Salem cottage, but not one she had ever seen in either timeline. The main room was much larger than the one she lived in with her folks. The curtains on the windows were green, just like Zack's eyes. Isis loved that color and would have picked those curtains herself if she'd ever have the chance to decorate.

She lifted her hands and noticed they were wider than she had ever seen before. They were adult hands. The burns on her skin no longer looked fresh. Most had even blended in with her tan complexion. The engagement and wedding rings on her finger were thin with sparkly diamonds around them. Isis reached to the middle of the table where round cookies sat in a clear bowl. She took one out and brought it up to her nose. From the meat and yeast-like scent, she realized they had to be dog biscuits.

Isis jumped in surprise at a head shooting at her from the left. Her mind raced to Valeria, or The Apprentice. This was neither of them. It was a brown beagle that raised its upper body and placed its front paws on Isis' lap. She let out a deep exhale. Excitement filled the beagle's wide eyes. He barked what sounded like a plea.

"I take it these are for you?" Isis held out the cookie. The dog took it in its mouth, ran under the table, and chomped away.

Heavy breaths and fatigue shot through Isis' body. Strange considering she was just sitting in the middle of this living room pretty much doing nothing. With her feet against the floor, she pushed herself and the chair away from the table. What she saw made her gawk. Her hands weren't the only part of her body that was wider. Her stomach was huge and round. It wasn't from overeating or developing body fat; that was made clear by the sudden kick she felt from the inside.

"Oh wow," Isis shrieked. "Oh, my…"

Standing from the chair proved to be a huge struggle. Isis needed to grab the end of the table to keep her balance. The slight nausea she noticed when she was seated increased the moment she stood up. She almost fell over when the beagle ran from under the table and zipped past her. Barking filled the room. A peek over her shoulder caught the animal jumping up and down by the front door, which then opened from the outside.

A young girl, who had to be around five or six

years old, stepped through the doorway, then pushed the door shut. Her skin tone was a few shades lighter than Isis' while her long brown hair was a perfect match. A green knapsack hung over her right shoulder. "Hi, Vegas!" She dropped to her knees and hugged the dog, who stopped his jumping just long enough to lick her face. "How you doing, boy? I missed you!"

Isis eyed the doors across the large room. One was wide open and led to a bathroom. The other two were closed. One of the closed doors was on its own wall to the left of the open kitchen. The other was on the kitchen's right. That door had a piece of brown construction paper taped to it with hand drawn flowers and the words "Hope's Room" in red crayon.

The little girl ran to Isis. "Hi, Mommy!"

"You're Hope?" Isis asked.

"What?" The girl's brown eyes slanted as if she were just shown an object from an alien world. Isis faked a grin in an attempt to alleviate the girl's concerns.

"Of course, I know who you are. I'm just teasing."

"Oh!" Hope giggled. "Mommy, you're so silly."

Hope placed her ear against Isis' stomach. "Hi, Harry," she sang. "I can't wait to meet you soon."

"Harry," Isis whispered.

Isis reached out and touched Hope's face. Her skin was so soft. "Don't you always ask me right now how was school?" the young girl asked.

"Um, right." Taking the cue, Isis asked, "How was school?"

Hope hurled her bookbag onto the table. "Really weird."

"How was it weird?"

266

"Teacher was saying weird stuff about you and Daddy." Hope looked up into her mother's eyes, or at least who she believed to be her mother. "She said in the future, you changed time and saved the whole world from an evil witch. Then you and Daddy did it again before we were born. She said she was a kid when you were a powerful teenage witch, but you gave up your connection to save us." She poked a finger against Isis' chest. "Teacher also said that you and Daddy used to teach all the witches, but you stopped to raise a family. Is that true?"

"I become a teacher," Isis whispered to herself. She felt some pride in saying that out loud.

Isis stared at the girl who would someday be her daughter. Hope. Wow, she was beautiful. More important, her face was vibrant and radiated confidence. She wasn't beaten down and loathed like Isis was at that age. She was living a good life, or she would in the future. Her destiny was not to struggle and suffer in a dying world now that The Apprentice's actions were halted. Maybe that meant Harry didn't have to die at fourteen. The future was now an open book for both of them.

"Mommy?" Hope's head tilted in confusion. "Did you really do all that?"

"Yes," Isis answered. "I guess I did teach witches how to use the energy." She must have. She would be very good at that.

"Then you stopped just for me?"

"For our family." Isis never thought she'd quit doing something she really liked, and she had to like teaching. But she did—or will—quit. Her priorities as she gets older obviously change. Perhaps that change

267

came the moment she saw such a pretty face that was her child.

"Well, that's cool, I guess." The girl sounded dissatisfied. "Teacher also said you taught all the kids before I was born. She said you were her teacher. You taught history, and Daddy taught…something with a T." Hope's face wrinkled. "I don't remember."

"Traditions?"

"Yes! That's it!" Hope flung a finger at Isis.

Vegas barked then ran to the door. Again, his excitement and the wagging tail shook his entire backside. The door swung open. Isis' head lifted as she watched the man she was destined to marry enter their home. She expected to recognize the face immediately.

But, when the gentleman she presumed to be her husband walked in, her mouth popped open. "Oh, my…no way!"

Chapter Thirty-One

From the ring on his finger, this was Isis' future husband entering their home. Of course, it was Zack, but not the Zack she knew. This one, with a much older face, wore a button-down white shirt that was well pressed. His blond hair was perfectly combed back with every strand in place. There was even some gel in that hair which was something Isis had tried to get him to use since the first time he took the stage with her family. He wouldn't even consider it. Apparently, in adulthood, he finally did.

The blue tie hanging from his neck threw Isis off. She rarely saw him wear a tie. In fact, he always complained they choked him during those rare occasions Isis, or any other member of the family, got him to put one on. Right now, Zack was wearing it like a champ. It matched the confident smile he had across his face. It was a smile he had whenever something exciting happened during his day.

"Vice President Daddy!" Hope ran across the living room to her father with as much excitement as Vegas.

"He's vice president?" Isis whispered under her breath. "Wow."

Zack dropped to one knee and gave Vegas a pet on the head, then stretched out his arms for Hope to give him a huge hug. "Hey there, Princess!" That hug showed off the compassion Zack had shown Isis for as long as she'd known him. Now it was for a product of their love. She wanted to run over and give him a similar hug, but she could barely keep her balance. Isis never knew what pregnancy felt like, but she had a hunch this baby was ready to come out any day now.

Zack stood and faced Isis with a huge grin. "And how are the two of you doing today?"

"We're good," Isis answered, although it was just an assumption.

Zack cupped his hand under Hope's chin. He tipped her head so they could make eye contact. "Princess, I need to have some adult talk with Mommy. Okay? Why don't you head to your room and listen to your music?"

"Does that mean I don't have to do my homework?" She flashed a wide smile.

"Not right now." Zack peeked up at Isis for confirmation.

Feeling a bit lost, Isis nodded. "You can do your homework later."

"But you two are going to Auntie Maya's president thingy in the Quad tonight, right? Who's going to look at my homework to see if it's right?"

The name *Auntie Maya* didn't slip past Isis' notice. That meant they stayed friends, and even grew closer. And she was New Salem's president? Turned out Maya was right all along, in both the previous reality and this one.

"Grandma and Grandpa will be here babysitting you tonight while Mom and I are at New Salem's anniversary celebration. Which is also called, what?"

"I know!" Hope raised both her hands in the air.

"It's called Tituba."

"That's exactly right." Zack patted her head. "But it's not just a president thingy. It's an all of us thingy."

"I like it when Grandma and Grandpa babysit me. Grandpa makes me fly!" Hope clapped her hands together. "Will Auntie Sacha and Carolyn be here, too?"

Zack cupped his hand across the back of Hope's neck. "Sorry, Kiddo, you know they're both part of Natasha's Task Force. That means they need to be at the bash as well."

"Oh, that's not fair—"

Zack playfully pressed a finger over Hope's lips. "But, since Auntie Maya and Uncle Jeb will be hosting the Tituba celebration, and since almost everyone wants to be there, they can't find a babysitter. So, Rex and Baby Kara will be here tonight, sleeping over. That means while the adults are having a party out there, you kids are having a party right here!"

"Can we stay up, go outside, and watch the fireworks?"

"That'll be up to your grandparents, but I have no doubt they'll say yes."

Hope jumped up and down. Zack held out his hands for her to slap them with her own. A tear rolled down Isis' cheek. Zack was such a good father; she saw it in the passion he displayed when speaking to their daughter. Wow, their daughter. Hope. She was like an angel in Isis' eyes. She could only wonder if she would turn out to be as good of a mom.

"Now, please head into your room." Zack stood up and faced Isis. "Give Mom and Dad some privacy."

"Okay. Come on, Vegas. Let's go listen to some

music!" Hope ran to the door with her name on it. The dog followed her and entered the room once Hope pushed open the door. Hope followed Vegas and pulled the door closed.

Isis wobbled toward Zack, who pressed his hands against her waist to provide balance. Walking was a far bigger challenge than she expected. Her body was definitely not sixteen. It was more like...actually, she had no idea how old she was in this moment. Whatever the age, she sure hoped her body at that point was better equipped to handle this pregnancy. It had to be since it was her second one.

"Hey." Zack touched her arm. "There's something I need to tell you."

Isis eyed Zack's hair. She touched the side of his head with her left hand, then ran her fingers through his short blond strands. It felt a bit slick from the gel. She still couldn't believe he was using it.

"What are you doing?" asked the confused adult Zack.

"Nothing." Isis quickly pulled her hand to her side. "You said you had something to tell me?"

Isis looked into Zack's eyes. He was older, but she knew his expressions so well. This one was Zack's concerned face. Whatever he needed to talk about, it was troubling. "Something is going on," she said. "What is it?"

He took a deep breath, then spoke. "There was a situation in the school cafeteria involving Hope."

"Really?" Isis peeked back to Hope's room. "She didn't say anything when she came home."

"I'm not surprised. She was arguing with her teacher who insisted she finish her lunch before leaving the table. Allegedly, Hope became agitated and flipped her tray over."

Isis threw Zack a suspicious glance. "How did you find out about it?"

"Jeb witnessed the incident. As the school's headmaster, he was obligated to call the president's office. Maya is at the Euro conference with Ambassadors Tia and Jasper. They decided to bring her so she could meet with various leaders. Since they weren't back yet, the call came directly to me."

Isis peeked over at the open kitchen. There was a phone attached to the wall near the refrigerator. It was just below their framed wedding picture. "If all she did was misbehave in school, why didn't they call here? Why did he have to call the president's office?"

"Isis…" Zack took her hands. She knew well how that always prefaced huge or upsetting news. "Hope never touched the tray. According to Jeb, her hands were under the table."

"But how could that happen unless…she manifested?" Isis dropped her jaw as far down as possible without falling off her face. She looked back at Hope's bedroom door, then back at Zack. "Isn't she, like, six years old?"

Zack's eyebrows rose. "She's seven, Isis."

"Right, right, she's seven. That's what I meant." Isis bit her bottom lip. "Still, I was the youngest ever to manifest, and I was nine."

"You're not the youngest any longer," Zack replied. "She has you beat by two years."

"That means she's going to be really powerful." Isis cupped a hand over her mouth. "We already know Harry's connection will be strong. It looks like we're going to have two powerful witches to raise."

"Yes, and you are the only one who can teach them how to control such strong connections. You're the only one who can understand what it's like to be so powerful at a young age."

Isis nodded. She understood, but she didn't want to make that decision on behalf of her future self. She had no idea what she would go through or what her outlook would be at this stage of her life. "Is that all that happened today?" Isis asked to change the subject. "You looked kind of anxious when you walked in. Was it just about Hope manifesting?"

"Oh yes, I almost forgot!" Zack's face lit up. He grabbed Isis by the shoulders and leaned in. "We got it!"

"Remind me?"

His head leaned to the side, but he quickly shook away the confusion. "The new resort in Las Vegas! We're signed on for four shows from Friday to Sunday every other week starting three months from now."

"Three months. That means you'll be here for..." She patted her stomach.

"Of course. There's no way I would miss Harry's first few months." Zack spread his arms as if he were taking in a spotlight. "But after that, our teen witches will be taking the stage for training. The manager even arranged to put us up in their suites for the days we are there every other month. Your mom and Sacha will be coming with us to handle the transportation, to chaperone, and help with the show. Honestly, I never thought this would happen. The manager didn't strike me as interested."

"But you did it," Isis said with pride. "You made

him interested."

"Truth be told, Maya was a huge help in getting us signed." Zack chuckled. "I swear, that woman could sell someone their own T-shirt while they're wearing it."

"What about my dad? Is he hosting again?"

Zack threw Isis another sideways glance. He placed a hand against the side of her face. "Isis, are you okay? Do you need to get checked out?"

Isis widened her eyes. "Um, no, no, I'm fine." She rubbed her huge pregnant belly. "I've been a bit forgetful on recent things. Pregnancy can cause that…I think."

"That didn't happen the last time." The concern was still in his voice. "Your dad insisted on staying back to help you with Hope and the baby." Zack raised a hand over his head and pointed down at himself. "I'm handling the hosting duties this time around. That puts me in a position to make sure the kids get in their practice but we can keep it low key enough that we don't overshadow the other Vegas magicians."

"Of course, I should have remembered that." Isis smiled big. "Dad's really giving up the mic, huh?"

Zack shrugged. "I know he says he's too old for it now, but I think he's secretly excited about spending that extra time with his granddaughter. You and Harry as well, no doubt."

"Wow!" Isis wrapped her arms around Zack's waist. "After all this time, The Witches of Vegas are back in business!"

"Yes, they are," Zack said, with a huge grin. He rubbed a knuckle under her chin. "And it was all your idea."

"Really? It was?"

"Ha ha, very funny, Isis." Zack leaned in for a kiss. His green eyes sparkled. They looked so familiar in the middle of that older face. Isis leaned in and puckered...

She was suddenly watching the couple from several feet away. Their embrace was passionate. The emotions radiating through Isis resonated on the matching face to her left. "Is this real?" Isis asked. "Is this my future for sure?"

"If everything continues on its natural course, and we believe it should, this is your future."

The adult Zack helped his wife to the table and onto a chair. He dropped to one knee and rubbed her stomach. In turn, she put her hands on his cheeks and leaned in with a grin Isis knew well, even if she had never seen it with her own two eyes. It meant whatever she was whispering was meant to tease him. His eyes rolled. Then they both laughed.

"So, do we enjoy Auntie Maya's president thingy?" Isis gave the other her a slight smirk.

Her own smirk suddenly looked back at her. "For about an hour. Then you and Zack spend the night in the medical center."

"The medical center?" Isis' head snapped back. "Why? What happens?"

"The next morning, Mom and Dad bring Hope over to meet her new baby brother who was born two weeks earlier than expected."

"Oh." Isis looked back at the older couple facing each other in their seats, hands clasped, and enjoying a friendly conversation. Adult Zack leaned down and placed an ear on adult Isis' stomach. The way they looked at each other with those googly eyes and huge grins meant to make each other laugh, they were still close and very much in love. In fact, she could tell from her face that older Zack made Isis as happy as teenage Zack made her feel now.

"Harry, he's born healthy?" Isis asked. "We're all okay?"

"Yes, almost everything goes well that night. In fact, Harry will be the last baby Doctor Mac delivers before his retirement."

"You said almost everything." Isis eyed her double. "What goes wrong?"

"Well, there is something…" The smirk grew into a full smile. "You do miss the fireworks."

Isis shook her head. She really didn't care for having her own sense of humor thrown back at her. She still wasn't sure if this was the actual her before the timeline changed, or was it a creation of the energy that simulated her personality? The question would probably linger in her mind forever. It definitely needed to go into her notebook.

"That glimpse." Isis scratched the side of her head. "I couldn't tell if my connection fully returns or not."

"No, you couldn't," the first Isis replied. "But what's life without mystery, right?"

Isis wanted to call her a smartass, but that would be self-deprecating. Plus, another, bigger concern popped into her head. The smile melted from her face. "What you're showing me about my future…do I have to keep it all to myself?"

"We know you could, but that's not a burden we'll leave you with alone."

She motioned over Isis' shoulder where the fog thinned. Isis was able to make out two people standing several feet away. One was Zack, who looked their way through widened eyes with his mouth hanging open ever so slightly. He'd seen it all from the sidelines, unlike Isis who experienced the moment. Domina hovered behind him. Apparently, she was his guide for this glimpse into the future. That made sense; the real Domina always felt more comfortable around Zack than anyone else in that timeline.

"The Other World," Isis said, still staring at Zack. "I'm thinking you could have separated it at any time, right? But The Apprentice had to get there first, and we both had to be back here."

"Yes. Events needed to play out as they did. You're both important to the future. The same with your children, your students, and their children as well."

"Harry saved Zack from getting killed when they crossed over for me. Did that really have to happen?" Isis tapped her chin, then eyed her older self. "Harry knew it would, which means you knew as well. You sent Harry to his death."

"With every move we made, future events kept changing, and we had to adjust." The former Wiccan vampire faced Isis. "At the time we pulled Harry, he was going to die, regardless. Now, thanks to you, there will no longer be a need to send him back in time, and he won't need to sacrifice himself. Time is flowing as it should without interference, which means there's also no longer a need for me, or for any of us. It is now time for our essence to become one with the energy."

Isis' head spun from Domina's conversation with Zack to her other self. The nonchalance she talked about having her existence erased caused her to jump.

"You're really going to die? Right now?"

"It's not exactly like that, and it really is okay." The manifestation's sly grin faced Isis. "Enjoy the rest of our life, Isis Quinn-Santell, which is now your life. You deserve it." She waved a finger between them. "We deserve it."

"That sounded like goodbye," Isis said. "Am I really never going to see you aga—"

Isis' eyes opened to see the dark ceiling of her bedroom. She sat up from the bed. Weird dream, but it felt so real. Too real. Could it have just been her imagination? There was one way to find out for sure.

Isis placed her feet on her bedroom's carpeting and ran to the window. It faced Zack's bedroom window in the cottage next door. She grabbed the curtains and yanked them open. She had to figure out how she would get his attention if he was still sleeping without shouting for him. With the energy, she used to send out a psychic signal to let Zack know she was at the window. But that was no longer an option.

As it turned out, she didn't need to. Zack stood in front of his window with the curtains wide open. She wanted to call out to him, ask if that was really him in the dream…or if it even was a dream. But she couldn't shout without waking up everyone within earshot. That included her folks in the other bedroom, and Sacha who should have been asleep in Zack's cottage.

Instead, Isis pointed to her eyes, then at Zack. He responded with a huge nod. His lips stretched into a smile. "Oh, wow, it *was* real," Isis whispered.

She ran two fingers down her chest to signify the tie on the adult Zack. She stroked those same fingers through her hair to reference the gel. His head shook back and forth, which made her giggle. "I know. Not yet," she said under her breath. "But soon enough."

With her right hand, Isis clutched her left wrist and brought both hands up to face level. She pressed her fingers together and folded her thumbs so her hands would make a heart symbol. In return, Zack tapped the center of his chest twice, then pointed back at Isis.

"See you in the morning," she whispered. "And then, for the rest of our lives."

Zack stepped back and pulled his curtains closed. Isis did the same. She skipped to her bed and dropped down. The back of her head hit the pillow. She focused on the final instructions from the first Isis. *Enjoy the rest of our life, which is now your life. We deserve it.* Yes, Isis did deserve it, and she planned to do just that. With Zack, with her family, and with their friends.

But oh, man, she couldn't wait to meet their kids.

Epilogue

Las Vegas…

With a sold-out audience surrounding him on three sides and hanging on every word he spoke, Simon repositioned himself on his metal stool. He cleared his throat and straightened his back while bringing the microphone up to his mouth.

"Based on the reactions you all had toward much of what I said tonight," Simon explained to his audience, "I suspect some of you may envy the idea that I am a vampire. But let me assure you that living forever is not always a happy existence. Quality of life does not come from longevity.

"As a vampire, I do not get to enjoy the finer things in life. I miss the sweet taste of food, wine, and physical relationships. For me, those are all things of the past that I experience only through memories. Believe me, I would not wish that on any of you."

Simon eyed his audience. From the height of the stage, he could see every man, woman, and child who paid their hard-earned money to hear him speak. It was a responsibility he took to heart throughout his talks. "So, my advice to you, my friends, is to enjoy your limited time on Earth. Cherish the moments that you have with your loved ones, and with yourself. Work hard, play hard, and make the most of it by enjoying life to its fullest. Enjoy it all in a way I no longer can. Allow me to live vicariously through you. Thank you all for spending this night with me and listening to what I have to say. Please take it all to heart."

The audience broke out in applause. Simon bowed his head, soaking it all in. Despite dozens of talks under his belt, the mental high he received from a sold-out crowd's ovation never got old. Of course, there were many in front of him that refused to believe he was anything more than a performer, certainly not a genuine vampire. But Simon appreciated them nonetheless.

He eyed the clock on the back wall. "Ooh, we went long tonight, didn't we? Unfortunately, we only have time for one question. Any takers?"

Several hands rose. Simon waved to a middle-aged man with black hair and glasses seated in the front. "You, Sir," he said. "So I may get to know my audience personally and intimately, I always ask that you please share with us your name and occupation."

The man stood from his seat. "My name is Harry Chen, and I'm a detective for the Las Vegas police department."

"Ooh." Simon pulled his head back. "I do hope I am not under arrest for the time I impersonated a live human."

The audience chuckled, as did Harry. "No, not at all. I'm off the clock."

"In that case, Detective"—Simon waved his hand—"please ask your question."

"It looks like the members of your former show, The Witches of Vegas, have left the stage. How do you feel about that, and do you see them ever returning?"

"Hmm, that's a good question, indeed." Simon

tapped the mic. "I admit, the departure of The Witches of Vegas leaves a huge hole in my heart, and the hearts of many, but I am sure they had their reasons. They were a family, and, in our time together, they treated me as one of their own."

Simon stood from the stool. "That is why I feel I can speak for them when I say to all their fans, thank you for sticking with us throughout their entire run. Thank you for your attention through the good, the bad, and everything in between. I know they appreciated all of you as much as you have appreciated them.

"I do not know if we will ever hear from The Witches of Vegas again. If not, I will truly miss them. And, of course, I wish them all the best."

Simon waltzed to the end of his circular stage. "And I wish you all the best as well, my friends. Thank you for listening to me and enjoying my stories. Everyone, take care of each other, and have a wonderful life."

The audience once again broke into applause. Simon took a bow and waltzed off the stage.

A word from the author...

The Witches of Vegas series is officially a wrap. What started as an idea that hit me on a Thursday at two o'clock in the morning turned into five great adventures in an award-winning series.

Now, on this final page, I'd like to thank everyone who encouraged and supported me throughout the entire process:

My wife Sue, who continues to be the best partner I could ever ask for,

My parents, Bev and Marty Rosendorf, who believed in me throughout all of my endeavors,

My in-laws who, along with Sue, were always my beta readers for each book before they hit the stands,

Dianne Rich, my TWRP editor who shared with me her love for The Witches of Vegas series from the moment she edited the first chapter,

My friends and colleagues, who were always the first to pick up each book upon their release,

All of my readers who, through their enjoyment and love for the characters, have inspired me to keep writing, even when my muse wanted to take a break. Their reviews have always helped improve my writing.

And, last but certainly not least, my friend and number one reader, Dore DeQuattro, who showed genuine excitement from the moment I shared with him the idea about witches hiding in plain sight as magicians on the Vegas Strip. His excitement grew with each new idea I shared with him and as they all formed the five books which make up this series. Dore even offered words of confidence and encouragement in our last conversation. May this great man rest in peace.

Thank you for taking this journey with me, through The Witches of Vegas, Journey To New Salem, Witch's Gamble, Witch Way to Vegas, and Wiccan Mirror. Keep an eye out for future projects. I'm sure you'll be hearing from me again sooner rather than later.

For more information, follow me on Twitter, @MarkRosendorf or check out my website, www.markrosendorf.com

www.ingramcontent.com/pod-product-compliance
Lightning Source LLC
Chambersburg PA
CBHW070059030726
47506CB00002B/517